Sin & Scales

Paradise Duology: Book One

MICHELLE EMMANUELLI

CONTENTS

Contents

CAPITAL
ARMYN
ORAN

PARADISE
KYRN
CAPITAL

Blind

Even if I come
with horns,
and a tail,
still
Your people
forsake You, putting
their glory over Yours,
and when they worship themselves
they worship me.

I

Between God and dragons, I wager my life He'd lose.

The last words of Papa's conversation with that horrid revolutionary echoed in Wynne's mind. She climbed the stairs to the Temple, her legs threatening to give out on her. Sleep eluded her last night, and tears loomed at the edges of her frayed nerves. But she needed to hold it together.

Lanterns guarded the marble steps, and when she wrapped the snakehead knocker against the double doors, the echo carried over the morning mist like a moan. Beside Wynne, her dragon shifted, shaking her silver hide and blinking blearily.

The twilight devoured any semblance of light. A silence reigned over the city, squeezing tighter with every hour that passed. Anxiety loomed in the hearts of shuttered homes, suffocating like the smoke that had drifted from the Armynian mountains two days ago.

Two days.

Could it really have been so short a time?

Two nights had come and gone since the wretched Armynian people had entered the kingdom of Paradise at the western border. She'd seen the fire that ravaged the neighboring kingdom of Armyn, the winged Armynian dragons that flew for safety like sparks flying from Papa's forge. And whatever curse they'd wrought upon their kingdom had come with them.

People sick, dying to the Armynian curse.

Papa among them.

Anger flushed through Wynne, and hot, frustrated tears pricked her eyes. If it hadn't been for that Armynian revolutionary that showed up at her door, Papa never would've gotten sick. A frigid wind snuffed out her anger like a candle, and she shivered.

Clutching her money purse, she wished for a moment that she hadn't kept this from Morgan. That he might be here, too. At least his presence would keep the cold from seeping through her bones, and his reassuring smile would chase away the tormenting voices of worry echoing within her skull.

The Temple door cracked open, and a golden sliver of light fell over the hem of her wool skirt.

She eyed the priest who answered—a rotund fellow with sharp eyes and greedy hands hidden in the folds of his white-gold robes—and bit back a frustrated sigh. Any priest would have been better than Eli. She tamped down the worry that wormed up her throat and plastered on a smile.

"Long live the King." Her breath puffed in a cloud of crystallized air.

Eli appraised her dragon, Armor, with a sweep of his eyes. Armor's smooth scales refracted the gold light, and the blatant vexation on his face softened to aggravation. Armor's pristine silver hide, free of molt or barnacles, had passed judgment today.

"I have an offering," she said quickly, bowing. She opened her palms as if revealing a great treasure, but it was just the sorry dregs of her savings in a velvet pouch: a couple dozen silver coins from the last few months' wages.

His eyes flashed at the jingle of coins. "What service do you require, Miss Mayweather?"

"It's not for me, but my father." She swallowed against the tension in her throat. She couldn't be turned away. "Please."

Eli opened the door fully, and the earthy, floral scent of incense washed over her. Though it was an offering to the King meant to bring peace, it only made her stomach roll.

"Come," he said.

Wynne glanced at Armor. "Stay, girl."

With a sigh, her dragon crossed her paws and lay down at the top of the steps, tucked in the shadows of a marble column.

Eli didn't wait, turning on his heel and disappearing into the wide Temple corridor. She trailed him to the sanctuary, where vaulted ceilings and carved pillars loomed over her, and she couldn't help the flicker of pride at knowing her dragon had never had to enter the Temple for judgment.

At least Wynne hadn't messed that up yet.

The priest's robes swished against the marble like the slow breaths of a sleeping dragon as they entered the cavernous sanctuary of the Temple. The chill of oncoming winter seeped through the thick stone walls, far from the blush of summer heat that warmed the Temple the last time she'd walked the halls for yearly penance. Two marble columns were carved in the shape of dragons, their empty, white eyes glaring at her as if in eternal derision.

Maybe that was the judgment she deserved after all.

But not Papa.

Eli stopped her in the middle of the room where a thin veil cut the chamber in two. He held out his hand, the smooth, ink-stained fingers betraying his duty as a scribe and healer. "What is your need?"

"A cure for the Armynian curse." She hesitantly handed him the coin pouch, along with a black dragonscale she'd plucked from Papa's dragon. No bigger than her thumbnail, but it glittered iridescently like a fish scale. "My father is dying."

Eli weighed the velvet pouch in his hand, opened the drawstring, and poured the silver coins into his other palm. He counted them silently, though she had already counted three times to match the current standards of the scales. Then he disappeared behind the veil.

Wynne inched closer, squinting to see beyond its folds. Darkness gaped at her in the hairline split, though she knew, somewhere beyond, the priest had placed her offering and the dragon scale on two great silver plates. They would tip one way or another, revealing her faults, or balance if the payment was enough to lift the curse put on Papa.

Anxiety twisted in her stomach. Had she done enough? Would the King have mercy on him? Even if she didn't deserve mercy, Papa should be spared. The sickness was not his fault. If that King-forsaken Armynian hadn't spewed his poisonous words into Papa's life, he wouldn't have been dying, his mind lost to delusion.

Beside her, Eli's dragon silently guarded the veil. The gray creature had Eli's beady eyes, and no doubt his master's penchant for gold. All dragons reflected the hearts of their masters. Just as Morgan's dragon, stoic and noble, followed him like a serpentine shadow.

After what felt like an eternity, Eli returned, and the frantic beating of her heart lessened. He peered at Wynne down his crooked nose, and with his dark eyes, he looked all the more like a greedy crow.

The thought was not amusing.

"It's not enough." He stretched out his hand with her empty purse.

Trepidation flared into panic, constricting her throat like a snake. It should have been enough, with her careful planning and sacrifice.

What would Papa think of her now? He might expect her to leave, to give up on him, but no. She wouldn't abandon him.

She swallowed hard past the lump in her throat.

"Can the High Priest hear my case?" Her fingers tugged at the collar of her cloak, the winter garment now all too suffocating. "If he could just hear me out, I know it would tip the scales. My father is innocent."

"No one is," Eli said, almost smug as he looked down his beak nose at her. "Come back when you have more than just a pittance. The Temple will hold your offering for the next penance."

Fear flared into fierce anger. She yanked her hood back and closed the distance to the priest. His dragon growled, looming down toward her as smoke billowed, but she didn't care.

She wouldn't fail.

She couldn't.

"I will speak with the High Priest. The Prince, even. The curse isn't Papa's fault, and if you don't do anything, it'll be yours!"

Surprise blazed across his features, but he quickly masked it behind his sniveling, priestly countenance.

"Do you really think your father is the only one?" He regarded her as if she was wasting his time, which only spiked her fury. "I did you a favor, Miss Mayweather. The high priest emptied the sanctuary to get some rest, consult the King in prayer regarding those winged Armynian rats. I didn't have to open the door for you."

Wynne's hands curled into fists at her sides. "Weigh it again. I'm sure it's enough."

"Not what you've brought."

The finality of Eli's tone cinched the terror that wove around her throat.

She had known better than to trust Eli.

This conniving, self-centered hypocrite had skimmed off the top. She should have counted the money out in front of him—especially after how she'd slaved at the tailor shop to gather it, taking double the orders and wearing her fingertips thin even over just two days. It *should* have been enough.

"But *that* might serve you well." Eli's eyes were fixed on something over Wynne's heart.

Her hand flew to her chest, fingers gripping the ring that hung at the end of a thin chain. In her burst of anger, her movements had yanked the chain out from its hiding place.

"No."

She had carried Morgan's engagement ring for comfort. Now, as Eli eyed her with a greedy light in his eyes, she wished she'd forgotten about it entirely. It shouldn't go to the hands of this wretched, good for nothing—

"Is it worth more than your father's life?" Eli leaned forward, lowering his voice to a gravelly croak, a poisonous mist curling around her.

If Armor were here, she'd wrap her tail around Wynne's legs to ground her. Or hold her back. Because now, all she wanted to do was yank the last wisp of his black hair out of his head and throw it upon the King's scales of judgment herself—

As if sensing her intent, Eli's dragon stepped between them, and she distanced herself slightly.

Her thoughts circled back to Papa, his rattling cough and the sickly pallor to his skin, and she broke the chain around her neck.

She held it out, turning her face away to the woven tapestry hanging on the wall.

The priest snatched the ring from her fingers.

Even though she didn't look at him, she knew what would catch his eye. The intricate craftsmanship, the emblem of the ox, the ruby eyes and ivory horns. Eli let out a bark of laughter. "Lord Delmar? With you?"

The derision in his tone made her snap a glare to him, but she pinched her lips shut.

He looked her up and down as if studying her with a new perspective, one that made heat rise to her cheeks. Wynne cocooned herself in the folds of her cloak.

She lifted her chin, steadied her breath. "Care to verify? I'm sure he'd appreciate the intrusion in his private affairs."

"You will have my discretion," the priest almost growled, "when your union is sealed." He tucked the ring into a pocket in his robes.

Before Wynne could say more, he disappeared through a part in the veil. Scales rustled against marble as Eli's dragon blocked the partition.

She could almost taste the smoke in the air from the dragon's breath. Its coat rippled, refracting the candlelight like the glare of sunset through stained-glass windows. Whatever pride she'd taken in Armor's scales soured into shame in her stomach. Beside this creature, Armor was a rat among silken cats.

And so was she.

Eli returned with a small brown package. The King's seal adorned the paper, a green snake wrapped around the judgment scales. He bowed contemptuously low. "May the blessings of the King go with you."

She snatched the package. "And with you," Wynne spat between her gritted teeth as she spun on her heel and left the sanctuary.

At least it was still early. She could catch a reprieve from her raging emotions in the quiet walk home, focusing instead on the whispering breeze and the murmuring insects being her only company.

She exited the Temple and froze. Voices shattered her hope for peace, and she shrank back into the inky shadows. Two sailors strode into the square, and she let out a breath only when they had passed on. She gestured to her dragon.

"Let's go."

Armor stood to attention, reaching just up to Wynne's elbow at her full height, and followed as Wynne bounded down the steps and slipped into an alley.

The package clutched to her chest, heart beating against the rough paper, she could almost hear Papa's words of thankfulness when he was healed. See the smile that crinkled the skin of his face, leathered from years of working the forge. Not the scowl that darkened his expression ever since the day Mama left.

By the time Wynne left the inner city, the sun's golden rays glanced off the watchtowers that guarded the capital's fortress walls. She paused at the inn a few blocks from home and looked over her shoulder.

With the city's sloping position on the seaside cliffs, she was high enough to spy the Temple and the palace. Fortress walls ended at the sea, where a ship bobbed like a cork. Sailors spilled out onto the port, leading a small trail up to the white marble face of the Temple, like starving pups coming to beg at the feet of a wolf.

While smooth cobblestone had paved the streets in the center of the city and colorful stucco buildings winked cheerily about the Temple square, only dreary wooden edifices greeted her now. Quaint shops were traded for mossy-faced inns and rough taverns, and the streets turned to muck the farther up she trekked, to where she had to hike her skirts up with one hand.

Papa's house was tucked behind a barren yard and pressed up against the city's wall. Two years ago, Mama would have tended to the house's mossy facade and weed-filled window pots and taken care to prune the rose bushes and uproot the dandelions. That had fallen to Wynne, until Papa's encouraging praise had turned sharp with bitterness. As she stepped to the door, she could feel Papa's rebuke tearing up her insides like shards of glass.

Armor scurried over the side of the house, digging her claws into the knotted ivy, as she went up the two stories and disappeared into the backyard. No doubt to see what mice she could catch in the overrun weeds.

In the kitchen, Wynne opened the package with trembling hands. A vial and a small parchment. Instructions. She memorized them.

She poked the dwindling fire in the kitchen and set water to boil. A strong gust of wind blew in from the back of the house, followed by Armor appearing around the corner.

"Wipe your paws," Wynne chided, snapping a towel in her dragon's direction.

Armor eyed the fire and blew smoke from her nostrils as if to say she would be more useful here. Wynne gave her dragon a pointed look, though she couldn't help the grin that tugged at her lips. "See if you can find Miro. He might have to take some of this, too."

With a huff, Armor padded from the room, leaving muddy footprints in her wake.

Wynne poured the vial into the pot. It turned purple, then deep magenta. It would be ready once it turned orange. It could be a minute or hours. Depended on how much Papa had grieved the King.

And if her sacrifice had been enough.

She sank into the chair at the table and covered her face with her hands.

The floor beneath her rumbled as heavy footsteps plodded toward her. Scales rustled against the hardwood as her dragon neared and dropped her head into Wynne's lap. Comfort filled Wynne as Armor's tail wrapped around her ankles, and she dropped a hand, running her fingers up and down the interlocking metallic scales of Armor's neck.

An image flashed in her mind, and her heart fluttered. The dewy grass, green from summer rain, yielded welcomingly to a couple. Wynne spotted herself through her dragon's eyes, silhouetted against the rising sun as she strolled with Morgan, hand in hand. Their voices were carried away by the caressing breeze, but his laughter still rang like music over the approaching dawn.

Wynne sighed, blinking away the memory. "Thank you," she said, smiling at her dragon, and relaxed into the chair, calming at the sound of the fire crackling.

A low growl reached her ears, and Wynne looked up. Papa's dragon, Miro, pushed through the weighted curtain that separated the kitchen from the hall and sniffed as he eyed the pot menacingly.

"Don't knock it over," she scolded at his dramatics, having to smile despite the weight pulling at her bones to get some rest.

Miro's gaze shot to her, and panic squeezed her lungs.

Though the bright hue of Miro's yellow eyes had dimmed since the curse, the most alarming change was how his entire body seemed to be molting. Large white flakes would break off him like a dusting of snow. Even if he was uncommonly large for a Paradisian dragon, one look from anyone would be a disgrace. With a paw, he scratched at the flakes and shook out his hide with a frustrated huff.

"Sorry, Miro," Wynne offered. If only she could get him out to the river.

It would be easy to get Miro out of the house but altogether impossible to sneak him past the guards stalking the top of the walls. From the allures and the watchtowers, she knew they could even spot shadows in darkness. It didn't help that she knew Miro could hear the babbling of the cleansing river just on the other side of the wall in her backyard.

She sighed. What she would do to find peace, far from Paradise...

Wynne turned her gaze back to the pot and glared at it, as if she could make the water boil alone. It turned a ruby color, like the ox's brilliant eyes in Morgan's signet ring—her engagement ring. A promise she would keep but might never be able to fulfill. She would find a way to get it back.

But before that, she would find the Armynian who made Papa sick. And it didn't matter if she had to explain the ring to Morgan if she could get the satisfaction of making this revolutionary give her father back—even if she had to drag him to the scales herself.

2

The pungent herb salve stung when Morgan Delmar slathered it on his forearm, and he winced as his fingers brushed the burns. What had he done to deserve punishment this time?

As he buttoned his shirt, he flinched at the sudden memory of Orgul's outburst four days ago. Derangement had glimmered in Orgul's expression, pupils so thin that all Morgan could see was the amber glow of his dragon's eyes like fire. When the spell passed, Orgul had reared back, shock seizing his reptilian features, and stalked off into the night to wallow in loathing.

Morgan tamped down on the resentment and let out a pent-up breath. It wasn't fair to blame Orgul for something he couldn't control.

Even so, he couldn't help but feel relieved that Orgul had disappeared this morning. His dragon had probably gone to the top of the walls around Paradise, the allure, and gazed down on the fields, now brown and desolate in preparation for winter. Maybe his dragon looked further west to the smoking ruins of Armyn, remembering how the kingdom had burned like hellfire when rebels overthrew it just two days ago.

Morgan often went there himself to gaze at the freedom he no longer had.

He turned at the creak of hardwood floors. A knock sounded. Morgan grimaced. He couldn't roll down the sleeves without bandages first. Maybe if he stood at an angle, Mother wouldn't notice—

"Morgan?"

He sighed. His sister, Addie. "Come in."

The door opened, and Addie was at his side in an instant, her brows knit. "Again?"

Addie was tall for her fourteen years, with slender features and a graceful manner, though she rarely deigned to show it. Her dark hair was often left cascading down her shoulders, as wild as the impish tilt to her grins when she hatched another plan. Though now her face was scrunched with worry.

On her shoulder, her own dragon perched, a golden-scaled creature that seemed too delicate to be a dragon. More like a bird, without the wings. Only the dreaded Armynians had wings, a feature that was more useful now than ever to determine their presence within the mining towns at the border of Paradise. A few had been spotted out west by the mountains, but rumors circulated they had even made it to the capital.

Addie plucked the salve from the dresser and frowned as she sniffed, her nose crinkled. She pursed her lips a moment before she dug her fingers into the cream and grasped Morgan's wrist.

"Hey, what are you doing?" He tried to yank his hand back, but the movement stretched his skin, and he winced. "I'm going to be late—"

"Good." She tightened her grip. "Just hold still."

He huffed and rolled his eyes. Fighting her would only make it worse. Even though her grip was tight, her eyes were bright with concern. She applied the salve, and he let out a hiss, this time at the pain that shot up his arm at her rough movements.

"What are you going to do about Orgul?" She released his wrist and took his other arm. Her gaze never left her work, though this time she was gentler.

Worry churned in his gut. What would he do indeed.

He let out a breath. "What I can."

Addie frowned thoughtfully, but her gaze still didn't raise to his. "What have the priests said?"

He didn't want to say. He'd been to the priests a dozen times in the last six months, and each time a different priest had accused Morgan of being the cause. Their accusations only further cinched the shackle of helplessness around his throat.

They would put him in chains if he returned. Branding him as the scum of the earth until he paid penance to the King for the sins he didn't even know he committed. If Father were still here, he might have some words of wisdom from his books, but Father wasn't here to decipher the most confusing passages anymore.

Father had always mentioned God, but Morgan had only ever been left with the distinct impression of being crushed by the weight of sin, gasping for breath that wouldn't come. Like a mouse trapped under Orgul's claws before his dragon devoured the miserable creature.

"Stay still for a minute."

Morgan let out a chuckle, trying to relax the tension in his shoulders. "Haven't moved since you came in, Adelaide."

She didn't bite at his attempt to lighten the tension, her lips pursing. Addie grasped the bandages from the dresser and wound the tan fabric around his arm with light pressure. "I'm glad you're all right."

Morgan shook his head, shaking away his swirling thoughts with the movement. He turned a mischievous smile to her. "Did you see Felipe yesterday? He came to the house."

Red immediately flushed Addie's cheeks. Her hands stopped their careful work. She raised her gaze to his, opened her mouth and shut it again, and turned hastily back to the bandages.

Good. A welcome change in the conversation now that it wasn't spotlighting him. "He was asking for you." He shrugged, letting his words hang in the air as her fingers slowed. "Something about needing your help?"

She dropped the bandages, the rest of the roll dangling to the ground. "W-with the festival?"

He grinned knowingly, and he laughed when she ducked her head. "Of course. Who else would he trust to organize the musicians and the dances?"

Addie grasped the bandage, finished the wrapping with trembling hands, and pursed her lips. She met Morgan's gaze again, her expression wary though her eyes lit. "When he comes again..."

"I'll make sure you know."

She nodded in relief. Her gaze flickered to the window now, but he kept his gaze fixed on her. Something else was on her mind, and it wasn't Orgul or Felipe.

She pressed her lips together, but not enough to hide her smile or the sudden excitement over her features that rivaled seeing her childhood crush. "Did you see the ship dock at the port?"

Morgan raised an eyebrow. No wonder she was up early, trying to catch a glimpse of their runaway brother. But it was hard to miss the loud shouts of sailors unloading imported goods over the quiet morning. "Ryder's not there, Addie."

She tugged on the bandage to tie it off, and Morgan flinched. "Sorry," she murmured, and started on his right arm. "I just miss him. Don't you?"

Morgan fought the urge to grimace. Not quite. His older brother had left a gaping hole in the family line, one that now yanked Morgan from his search of history to the stark present. He would rather explore the founding of the four kingdoms than sit before the council's critical eye. But Addie had no inkling of the shadow Ryder cast on Morgan's footsteps.

He knew the council expected him to have Ryder's quick ideas and decisive action, but there was always too much to consider. It suffocated.

Besides, it didn't matter if Ryder showed up today. Or any day. What mattered more was the second ship bobbing on the horizon miles away. The passenger ship that would be his freedom to live in peace, without the weight of insurmountable expectation.

"Maybe he'll come back," Addie offered.

Maybe so, but to get back into the fold of the community would require a humility Ryder didn't possess.

"Want a scone from the kitchen?" Her voice was cheerful, though her eyes betrayed her concern for him.

He chuckled. "Thank you, but I have to go." He pressed a hand to her shoulder. "Stay out of trouble today."

She made a scrunched-up face as if she was annoyed, but by the way her eyes sparkled, he knew she didn't mean it. "Don't I always?"

By the time Morgan made it to the cobblestone streets, the sun was already cresting the tallest mast of the ship. With golden rays hitting the marble of the Temple directly, it almost looked beautiful, a beacon of hope for the people. But Morgan knew of the darkness that slithered below the unshakeable foundation.

The Temple square boasted a large fountain that hushed the whispers of passersby in the gentle tinkling of the water. A favorite place of Wynne's, where she had poured out her heart to him many times, but a place he wished he could avoid. The ox statue in the center of the fountain, fitted with ruby eyes and ivory horns, leered over him. Just another reminder of his family's forced service to the King.

Trepidation pressed on Morgan's chest as he entered the Temple, where vaulted ceilings whispered and shadows breathed. Curtains swayed with passing servants and their dragons, closing back and snuffing out whispers of conversation.

Morgan glanced about the sanctuary, sensing Orgul's presence, and amber eyes blinked out of the corner. His dragon melted from the blackness.

Relief at the sight of his dragon loosened the tension from his shoulders, but not by much. Orgul's obsidian scales and sandpaper skin were softened by slender features and long neck that arched over the passing nobility. His amber eyes glinted in the candlelight, but they held no hint of derangement now, only remorse.

Orgul dropped his head, and Morgan reached out a hand in forgiveness. He wished he had more time, but he was already late to the council. Morgan turned to the Temple veil.

The curtains swayed, and the embroidered green snake, poised to strike, came alive on the crimson silk. Tension twisted Morgan's gut as the snake's ivory fangs flashed in warning.

No, he would not let fear bind his heart. He'd seen those piercing eyes before, even as they'd overlooked him in disdain. He would not fear the serpent king.

Morgan steeled his shoulders and stepped forward. Scarlet curtains pulled back with a soft swish as they entered, and he had the familiar feeling of being shut in a cage.

A cavernous hall of white marble greeted him as he spotted the Prince on the dais. Rainbows fell across the worried faces of the council through the morning sunlight in the stained-glass windows, a picture that only Father would have considered humorous.

Lord Henry Soam stood at the Prince's right hand, chin raised with all the arrogance of being the Prince's only son.

The high priest stood at the opposite side of the Prince. From there, a few more province leaders populated the sanctuary. With relief, he spotted Lord Ashton, whom Morgan considered to be the most reasonable of the nobility.

Morgan bowed to the Prince as he entered and stood beside Lord Ashton. Orgul fell in line behind him, like all the dragons who stood behind their masters like colorful shadows. Each one was wingless, in Paradisian fashion, and free of any blemish or molt that may have betrayed their master's wrongdoing.

His eyes stopped on an unfamiliar red dragon across the room, sitting at its master's feet. The stranger had dark curls and golden, calculating eyes. Though his clothes reflected the formality and colors of a captain in the army, this man was different. The man's dragon shifted, and cold shock fell over Morgan as he spotted the tattered wings. An Armynian.

Why in the world would the Prince have an Armynian within the Temple?

Before Morgan could turn to ask Lord Ashton, the Prince raised his staff lazily in the direction of the council. "Greetings, council and guest. We come today to weigh the case of Gareth Sere. He stole from the Temple, and now we'll see if he's served his penance."

The Prince's voice droned as if he'd rather rush through the trial and get to the heart of what was on his mind, but the high priest moved with the deference of a man who relished power.

The high priest gestured grandly to one of the guards. "Bring him in," he announced. "Let him be weighed."

Morgan's gaze went to the giant scales behind the Prince; the plates were wide like serving platters for a gargantuan creature. He shuddered.

The curtains beyond the scales parted, and a sailor entered. Limp, greasy hair fell about his shoulders, but his gaze fixed on the Prince with startling fury.

Chains bound the sailor's arms, winding up to his elbows like silver ivy. The metal glowed white, and the man grimaced as if they burned.

"Move it, sea rat," the guard beside him snapped, and the sailor begrudgingly lowered his gaze in submission.

The sailor fell back to stand beside the scales.

Heat creeped up Morgan's neck as the judging eyes of Lord Soam turned his way. He raised a brow, smirking at Morgan as if reminding Morgan of his brother's trial and his family's disgrace.

Not for the first time, Morgan wished that he could be anywhere else but another trial. A daily occurrence now, usually with two or three condemned, but only one sentence ever mattered to him.

The man's dragon lumbered in after him. Its blue coat was peppered with barnacles, and it left behind a dusting of scales as it approached judgment.

"We may hear his defense or repentance once the scales speak their piece," said the Prince.

With a gesture from the high priest, Gareth stepped up onto one plate, and it sank to the floor with his weight. His dragon went to the other side. Despite the dragon being double the man's size, the dragon was only slightly heavier than the sailor.

A hefty price to pay, but not impossible.

"You may speak your defense, sailor," the high priest said solemnly.

The sailor crossed his arms. "I have nothing to say to you or your wretched Prince," he snapped.

As the man spoke, the scales shifted, and the dragon's weight pulled further down. The sailor paled, but held his ground. Just like Ryder had when he had been on trial...though Morgan doubted this man would suffer the same consequences—even if he had just spoken words of treason against the Prince.

The high priest went on unperturbed. "What payment will you find to appease your sin? Will anyone step forward to pay your debt?"

The man was silent. Not one council member moved, and neither had any family relation come on the man's behalf. A few eyes went to the strange Armynian, as if he could have been the witness that came to pay the sailor's fine, but he didn't stir.

The sailor's fate was sealed.

"You are sentenced to two years serving in the King's guard." As the Prince spoke, the scales tipped and balanced. The judgment was decreed. "Now get him out of here," said the Prince, irritation in his voice.

"Get him out of here," echoed the high priest to the escorting guard, and waved the newly sentenced guard out of the room.

A twinge of guilt plucked at Morgan's heart. Morgan was on the Prince's council, a position of high regard among the people of Paradise, and yet he could do nothing against the Prince's decree.

The Prince's words were those of the King.

And the King's judgment was law.

When the Prince looked satisfied that the intrusion was out of the way, he turned to the council. The air in the room turned tense, like electricity crackling in the air before a lightning storm.

"Armyn has suffered a loss that will not be repeated." The Prince crossed his arms, his voice pitched low like a snake's rattle. He lifted a hand to the Armynian captain, who wore a somber expression.

"I'm afraid the reports are true," the captain said. "Our temple has fallen, and our King is slain."

Gasps greeted the news, followed by incredulous murmurs from Lord Soam. The Prince raised a hand for silence, eyes flashing. "Continue."

"This was done by those within the Temple—"

"Your own priests?" finished Lord Soam with a hiss, throwing a pointed glare at the Armynian captain.

"Yes." The Armynian grimaced, though his eyes flashed in anger. "We discovered too late that lies were being taught rather than the King's law. They destroyed our Temple, but they are not finished. They will come for your King next."

Lord Soam took a sharp breath. "Never."

Another council member responded with similar anger, and more joined in. The voices grew to a roar, and Morgan fought a headache. What he would give to be sheltered in his study, poring over tomes, as Wynne stitched away at her work, nestled in an armchair—only hearing of the chaos with Armyn and not being remotely connected to it.

At least Morgan's presence was all that was seemingly required of him today. Where he normally might've been called upon to speak on foreign politics, he had been overshadowed by the fall of Armyn.

Morgan fixed his gaze on the Prince, unwilling to look at the captain standing across from him.

Lord Soam's voice cut over the chaos. "Why are we even trusting this Armynian to be in our presence? Tell us, captain, why are you here?" Soam laid a hand on his sword. His dragon tensed as if to strike. "Speak wisely."

"I am here to help you." The captain raised his hands, palms out, anger blazing across his features. "Unless you would rather those wretched revolutionaries break through your Temple."

"You could be with them," snapped Soam.

"I am not."

Wings unfurled, and the red Armynian dragon raised its haunches as if to launch across the sanctuary.

"Enough."

Soam's dragon froze, smoke billowing from his nostrils. The Prince dropped his hand, but his scowl remained, fixed now on Lord Soam with withering intensity. "Do you not trust the King's judgment?" He spoke the words as if they were acid. "The captain has proven the King's trust in this short acquaintance, even though he has yet to earn mine. He has caught one of these revolutionaries. Bring him in."

He gestured to the guards, and they brought another figure through the curtain. The man's arms were fully chained behind his back, as if his skinny frame could be a threat against so many dragons.

"Can they be redeemed?" This came from Lord Ashton, who stood with his hands folded placidly. "If they have been mistaken, maybe they can be taught anew."

"Our people come first," answered the Prince, an edge to his voice that led Morgan to think the Prince would not offer the revolutionaries mercy even if they did surrender. "The Armynians have brought a curse to Paradise. Those renegades push their heresy and their sins upon our people, causing sickness and delusion. We must focus on the remedy."

"But how do we know they are not part of the solution?" asked Lord Ashton.

"Their sins are not those that can be paid, Gerard." The Prince scowled. "They have killed their dragons, the very reflection of their souls, and they will not stop there."

A murmur rippled across the council. Even the dragons shifted, scales rustling against the stone floor.

"They must be stopped from entering the city. They must be struck down." The Prince raised his staff. "They will not stop until they continue their march beyond the veil."

"There are some Armynians in my province who are peaceful." Lord Ashton adjusted his cravat. "They crossed the closest border and are content following our laws and customs."

"They will not be content forever. We need to strengthen our defenses," said the high priest confidently, stepping forward. "I will order the mines to double production. We will need shields and armor for the army—"

"That will not be enough." The Prince's gaze snapped to the high priest. "Your weapons of iron are not strong enough for the steel these revolutionaries have. This cuts through dragonscale."

The council gasped, but Morgan pursed his lips. Impossible.

"See for yourself." The Prince waved a hand in prompting. One guard removed the revolutionary's tattered cloak, revealing something shiny and brilliant, refracting light in a way that made Morgan's stomach lurch.

His eyes recognized it before his mind ever caught up, and he heard a few intakes of a breath around him. He was glad now, for the first time, that he'd feigned his emotions before the council for the past two years, or he might have gasped, too.

"Dragon skin." The Prince grimaced, red tinging his cheeks as he steepled his fingers. "They have turned the very gift of our King into a mockery. They will not bow at your skill, Anias."

The high priest drew an ornamental dagger from his side. "He most definitely will," he snapped. In a moment, the high priest had swiped the dagger, and the revolutionary raised his arm to block it. Where the dagger hit the dragonscale, it shattered. Metal shards clattered against the floor.

"You are deceived." Now the revolutionary spoke, and a power seemed to emanate from his voice that turned the winter chill into a blaze of heat across Morgan's skin. The dragons froze, though some looked ready to pounce. "God will not be mocked," he said, eyes on the Prince. "Your time as the ruler of Paradise will come to an end."

The Prince flushed red.

"Indeed," he went on, "your reign has already come to an end."

Morgan's eyes were trained on the Prince, on the tic in his jaw and the sudden starkness of the white streak in his black hair that matched the ghastly pallor of his face. Even Lord Soam regarded his father with veiled apprehension, watching for the Prince's reaction.

The Prince's knuckles were white as he grasped the revolutionary's dagger, the metal glowing faintly.

Without another word, the Prince moved and sank the revolutionary's dagger into his chest right through the dragonscale. The revolutionary collapsed. Dark red blood pooled out of the wound, looking for all the world like a dragon was bleeding out on the white marble stones of the Temple.

"You can't do that," the high priest protested, his pudgy face reddening. "The revolutionaries must be tried and sentenced—"

"Any and all revolutionaries found within the borders of Paradise will meet the same fate." The Prince adjusted the cuff of one sleeve. "You are dismissed."

3

MORGAN DRAGGED HIS HEELS as he walked through the Temple square. The hum of the market only made his head pound. Citizens laughed, completely unaware that the Prince had just exacted judgment without a trial. Though Morgan knew firsthand that trials were never fair.

Colorful awnings on the vendor stands and the salty sea breeze made the morning walk aggravatingly pleasant. He could just imagine Wynne leading him through the market like a butterfly flitting between flowers, and how her smile would enchant everyone who saw her, only to astonish them when she haggled prices.

But now, since he'd been catapulted into the Prince's council, whenever she noticed she was gathering attention, she would curl back into herself, wrapping the shadows about her like a cocoon, and his heart would twist with guilt.

He found the quaint entrance to the tailor shop and strode in. A startled set of blue eyes fixed on him when the bell announced his arrival. Orgul stayed outside, too large to enter the cramped establishment.

"What could such a gentleman be needing today?" Wynne smiled, stitching colorful island pearls onto a blue gown.

His eyes flickered to the empty spot at Wynne's feet where Armor usually lay. "Some company from his bride to be," he said, flashing a grin and bowing slightly.

"You'd better snatch him up, Mayweather, before I do," said Wynne's friend, Juniper. Wynne shot a mock glare her way, and Juniper raised her hands in surrender, grinning. "I'm just saying."

"I'd be surprised if he could put up with your mouth for too long," she quipped back, though her eyes didn't meet his again. "I'm blessed he even tolerates me as much as he does."

The somber tone of her voice sent a flash of alarm through Morgan. His pulse quickened. He studied her as he gestured to the gown she worked on, her fingers moving nimbly. "Who's this monstrosity for?" he teased.

Wynne rolled her eyes, a grin still brightening her face. "Who else do you think gets pearls from Mandor?"

"Lady Soam?"

"You got it." She set down the pearls, though her hands trembled slightly. "What a bore it must be to be the wife of the Prince. She has to be one of the only people I know who would enjoy the attention." Her fingers fumbled on a stitch and the needle sank into the flesh of her finger. She winced and drew her hands back.

He knelt before her as she brought her bleeding finger to her lips. "Wynne, what's going on?"

Fear bubbled in his chest. He glanced up at Juniper, who took the cue and ducked into the back room of the shop. Now that they had the privacy, he could see Wynne's walls come down in the way her smile shattered and her eyes dimmed.

"I'm sorry, Morgan," she said. "I...I don't have your ring."

"Did you lose it?"

She bit her lip and shook her head, her golden curls bouncing. "I had to trade it," she whispered.

Trade it. He leaned back, mind churning as he watched her fingers pull at a loose thread on her sleeve.

"I didn't want to." Her head shot up, her eyes full of urgency as her hands found his. "I'll get it back, I promise."

The tremor in her voice startled him out of his shock, and he squeezed her fingers as protectiveness reared in him. "What can I do to help, Wynne? What's going on?"

She took a trembling breath. "It's Papa. He's sick." A flicker of anger passed over her features before the urgency returned. "The priests gave me a cure... but I don't know if it will work."

Morgan tensed. His mind flooded with images of Father on his deathbed. The ghastly pallor. The rattling cough. How he'd pored over his Symaran history books until he couldn't even see and Morgan was left to decipher the text and read it aloud. And yet the difficult passages had never revealed 'the five arduous steps to heaven' that Father had sought to remember from his youth.

"It will," he said, squeezing her hand. "And if it doesn't, we'll figure something else out. Together." He lifted their hands to his lips, and he caught the ghost of a weak smile grace her lips.

She wrapped her arms around him. She mumbled something into his chest, but he heard the words as clearly as he could see the sunlight streaming through the windows.

I love you.

He pressed a kiss to her temple. "And I love you."

When she finally pulled back, he flashed her a grin. "Where's Armor? I would have thought she'd pushed me back by now."

The color that had returned to her face paled slightly. "She's at home."

With Wynne's father.

"It'll be all right, Wynne," he said. "You'll see—"

"Open your eyes, Paradise! Sin looks for a chance to devour you!"

Morgan froze at the voice that cut over the square. Wynne twisted out of his grip and rushed out the door, and he followed outside. A man stood on the fountain's edge, raising his arms to the people. A few gazes turned curiously to the man, but Wynne's eyes were fixed with something akin to hatred.

"No payment can save your souls!"

The sea breeze carried his voice, and more heads turned, but Morgan's gaze was caught by the rainbow sheen of the man's cloak. Even if he hadn't heard blasphemy from the man's lips, Morgan would know exactly who it was by his dragonscale coat.

An Armynian revolutionary.

Wynne's hand clamped around his arm. "That's the man," she hissed. "He cursed Papa two days ago."

Black moved beside Morgan, and he glanced over. Orgul had trained his gaze on the revolutionary, tensed as if to pounce, and straightened to his full height, arching over the crowd.

"Your King is a liar!" the revolutionary's voice boomed.

More heads turned toward him.

"Get out of here!" a fabric vendor shouted.

"Guards!" a few voices called, echoing.

More people in the crowd snapped to the revolutionary. Whispers and shouts and jostles passed through as some hurried away and others pressed in closer. A few sailors brandished daggers, silver catching in the cheerful sun.

"Let's get back, Wynne." Morgan tried to lead her away, but she held her ground.

"I'm going to catch him myself," she said, taking a step forward with the swell of the crowd. Morgan was forced to follow.

"We serve the true King!" yelled someone in the crowd.

A dagger sailed and the revolutionary ducked, losing his balance and stepping down to the cobblestones.

Morgan shoved Wynne behind him at the glint of the blade flying through the air, ignoring her protests. Even so, the crowd around them surged forward.

Closer now, Morgan caught a glimpse of fear over the revolutionary's otherwise sturdy frame. His chest seemed to heave in large breaths. "Can your King save you if he's already lost the war?"

The revolutionary's voice rang louder even as the crowd rumbled. Dragons snarled, standing to intimidate the revolutionary, but the group thinned as vendors shut their carts and people fled to avoid being involved. Those who stayed protested loudly.

Morgan was frozen. His heart drummed in his ears, and his mind whirled.

"Curse you!"

"Faithless outsider!"

"You'll never get past the gates to heaven without the King!"

The voices roared and jeered.

Morgan tensed as he spotted the guards corralling people to the edges of the square. They roughly shoved people aside, and defensiveness reared in his chest.

"Let's get a better view," he said to Wynne.

He ducked his head, pulling up the hood of his cloak, and blended into the scattered crowd, tucking Wynne to his side. Orgul followed them, but his dragon didn't catch any attention from the crowd riveted to the commotion at the square.

Jumping back when a carriage stopped at the congested street, he heard the distinctive sneering voice of Lady Soam. Turning into an alley by the Temple, he hid in the shadows as the rising sun spotlighted the events playing out at the fountain. Wynne's hand was a vice around his own, cutting off feeling to his fingers.

A priest stormed down the Temple steps, white robes flashing like thunder. "Heresy!"

The crowd, now at the edges of the square, echoed the priest's accusation, coming to a roar when the revolutionary spoke again.

"I was lost once, but my eyes were opened. Look!" He raised a white scroll about the size of his forearm. "The priests know the truth, but they hide it! If you would listen, you would know how lost you really are!"

"Twisted words!" shouted the priest.

"Your own hearts condemn you for your sin! Your dragons would rather you die than have you pass the gates of heaven! No payments or pious rules will save you—"

"Guards!"

The priest's dragon was stretched to its full height, roaring, and the revolutionary's voice was lost. With a jolt, Morgan realized the man was shaking. Could this pale-faced revolutionary really be a part of the rebellion that took down Armyn?

The guards jostled closer to the fountain, their dragons forming a scaly shield at all points of escape.

"Get back!" one guard shouted.

"Touch him and die!" a voice came over the rest, and a shadow flitted overhead before a white-scaled dragon touched down on top of the ox of the fountain. The source of the voice was a second Armynian, who dismounted his dragon and jumped down to the revolutionary's side.

Though his dark brown hair was streaked with gray, the glint in his eye and the strength to his steps was as youthful as a new guard conscripted into service. The man glowered at the guards and stretched his arm out before the revolutionary. "This man is worth more than all the frauds at your Temple put together!"

A few guards tensed. Others drew their swords. Dragons hissed and smoke billowed as many prepared to roast the two Armynians then and there.

But the priest moved first. Yellow flashed from the priest's dragon as fire soared over the guards.

The revolutionary ducked, losing his balance, and the nearest guard grabbed him. The second Armynian drew a sword, the metal glowing white, and swept it over the nearest guard, who tumbled back to avoid the blow at his neck. The revolutionary fell back into the fountain, and the Armynian hauled him up.

The guards surged forward into the fountain. Swords clanged, and voices shouted angrily, spearing Morgan with trepidation.

Wynne grasped his arm. "I have to go."

His gaze shot to her and he jolted. Her features were pinched in worry, her brow furrowed in a way that twisted his stomach like a thread of thorns. "Wynne—"

But then she was gone into the edges of the crowd. He started going after her, but a sudden commotion made the crowd swell between them and he was pushed back into the alley.

The Armynians had taken flight on the white dragon. Now they soared overhead, and the barricaded crowd gasped and ducked.

The guards barked orders and some chased the Armynian shadow on foot, but whatever tense chokehold had been on the crowd snapped.

Whispers erupted between the passersby. Vendors opened their carts, absorbing the gossip as the crowds began to melt into the streets. Priests disappeared back into the Temple.

And Morgan remained enveloped in the shadows of the alley, mind reeling. Two revolutionaries in one morning. And then the Armynian on his dragon. Why had he not killed his dragon if he seemed to possess a weapon with the same metal as the revolutionary dagger in the Temple?

But something else tugged on his mind that dispelled his current thoughts. Wynne. Worry wormed through him, and he stepped into the square to follow the direction Wynne had gone.

The sun on his back was like a spotlight, and he walked slowly, shoulders hunched, scanning the square for any council member who might engage him. He made it to the far end of the square without anyone speaking to him and let out a breath of relief. He could make it after Wynne now without being stopped.

A shift of movement caught his eye in the shadows of an alley, and a familiar gray dragon inspected him. With foreboding horns and eyes so white they looked like stone, Eli's dragon towered over most. Its penetrating eyes seemed to pass more judgment than the priests.

Morgan felt a glimmer of satisfaction to know Orgul loomed a foot taller than this reptile.

Eli stepped into his path, wearing his white and gold robe with emeralds dangling about the cuffs of his long sleeves. "How are your burns healing, Delmar?" His black eyebrows went almost to his hairline with feigned concern, though his grin reflected only malice.

"Fast enough."

"If you require some more substantive measures, chains would work nicely—" Eli waved a hand freely.

"No."

Morgan's gaze fell on gold around Eli's finger, and something tugged at his insides. Before he could look too closely, Eli tucked his hands into the folds of his robes.

Eli scowled, eyes casting about as if to see if anyone was watching them. His voice pitched low. "You are willful, and your dragon is the worse for it."

"I'm not here for advice." As Morgan spoke, Orgul let out a growl at his side. Morgan looked past the priest and crossed his arms. "Can I help you? I have somewhere to be." Wynne's worried face flashed in his mind.

Eli scoffed. "Symarans. Just like your father, *Lord* Delmar."

The way the priest said his unwanted title only made Morgan want to smack the smug grin off his face.

"He deserved to die the way he did," Eli said, waving a hand. "Symarans and their King-forsaken rules."

Something red glinted off Eli's finger.

Recognition almost sent Morgan reeling back a step.

An ox's ruby eyes glowed in a gold signet ring. His ring.

Even though he'd known of Wynne's sacrifice, seeing the ring on Eli's hand was enough to send a wave of anger through him. The priests' arrogance knew no bounds if they paraded the people's desperate offerings as their own wealth.

To only fuel his anger, the priest grinned as if he had the biggest treasure held ransom. "Wouldn't you know, Lord Delmar," he said, "that your beloved made a deal?"

Before he could think, he'd grasped Eli's wrist. "Give it to me." He could give Wynne any other ring to symbolize their engagement—indeed, he'd even started thinking of where to get one—but he couldn't leave the ring in Eli's hands. Not when it was Father's and the priests had all but killed him.

"It was given as an offering to the King," hissed Eli, his breath sweet with wine, "and you well know the priests are to live off the people's generosity."

"So you flaunt it?" Morgan let go of Eli's wrist and crossed his arms. His face burned. "You are called to be humble and honest."

"And you are sinful. Like your father. Take the loss as retribution for what he's done." Eli straightened his robes, the emeralds clinking as he moved. "I could be persuaded to part with it…"

"No." Morgan straightened, anger churning in his gut. He tucked his hands in his pockets. "Keep it. I have something of far greater worth."

And with that, Morgan turned on his heel and left.

He only made it a few more streets before a sneering voice stopped him. Lord Soam.

But even as the Prince's pretentious son needled him about the events at the square, he could only hear the beating of his heart in his palm, his fingers wrapped around his engagement ring.

4

WYNNE STUMBLED AS SHE rushed into the kitchen, catching herself on the counter. Armor sat by the fire, her blue eyes fixed on Wynne.

"Thanks for letting me know, girl," she said, moving to grab the pot.

The orange potion reeked as Wynne poured it into a mug, and she tasted bile even as she scraped butter onto a stale chunk of bread and took a few sips of her warming stew to mask the stench. A sad stew, with tough rabbit chunks and mushy vegetables, but it would do.

She chewed on her own piece of bread, but her stomach churned. Her vision blurred with tears that threatened to drown her.

Morgan's understanding had almost undone her at the tailor shop. At least there, among the fabrics and her friends, they didn't have to hide their engagement. She didn't have to hide who she really was just to please the judging eyes.

When she met Morgan three years ago, he was just a scholar. The younger son of a lord, and thus, free from the constraints of higher nobility. While Morgan's older brother would have been locked in the Prince's council room for days on end, Morgan had had liberty to do with his life what he wanted. And he'd chosen to build a future…together.

A future put under pressure when Morgan's brother was convicted and all eyes turned to Morgan—and then her.

But she and Morgan could be free of the judgment of Paradise.

If only the drink would make Papa better, they would all leave within a week to the island shores of Mandor. As they had planned.

She grasped a folded note from the kitchen counter. "Can you bring this to Juniper?" she asked Armor. "I need to stay here with Papa, and I need her to cover for me." Armor grumbled, annoyed with the mundane quest, but the dragon let Wynne tie it discreetly to her front leg.

Wynne had written the note before heading to the shop this morning, and she knew her friend wouldn't interrogate her sudden departure from the shop now. Juniper would defend Wynne's absence to their boss without even needing an excuse, but Juniper would worry if Wynne didn't return without some kind of notice. Armor left.

Collecting everything onto a tray, she maneuvered to the stairs. At the top, Wynne pushed through the weighted curtain into Papa's room and set the tray beside him. He didn't stir beyond a few shallow breaths, but Wynne was aware of yellow serpentine eyes piercing her from the shadows at the dregs of the firelight.

Papa's dragon, Miro, peered at her from his nest of flakes, eyes dull, hardly stirring when she swept the broom across the floorboards to collect the dry scales. The dwindling fire stirred to life when she dumped the flaky scales, but the flames didn't warm her.

Cold invaded her bones. She shivered and settled into the rocking chair by the fire—once Mama's chair, though it was far too rustic and base for Mama's tastes in the end.

Papa's chest rumbled with shallow breaths. His dark brown hair was peppered with gray like a sprinkling of snow on the horizon—and in the moments where he was awake, his sharp blue eyes were listless. His cheeks, usually ruddy with exposure to heat from the forge, were pale and gaunt now.

Studying his face, the slight rise and fall of his chest, the gentle rhythm of life slipping away, she couldn't help but remember his wager with God. And she wondered who would win.

The food steamed from its tray beside Papa, but he didn't stir or wake up, and she wouldn't steal whatever restless sleep he could get.

She busied her twitching fingers by stitching the buttons on the order she'd received from Addie. Her friend had wanted a crimson gown in preparation of the harvest festival to be held in the Ashton province next month. All that was left, after she finished the buttons, was to add the delicate lace, a special order that should have arrived from Armyn already if it weren't for the chaos.

She grasped a few buttons in her palm and tucked the rest into her pocket, her fingers brushing the drawstring of her velvet money purse. Empty now, but maybe it had always been. Wynne winced. Her hopes hadn't been dashed at the Temple; she hadn't any to give up.

Papa didn't wake even when Armor returned half an hour later, grumbling still about being sent on a demeaning task. Still, she settled at Wynne's feet, though not without a swat at Wynne's leg. The morning sunlight brightened into noon, then golden afternoon rays bled into dusk. Eventually, she had to sit closer to the fire and work by firelight.

"What's this?"

Wynne shot up at Papa's gravelly voice. His cloudy eyes were fixed on the drink beside him.

She lowered her work in her lap. "It will make you feel better."

He scowled and turned his head her way, as if he were directing his almost sightless eyes to her. "I don't want charity."

Wynne matched his scowl, though she couldn't help but fear he'd hear her heart beating out of her chest. "Morgan didn't buy it."

Papa didn't need to know how she got it.

He lifted the cup. Sniffed it. With all the burnt porridge and underbaked bread he'd eaten in the first year after Mama's absence, Wynne knew he'd stomach whatever she made. Even this.

The wary expression in his eyes faded slightly when he glanced back in her direction. He didn't ask, but maybe he knew its purpose. Maybe he was just as afraid as she was. Even so, he drank. Orange dribbled down his chin, but he finished the last drop.

Papa grumbled something under his breath, which Wynne decidedly ignored, and he looked out the window, where the setting sun cast its somber rays over the garden.

The garden had once been the facade for a beautiful family, but only for those not close enough to see the pests consuming the plants from within.

Mama had often sat at the edge of the yard, humming as she listened to the babbling river just on the other side of the fortress wall. Wynne had tended the garden beside her while Mama wove stories about life outside the walls of the city, about a life bigger than the borders of Paradise.

A place where the weight of guilt wasn't quite as burdensome beneath a sapphire sky as the rough waves of the pier.

Maybe the tropical splendor of Mandor was what Mama had longed for.

Or maybe it was the Duke who bought her love with riches.

She hadn't even packed her bags the day she abandoned them—why would she have needed to when being a duchess would have given her everything she wanted?

Wynne swallowed the bitterness that threatened to choke her.

"How was the shop?" Papa studied the garden outside, jaw working steadily on the hard bread.

"Busy." Wynne examined the stack of letters on the mantle. Her stomach sank. Another letter from the collectors. "Nabor requested I collect some Mandorian fabrics at the pier later."

That wasn't true. But it would be an excuse to disappear if Papa's words turned harsh.

"Alone?"

Wynne caught the warning in his gruff tone. "Yes."

Well, Armor would be with her, but Armor wasn't Morgan. And that's what Papa really wanted to know.

"You don't belong with him."

"And where should I be?" The venom in her voice made Papa straighten, and guilt made her words taste bitter. She leaned forward, elbows on her knees, and tried to soften her tone. She didn't want to make him more ill. "He's weighed on the same scales by the same King. Just like you and me."

"He has enough to cover his wrongs." Papa sat further up, his face morphing into an angry mask in the firelight. "I've seen him and his family. They clothe themselves like peacocks! You should be here—"

"Doing what?" She raised a collection letter, steadying her breath at the worry that wound around her throat like a snake. "Papa, if you would let me—"

"No."

Papa's gaze shot back to the weeds, as if he would try to throttle them out of the ground. Or torch them. Or maybe drown them with the same heavy liquor he downed every weekend at the tavern.

"We could have enough if you would just—"

"Wynne."

Anger coursed through her like fire, and she shot to her feet from the rocking chair. "Then pay this yourself." She tossed the collection letter to the foot of the bed.

His eyes widened, enough for her to see the guilt emanating from the cloudy blue, but then her vision blurred with her own tears. She swiped at them with the back of her hand before they could betray her.

The furrows in his brow softened, his arm reaching out. "Wynne, I—"

She let out a breath, remorse clawing at her insides. She shouldn't have blown up at him; she was supposed to have helped.

Stepping forward, she grasped his hand, trembling and cold, and squeezed it.

"I'm sorry," he whispered. "I don't deserve you, my starling. Please forgive me."

His words unraveled that thread of self-loathing coiling in her insides.

"I'm not going anywhere," she said. Not like Mama.

"I wouldn't blame you if you left a wretched sinner like me."

She grimaced at his words. The turmoil that had plagued him ever since he spoke with the revolutionary was almost as bad as his sickness. Nothing she said could ever alleviate his fears, the burden of his sin so heavy it seemed to crush the air from his lungs in the coughs that rattled his frame.

"You're going to be fine, Papa," she said. "The King will forgive you." But even her own words were hollow to her ears.

"No, no," he murmured. "How could such a perfect King find it in his heart to look at me?"

She didn't know the answer, and she didn't speak. Mainly because she didn't know how the King of Paradise could even be considered perfect. Demanding and lawful, yes, but not good. Pressing a kiss to his forehead, she left the room.

As soon as the curtains closed behind her, she spotted Armor looking up at her from the foot of the stairs. "Come on, girl," she said, meeting her at the bottom and slinging her coat over her shoulders.

The frigid ocean air bit her cheeks—even more now that the sun had set, and the stars blinked into existence. Her skirts whipped about her legs, both from the strong winds and the run that had taken over since she rounded the corner.

The moon, white and clear, hung like a spotlight as she wove through tight alleys to the one place where she knew she would find peace. The place where she'd met Morgan all those years ago, where they would meet and talk, where she fell in love with his heart.

Her feet carried her on their own, as they had in the years since Mama left, to the fountain in the Temple square.

A life-size statue of an ox stood above the fountain, poised to charge at an unseen enemy. The fountain's stone bowl was large, with a rim just wide enough for a toddler to sit and kick her legs against the faded carvings on the rock. Real ivory replaced the stone horns of the creature, and its eyes glinted with the same ruby of Morgan's signet ring.

She sat on the fountain's edge, facing the taverns that brimmed with drunken sailors, their raucous laughter carrying over the crickets and rustling leaves.

Papa had been right about the Delmar family's wealth, but he refused their generosity. And even she wouldn't go so far as to beg for help. Morgan's mother would take it as another grievance, just like Wynne's low-born position and disgraceful runaway mother.

She brushed her fingers against Armor's smooth plating, grateful that her outburst toward Papa hadn't carried much weight in the King's eyes.

"What do you think of the reward?" a slurring voice cut over the stillness of the square, and Wynne spotted two sailors stepping out of the tavern.

The older sailor laughed bitterly. "I'd rather put my efforts in working off my debt than chasing some ghost." He tugged at his sleeve, metal glowing faintly from under the cuff of his sleeve.

"Capturing the revolutionary would be enough for me," said the first sailor, crossing his arms. His dragon, about Armor's size, had scales that were already dulling.

The older sailor scoffed, downing his drink.

The young sailor shoved him. "You just want me to believe you don't want him."

"I'd rather not compete with the entire kingdom for one man's soul. He's..." The voices trailed off as the two sailors continued down the street.

Silence reigned over the square once more, but Wynne's mind whirled with possibilities. The revolutionary's capture had a reward. It would be enough for Papa if she could just—

A sudden splash made her push off the edge of the fountain.

She wrapped her coat tighter around her shoulders, her gaze glued to the figure who stumbled out from where he'd tripped into the fountain. The man sputtered, shaking the water from his hair, but by the hunch of his shoulders and his muted coughs, Wynne guessed that he preferred to go unnoticed.

But she wouldn't be here long.

Wrapping her cloak about herself, she turned to go, but the man's voice rang out in a whisper, and she froze.

Morgan left the manor moments before dusk. He tucked a thick iron key in his pants pocket and relaxed his shoulders.

After getting home from the Temple this morning, he pored through all of Father's books from Symara. He found some interesting passages, but they were hard to decipher, and he couldn't risk having the tome out for long periods in case Addie stumbled in and began her usual curious interrogation. Thankfully, that fear was alleviated when Felipe Ashton came, and she was caught up in the excitement of festival planning.

But even though his investigation had stolen his entire morning, it had yielded no answers.

Nothing in the book had talked about the sickness that had taken Father... He'd only found something on a deity named God, a King whose Son was the Prince of Peace, some kind of redeemer. Morgan had understood little else. The ink was faded beyond comprehension, or maybe that was the exhaustion blurring the words before his eyes. Morgan's questions swirled in his gut like coiling snakes. Why would Father have kept these books? And how much did they have to do with Father's dislike of the priests?

That feeling of walking into a serpent's den hadn't subsided, only worsened, as he walked down the darkened streets. The buildings closest to the Temple were built of stone and clay, all with dragons in mind. Grand arched openings, at least ten feet tall, accepted some of the largest dragons in Paradise. Wide streets provided ample room for passing dragons and horse-drawn carriages. But the luxury of space was reserved for the wealthy, and most homes in the outskirts of the city were cramped, the streets there closing in like a dragon's clamping jaws.

At least in the lurking shadows, he would only be another sailor, with a white shirt and brown pants, though perhaps wearing a nicer pair of leather boots. He didn't need more rumors to reach the priests or the council.

Voices echoed between the buildings, but the salty breeze brought a sense of familiarity as he walked the upward-slanting streets. He could almost be strolling down the beach, Wynne at his side, the stars twinkling in the midnight sky.

A vicious thought struck his mind. Had their wedding been delayed so far that she no longer wanted him?

He shook it away. No. She would have told him. Even in all the trials they'd faced over the last three years, Wynne was the one constant that stayed firm. Always hopeful. Always strong. Refreshing like a summer monsoon over the scorched desert kingdom of Symara.

His footsteps clicked against the cobblestones as he walked, forcing a calm countenance. His nerves had settled since he'd reluctantly locked Orgul up in the cellar. He didn't need Orgul to have another spell and hurt Addie. Or Mother.

He grimaced as his thoughts went to Mother and how she'd interrogated him after dinner. He'd been hoping to avoid detection, but she caught him outside of the seclusion of his study with a freezing look. Even Ryder's trial was nothing compared to the expression of disappointment on Mother's face when Morgan told her what had happened.

"They should have had a trial," he'd said. "The Prince was out of line—"

"Silence, Morgan, or you'll speak treason," she had hissed, glaring at Morgan over her second glass of wine.

"As if that's your greatest concern, Mother." Morgan laughed bitterly, anger flaring in his chest. "But I guess you got your way with parading your son in front of the council. Ryder wasn't enough of a disgrace for you."

Mother slammed a hand on the table, sloshing wine over the rim of her glass. She downed the third cup. "You're too much like your father." She had spat the last words. "You must serve in the Prince's council, and you will fulfill your obligation until the day the King releases us. Our family will not lose another to disobedience."

"We won't."

Then he'd gone to lock Orgul up in the cellar, but not before Orgul fixed him with a look of sorrow. He needed a solution for his dragon's fits, one that didn't involve humiliation before the priests.

He still winced at the memories that Orgul had thrown in his face when he burned Morgan four days ago.

Blue sky and mossy docks, a bobbing ship spewing sailors. Cold hit him like the icy winter sea. Ryder's tall frame eclipsed the sunlight that scowled down on the lifeless body floating in the foamy water. His brother's dragon whipped her spiny tail across the onlookers.

He could almost feel the sticky blood on his fingers still. Adelaide had run to Ryder's side, but no one had come to him. Not even as he lifted the dying sailor out of the water and tried to stem the red tide gushing from him.

It had been Ryder's crime, but Morgan paid the price.

He scoffed under his breath. Renown had a funny way of being infamy. Being catapulted into Ryder's position had stolen Morgan's future. And now, even though Ryder had been sentenced, Morgan would pay for it.

He always did.

But maybe Ryder had been right about one thing. For every word Morgan spoke, public or private, his dragon broadcasted his failures.

Ryder had called it a curse. *Why bother trying to pretend I'm better than everyone? I might as well live up to what you believe of me. I'm a scaly, miserable creature.*

It hadn't been hard for Ryder to convince the public of that before throwing off his responsibilities to Morgan.

As Morgan strode down the streets winding toward Wynne's house, his skin prickled with apprehension. Dragons cast shadows against the walls like sinister wraiths stalking the twilight. Flickering lanterns hung above taverns filled with raucous laughter. Even off-duty guards could be spotted among the crowds.

Then a figure caught his eye, and he jolted. Wynne.

She was wreathed in a dark robe that obscured her features, but Armor's chrome plating was unmistakable. Wynne moved nimbly, footsteps padding silently, her head bowed. She disappeared into an alley.

He waited two minutes and followed her route.

Where was she going?

Morgan had enough sense to walk noiselessly, a talent well-practiced when Mother entertained visitors from the nobility or the council. And it seemed Armor's attention was captured elsewhere as Morgan lagged a few blocks behind, hiding behind groups of boisterous sailors as he followed Wynne to the center of town.

The Temple was eerie, bathed in the silver moonlight. Between the buildings to the east, Morgan caught glimpses of dark waves glimmering at the pier. Somehow, perhaps because of the Temple's stony face glaring down on the fountain square or maybe because word had spread about the revolutionary, the square was deserted.

Wynne leaned over the water as she sat on the fountain's edge, her frame teetering with the breeze. His mind flashed to their early days in courting, when her laugh was as carefree as a sea breeze and his shoulders weren't hunched with the burden of his family name.

A splash broke the silence. Wynne jumped up, surprise blazing across her features as a stranger stumbled out of the fountain.

Grasping his sword, Morgan pressed as far out of the shadows as he could without being spotted and watched the familiar figure with a deadly aim.

5

"Hello." The whisper over the quiet courtyard raised her defenses, and she stepped back.

Why did she know that voice?

"What do you want?" she hissed, heat flaring into her cheeks. Her eyes scanned the square, but even though guards milled inside the tavern, she doubted they would reach her if necessary.

The stranger drew a hand through his wet locks, and in the shadow of the fountain's ox, all she could see was the whites of his eyes and the flash of his teeth as he offered a weak smile. A gray cloak hid him from his collar to the tips of his boots. "I'm not sure. He didn't tell me I'd find you, specifically, but I'm here to help. I'm Killian."

She scoffed, alarms ringing in her skull like the watchtower whistles when a fugitive was loose. "You're a madman. Do you want to freeze to death? Do yourself a favor, Killian: get a pint of poison at the tavern, and leave me alone." Tightening her cloak about her, she reached for Armor at her side.

Killian stepped forward, and Wynne tensed.

"Keep your distance, revolutionary," a voice cut through their conversation, and Wynne's heart fluttered in recognition.

Morgan stepped from the edges of the square and strode to her side, a hand at his hip. He looked for all the world like a sailor, his dark curls falling upon his forehead. The scar that cut across his jawline stood stark, bathed in moonlight, and silver glanced off his sword as his cloak shifted.

Then his words hit her.

Revolutionary.

At Morgan's approach, the man stepped back, moonlight illuminating his shockingly familiar features. Of course, she would never forget the face of the man who cursed her father with talk of some God.

And now she had a name.

Killian.

Fury blazed through her as she stared at the man who had ruined her life. It was impossible that she once believed him to be an earnest refugee from Armyn—before the news spread of the kingdom's true devastation.

Wynne had no doubt that Killian had orchestrated the downfall of Armyn, and that whatever honest charm rang in his voice was nothing short of poison.

At Morgan's approach, Killian stepped back, fear arching across his features, and Wynne couldn't help the glimmer of satisfaction that emerged from her anger. When Morgan's arm went around her waist, she realized with a jolt that she'd been trembling. She pulled her thoughts from the safety of his embrace to Killian, now at least an arm's length away.

She let out a mirthless laugh. "May I ask why I'm graced with the presence of the King's most wanted tonight?"

"I'm here to help. To bring healing for your father and—"

"Healing? My father is *dying* because of you. Tell me, great revolutionary, how will you save him?" The anger, now mixed with fear at Papa's state, churned in her gut. But she managed to keep her voice low, though taut like a thread stretched through a hole too large to mend.

"That was not my intention. I'm sorry." The compassion and remorse in his words only grated her further. This man didn't have the right to say anything about Papa. And she wouldn't let him leave until Papa was healed.

With a flick of her hand, Wynne gestured to Armor, who slunk back into the shadows at the edge of the square.

She should yank on a guard's arm right now and capture Killian—but Armor wasn't in place yet. And if Killian was caught by another, who was to say whether her triumph would be given to someone else?

She crept to the edge of the ox's shadow. "The priests gave me a cure. What I paid should be enough. What will *you* do?" Her words came out sharp as a needle, and Killian winced.

Beside her, Morgan tensed, and with a glance she spotted the confusion written in the lines of his frown. He had untangled his arm from her side, even as he'd approached Killian, and now she grasped his hand and squeezed.

She met his gaze and mouthed, *Trust me.*

He leaned down, his breath tickling her ear. "I will follow your lead, my dear, but be watchful of the stars."

Morgan's voice was strained, though he was as steady as an anchor beside her. His eyes reflected the deep blue of midnight above as he scanned the skies.

"Then help me capture him," she whispered so softly she was sure he barely heard it, but he nodded in understanding.

"I am not a liar."

Their gazes shot back to Killian.

His weight shifted from foot to foot, but his voice remained steady, despite the flash of the whites of his eyes. "But if you listen, you might just hear the truth. Your father's ailment is not of this world, but I can help you find healing for him beyond this lifetime. The price has already been paid by—"

Hope flared to life in her chest.

"You will redeem him? You'll give your life on the scales for him?"

Beside her now, Morgan's expression registered worry, though it would be unreadable to anyone even in the brightest daylight. He had the same distrustful look as if he were scrutinizing Lord Soam, only the dread in the creases of his brow made unease roil in her empty stomach.

But she knew what she had to do, and Armor was finally in place.

"Now!"

Armor leapt from the shadows to the left, snapping at Killian's heels. He reeled back, stumbling, and her dragon jumped up to knock him down. Her claws sank into his cloak, but Killian twisted and it pooled at his feet, entangling Armor in the coarse wool. A second cloak below it glinted, refracting light.

He bolted into the shadows of the alleys.

"Come on! He can't get away." Wynne started after him, weaving through the spiderwebbing streets and crates and clotheslines. Her heart drummed in her ears as she kicked up her skirts. She caught sight of Killian as he ducked left into another alley, and she followed, narrowly avoiding slamming into a drunken sailor.

A growl alerted her to Armor at her heels. "Go ahead, girl. Corner him."

Armor bounded forward, nose in the air, and Wynne hoped it was enough. Her dragon was no scent hound—and a glance from any respectable citizen would be a disgrace if she used her dragon as a dog—but she had little choice. Armor darted off into another alley, and Wynne followed.

"I think he's heading to the western gate," Morgan whispered, breaths short.

"How do you know?"

He pointed, and she glanced up just as a white shadow passed overhead. Cold fear speared her heart.

"Come on." He ducked into another street, and Wynne crept behind him.

Stealing another look up at the sky, the winged dragon had disappeared, but she didn't believe it was truly gone.

An image pressed onto her mind, and Wynne stilled. She saw Armor, her silver paws thundering against the cobblestones as she tracked the shadow flitting before her. A building rose on her right, and recognition struck Wynne with a jolt. Killian turned into the street beside an inn—one she passed by every day.

Blinking away Armor's sight, Wynne bolted after Morgan, her feet guiding her on the path she'd walked for twenty-one years now.

"I know where Armor's trailing him," Wynne hissed as she reached him, and Morgan spun to meet her, eyes wide with surprise. "Home."

She led the rest of the way, weaving through the streets as anxiety wound up her legs and almost cinched the breath from her throat. Passing the Jubilee Inn, she spotted the overgrown grass of home and a flash of silver as Armor swiped a paw at a figure.

Killian was backed up, pressed against the wall of her house, hands up and mouth moving as if he were speaking, but Wynne couldn't hear him over the pounding of her heart until she stepped onto the footpath.

Morgan bounded a few steps ahead of her. Armor moved aside at his approach, though her tail still whipped from side to side and her blue eyes flashed like fire.

"Remember this place?" Wynne gestured to her house, her voice hard. In the moonlight, the ivy creeping up the front looked all the more like dark fingers trying to pull the house into the depths of a grave.

Killian raised his hands in surrender, chest heaving.

"I will give you one chance to reverse what you've done, Killian,"—she spat his name—"before I drag you to the King myself."

She sensed Morgan's eyes on her, but she stepped forward and unlocked the door, pushing it wide. Killian met her gaze with a wary look.

"Go." She gestured to the stairs. "You can't miss it."

Papa's coughs reached her ears, rattling the suddenly still air.

Killian let out a world-weary sigh and stepped over the threshold. "I will try, but I can't promise to understand all of God's ways." Armor followed him as he entered, up the stairs, to Papa's room.

With the revolutionary now secured by Armor, the sudden weight of Wynne's life threatened to fall on her shoulders. Heat crept into her face, her head throbbing and her palms tingling, but she shook it off. She couldn't give into her emotions, not now.

Not yet.

Spinning on her heel, she slammed the front door, locking the bolt, before she flew to the other side of the house and secured the back doors, guilt gnawing at her insides.

Papa's dragon lifted his head from his resting spot before the stove, blinking lazily at her as she went for the kitchen. At least the shadows of the fire seemed to mask the uneven flakes that coated his skin.

She was halfway to the pantry when Morgan gently grasped her arm.

Had he been talking? The blood pounding in her ears had drowned him out.

But her gaze was drawn from his face down to his hand, where his finger glittered with the unmistakable ruby and gold of his signet ring.

6

MORGAN TOOK WYNNE'S ELBOW and led her to the cramped kitchen table, where she fell into a chair like a stone in a well.

He studied Wynne's expression, the muscle clenching in her jaw, but he couldn't make out what was going on in her head. Her emotions were as tightly sealed as the scales along Armor's back. Her knuckles were white as she grasped his signet ring—their engagement ring—but her gaze was far away.

She hadn't appeared to have heard him calling her name when she locked the door. She'd almost caught his hand in the crack. And she breezed by the kitchen, where her father's dragon lifted his head in greeting, though his eyes seemed glazed over with some kind of sickness.

Morgan winced at the memory of her scathing words to the revolutionary, and how her voice had trembled. She'd carried the weight of her father's life for two days.

And now that he was here, he would carry it with her...if she let him.

Unruly golden curls fell over her face, and he fought the urge to tuck them back, help her in some way.

He stood, grasping a mug from the shelf, retrieved water, and placed the cup before her. She reached for it, and when her fingers brushed the back of his hand, they felt like ice. The dull sense of dread that built up in him became alarm that pounded in his skull with every beat of his heart.

"Drink, Wynne. You need it."

When she didn't move, he leaned forward, planting his elbows on the table, and waited.

After what seemed like an eternity, she raised a hand, smoothed her hair back, and met his gaze.

Her eyes were bright with tears.

"Wynne—"

She opened her mouth, and he silenced. She raised the mug to her lips and swallowed, then spoke. "I'm sorry, Morgan. You shouldn't be here. You shouldn't have to deal with this...with me."

The last two words were but a movement of her lips, but he heard it like a ballista going off. His chest tightened, the words catching in his throat. "I'm here, Wynne. We'll figure it out together, like always. What do you need?"

Had it really been two years since he was appointed to the Prince's council? They'd walked on the beach, sheltered by the whispering scuttle of hermit crabs and the sheer cliffs, as they'd tried to picture how their lives would change in his new position. He had tasted the salty sea foam as they'd promised they would get through it together.

But the weight of expectation came down on them anyway, and two months ago, they had started plans to leave it behind. Now, nestled in the letter inside his desk were their tickets out of Paradise: four boarding passes on the next passenger ship.

It didn't matter if Ryder docked on this ship or not, because Morgan and Wynne would be gone. And if Ryder was in Paradise, then Mother would have her replacement.

But would Wynne change her mind now that her father was ill? Maybe he had enough time to get another set of passes, to give Wynne's father time to heal—but would Elwin leave his home on the off chance that his wife might return after five years?

Wynne swiped tears from her eyes, and Morgan's heart broke.

"I don't know what to do anymore," she whispered. "Papa's dying, Morgan."

Empathy tore through him. He grasped her hand, his other hand going to brush a tear from her cheek. She leaned into his touch, letting out a shuddering sob.

"What does he have?" He chose his words tentatively, and he held his breath while she collected herself enough to speak.

"I don't know." She shook her head. "We didn't know what was going on with Armyn, but we let *him* in when he asked if we could spare a meal."

Her voice took on a note of bitterness.

"I went to prepare the food. He had that scroll, but I wasn't paying attention. He must've cast some kind of spell. I only heard the end, where Papa made him leave the house. I've paid all I can, but he isn't getting better." She buried her face in her hands.

Her words sent his heart to his throat, and memories flooded his mind. Father's illness had been sudden and swift. He'd been gone within a week, and his mind had been ravaged by guilt and self-loathing. He became the kind of man that only recognized his wretchedness but couldn't see the light.

Wynne trembled after she spoke, her body shaking as if trying to force her to clamp down on her vulnerability. She'd said more than she meant to, but his soft gaze held a reassurance truer than any words or promise.

Morgan leaned forward, kissed her forehead. A flush of warmth went through her. All at once she might have been standing on the pier on the night he proposed, his weight shifting from foot to foot, an uncertainty in his gaze she'd never seen before—and then the sparkle of joy like stars in the night when she accepted.

But there was no joy now, just worry that bled into anguish. "I'm sorry," he whispered.

He stood when she did, and she reached for him, constricting her arms around his frame as if she could somehow say something to make everything better. He hugged her back, and she buried her face in his chest so she could hide from whatever expression might be playing on his features.

Would he ever go back to the way he was before?

His expression had darkened like the gloomy dungeons below the city. His smiles were tinged with a strain that hadn't been there before, his gaze often lost to whatever secrets he'd learned in the depths of the Prince's court. A pressure had fallen to him, one that made her boil with hate for the one who caused it all.

Ryder.

And now, Killian, for what he'd done to Papa.

"Has Elwin said things?" His voice was quiet, thoughtful. "Strange things?"

She drew back, surprised. "Yes," she said slowly. "Papa goes on about sin and judgment...and *God*." Papa's weak coughs sounded from the second floor.

Morgan's expression was drawn with concern, brow furrowed. "He sounds bad, Wynne."

That almost undid her.

She didn't need to hear her mistakes all over again. All the things that she'd messed up since Mama left. All the things that she should do better, that she was never going to be enough to handle anything on her own.

Bitterness and panic surged in her throat like bile. "And what? Would you have paid my father's debt? Pleaded with the Prince himself for the King's mercy?"

He jolted as if struck.

The ring seemed to burn hot in her hand. "I didn't want to trade the ring, Morgan. I had no choice."

He let out a breath, and his facade softened. "I know. It's all right."

The warmth of his gaze, the understanding, now stoked a self-loathing within her.

She wasn't perfect, as much as she tried to be.

She would never be a lady like Morgan's mother, who handled every hurricane like it was a whisper of a breeze. Wynne was too unstable, uncultured. Crass.

She would only ever be seen like her mother, a selfish woman that left her family for wealth.

So why even try?

His expression shifted now to something akin to surprise, brow furrowed in thought. Whatever response he was going to give trailed off as he suddenly turned his gaze to the ceiling.

Shingles creaked on the roof above in a steady clop—a dragon. Glass shattered, and harsh whispers reached her ears from up the stairs.

Papa.

Wynne jerked forward, and she tripped over her skirts that suddenly curled around her legs. Morgan was there to steady her, and when she reached the base of the stairs, he let her pass. Lantern light illuminated the sword that glinted in his hand, and when she met his gaze, he nodded.

"Go to your father. I'll attend to the guest on the roof."

Morgan carefully opened the window on the landing, twisting to latch onto the ivy and haul himself upward.

Wynne pressed her ear up against the curtained door of Papa's room. Miro stood beside her, his head just looming over her shoulder, a low growl in his throat.

A wind stirred and parted the curtains, the cold wrapping around her, and Wynne spotted two figures over Papa's bed, one on either side.

The moonlight illuminated a cascade of glass shards along the floor from the broken window. Killian spoke in hushed tones to another man, burly and well-built—the Armynian from the square.

Blue eyes blinked out from the recesses of the dying hearth. Armor looked at Wynne. Her dragon must have hidden when the Armynian broke in. Wynne lifted a finger and mouthed, *Wait.*

"You hypocrite." The man jabbed a finger at Killian.

Killian raised a scroll in his hands, the paper glowing faintly, spotlighting the grim determination on his face. "I need to pay my debt, Horia. God brought me here again—"

"Oh, shut it," Horia scoffed. "Don't call yourself a saint only to go back on our deal. What was all that about defying death at the hands of the King for a new life?"

Killian stuffed the scroll in his satchel. "You don't understand."

"Enlighten me, O wise one." Horia put his hands together, bowing, and Killian's expression hardened. "Oh? Shouldn't a sniveling priest have patience with someone lost like me?"

"You don't care about what I have to say," Killian snapped back. "Only how you can use me."

"I don't care? I risked my life for you earlier, and you can call it the grace of God that I found you now before these sheep turn you in." Horia waved a frustrated hand in the air. "I can't help you if you flirt with death."

"At least I know where I'm going."

"Spare me the sermon, Killian. Let's get back to camp."

Horia turned back to the window, where a shadow eclipsed the moonlight. Flapping wings. An Armynian dragon.

Wynne fought the panic that threatened to seize her breath. This Armynian was, by the sound of it, involved with the fall of Armyn. She'd only heard snippets of rumors, but they were coming true before her eyes. If Armyn's own priests had started the revolution that burned the kingdom, what other rumors were true?

Killian didn't move from his spot. "I'm not going. Not yet." He sighed, waving a hand at Papa. "Just let me see if I can help him."

Horia pulled back his cloak, and moonlight glinted off a dagger at his hip. He drew it, stepping forward to Papa's bedside. "I can help him right now."

Killian scowled. "Horia."

"He's better off dead than putting his trust in a King who doesn't even know his name." Horia's dagger hovered over Papa, and Wynne tensed. She should run forward, attack, but he was too close to Papa. She wouldn't make it.

Meeting her dragon's gaze, Wynne flicked a hand toward the man. Silver flashed and claws scrabbled on the wood as Armor shot forward, snapping at the rebel.

Her claws found purchase on the man's leg.

Horia struck out with his dagger, and Armor let out a yelp and reared back. Hot blood dripped from where the dagger had pierced her shoulder, and Wynne gasped.

Impossible.

Armor growled, pressing forward again as Miro emerged from the curtain and met her advance. Horia was pinned by the window, sidestepping Armor's lashing tail and Miro's snapping jaws.

Wynne slipped behind the dragons, flying to Killian's side, and grasped his arm. "Come on." She should have taken him to the Temple when she'd first cornered him. And she wasn't giving up now. If she couldn't get Killian to the Temple, she would at least stop this rebel from taking him.

"Get him out of here, Armor," Wynne commanded as she yanked Killian toward the door, away from Horia's clutches.

Horia struck out again, but Armor was ready. She tackled him, and he stumbled back against the wall. His dagger flew from his hand, clattering to the ground two stories down. Papa's bed shook with the force of the impact beside him.

"Good lizard you've got there." Horia rubbed his arm. He offered her a nod as if impressed, and she scoffed. "But you've still got a lot to learn." With one movement, he was on the windowsill, then he disappeared up onto the roof.

Wynne turned to Killian, who grasped the scroll in his hands as if it were his lifeline on the stormy seas. "Let's go. You owe me."

"He's not do—"

A shadow darted through the broken window, and Horia's white dragon shot across the room. Wynne ducked and Killian jumped out of the way. The dragon slammed into the wall, rattling the house's wooden structure.

Smoke rose from Armor's nostrils as she prepared to let out a burst of flame. "No!" Wynne shouted. "You'll set the house on fire."

The white Armynian dragon shook its head from the impact, then fixed its gaze on Killian. She grasped one of Papa's swords from the mantle and stepped in front of the revolutionary.

The dragon lunged. She twisted away from its oncoming claws and thrust out the sword, cursing the sudden tightness of her dress as her movement almost tore the seams.

The metal sword shattered, clattering onto the wooden planks in pieces. The jolt sent a painful twinge through her arms.

The creature stood between her and Killian. It rounded on her and eyed the window. Its only means of escape.

She raised the broken hilt of the sword defiantly.

Suddenly her feet were swept out from under her by a swipe of the creature's tail. She hit the ground, hard, her shoulder aching, head spinning. By the time she was back on her feet, Killian was gone.

Panic constricted Wynne's throat.

Then a rustling above her caught her attention. They weren't gone yet.

Morgan's voice, strained, reached her ears. Her heart warred between relief and worry.

With a glance back at Papa to make sure he was still breathing, she rushed to the window.

"Miro, guard Papa. Armor, follow me."

Wynne sat on the windowsill, then twisted to dig her fingers into the winding ivy. It held her weight, and she let out a breath as she started upward. Over the pulsing of her heart in her ears, she heard the clang of swords.

She hauled herself higher so she could spy over the edge of the raingutter.

Morgan fought with Horia on the roof, metal clashing and stone cracking as broken shingles rained down. With a deep breath, Wynne yanked herself onto the roof, her body pressed to the cold, damp tiles, and scanned the skies.

Where was Killian? The dragon?

A lantern flickered on the city wall high above, and a thick rope ladder fell down to the roof. A figure grasped it.

Killian.

"Wait!" she shouted, rising to her feet. The slant of the roof made her almost lose her balance, and by the time she glanced back, he was already climbing the rope ladder as it swayed in the wind. "Killian!"

A dragon's screech tore through the air, and Wynne glanced over her shoulder to see the Armynian dragon's claws extended for her. She ducked, but the claws never made impact.

Armor rammed into the Armynian dragon, and the two went barreling over the roof of the house. Smoke billowed as Armor's blue flames spewed from her mouth. Wynne knew she should help, but she couldn't let Killian escape.

She needed him. He had to fix Papa.

She launched herself forward, grasped the ladder, and started the climb. Her position was awkward, and her legs went wayward with each step she climbed. Then weight joined her below and the ladder straightened.

Morgan, his shirt sleeves glowing white in the moonlight, was holding the rope to steady her. Miro fought with Horia, avoiding the arc of his glowing blade.

"Climb!" his voice called up to her.

She ascended, keeping a steady rhythm. Nearby buildings flickered with silhouettes. There was no escaping the rumors now.

Below her, she heard Armor's growl and the flap of dragon wings. The rope went slack and Morgan's voice rose up in a shout. She glanced back down.

He stood, a few feet from the rope, hands up as the Armynian dragon snapped his sword in its jaws. The dragon lunged and Morgan kicked.

Too late.

The dragon's teeth clamped around his calf. He screamed, and she almost lost her grip. She judged the distance below. She could jump, reach him—but Killian would escape. Papa's healing, gone.

Steeling her nerves, Wynne resolved to let go of the rope and—

"Go!"

Morgan's voice sent a wave of energy through her, and her grip tightened. She forced herself to climb. Dragon growls and snarls sounded below her as the battle continued, but she couldn't lose focus. Killian had reached the top of the wall, disappearing over the edge, and she quickened her pace.

When she was halfway up, she looked down. Miro snapped at Horia, holding him back from the rope, until he swung his blade and Miro reared back.

The rope tensed below her at added weight, and she spotted a sailor's shirt, glowing white in the moonlight, as Morgan climbed up after her.

Her fingers curled around the wall's edge just as smoke reached her. Fire! She scrambled onto the allure of the wall, the thin walkway no more than three feet wide, and glanced back. Her eyes burned with the acrid smoke that consumed her house in blue flames.

A hand reached over the ladder, which swayed more precariously as the flames licked higher. Smoky tears blurred her vision as she grasped Morgan's hand and hauled him over the edge.

"Papa!" she called down, terror freezing her in place.

Arms wrapped around her waist to pull her back, but she shoved him away and watched, breathless, as Armor broke out through the shuttered window of the kitchen. She shook cinders from her scales.

A smoke-covered figure followed, reaching back to haul something out. Papa! The figure half-carried, half-dragged Papa out of the house and away from the fire before falling on his knees. He turned his face up, as if searching, then his eyes met hers—Morgan.

Wynne gasped.

Morgan had saved her father. He tried to stand, but fell when he put his weight on his left leg. He looked somewhere below her on the wall, fear morphing his features, before he shouted something to her. She could only read his lips.

Run.

The man she'd thought was Morgan yanked her back just as the Armynian dragon swooped up along the wall. It snatched Killian and arched high above them.

She broke free from his grip, reached for the rope. She needed to get back, get down, but the man beside her shoved her aside and severed the line. "Time to go."

He pushed her again, and she barely caught her balance against the outer parapet. The river running by the wall churned dark and malevolent below. Smoky tears still blurring her vision, she didn't even catch a glimpse of the interloper's face before he shoved her over the edge.

A scream caught in her throat, her stomach flipping somersaults in her belly, as the ground came up to meet her.

Freezing water closed over her, the terrible current of the river dragging her down, down, away from the city and the smoke that consumed her life. She kicked and flailed to the top, but the weight of her skirts threatened to pull her down.

A sudden bend and the current pulled her under.

Panic clawed at her throat.

The river's icy fingers wrapped around her limbs, yanking her further into the current. She flailed, fighting her skirts and the burning in her lungs, but the current only pulled her deeper.

She sucked in a breath and choked on water.

Hands gripped hers and hauled her up, up to the blessed surface. She collapsed on the sandy shore and retched water. Cool air burned her lungs, but she was alive.

Panting, coughing, Wynne collected herself enough to look up into the face of the man who'd shoved her over the wall.

7

Wynne staggered to her feet, fighting another coughing fit from the water burning her lungs. Hot fire rushed through her as her gaze fell on the sailor. "You," she seethed. "This is *your* fault. Without you, he wouldn't have gotten away."

The sailor was shaking the water from his dark hair, unbothered by her words. In his sailor garb, his features darkened by twilight, he looked like Morgan—and it made her angrier.

A shadow flitted over them, and rough hands gripped her arms as he yanked her back into the forest cover. She fought his grip. "What are you—?"

"Shut it, sweetheart." His breath curled around her ear.

She spun out of his grasp. "You shut—"

He glared at her. "Quiet."

The murmur of wings flapping stole her attention from him. She pursed her lips, but not because he told her to, and followed his gaze to the open clearing where he had dragged her from the water. The Armynian dragon, white against the dismal darkness, alighted on the riverbank.

Killian scrambled out from under its claws, lurching away from the creature and Horia. Heat flushed through Wynne at sight of Horia and the memory of how he'd held a knife to Papa as if his death was inconsequential.

"You better shut your mouth, Killian, or I'll drop you back in the square myself." Horia scowled. "It's a bit too late for you to play the hero."

"Then leave me. We're done." Killian unlatched his satchel and threw a glowing scroll back at him.

"They're going to catch you." Horia stowed the scroll in a bag at his side. "And then you'll see where your life ends."

"Better than the path you're taking." Killian crossed his arms.

"We have the same goals, zealot," Horia snapped. "Different means. I arm the people, you strip them of their power."

"Killing the Kings will not save the people from destruction," said Killian. "It's a false hope! Give up on this plan. See reason, Horia—"

"I would ask the same of you." Horia mounted his dragon. "You know where to find us when you realize your mistake."

With a click of Horia's tongue, the dragon was in the air. A cold gust of wind buffeted Wynne as the creature swooped low over the forest cover and out of sight.

Killian kicked at a stone on the ground, frustration hunching his shoulders. He was grumbling something to himself.

A gleam at her side made her keenly aware of the sailor beside her once more. With a careful glance, she spotted the glint of a blade in his hand and the dangerous gleam in his eye.

Icy fear washed over her. If she had to fight this sailor for the revolutionary, he would win by strength alone. Would he raise the blade to her throat if she stood in his way?

If Morgan were here, he would stand between hell and destruction to help her. She spotted the same determination in the sailor's expression, but she wouldn't let it phase her. No, she'd already made sacrifices to be here, so close to getting Killian back to the capital for her reward, and she wasn't about to back down.

She pitched her voice low. "He's mine, sea rat."

"Who's there?" Killian raised his arms defensively.

She stepped from the brush, and Killian's arms fell to his sides. "What do you want from me?" The edge of suspicion in his voice had soured to defeat, his frown betraying worry.

"You owe me." She advanced, glancing over her shoulder but not seeing the sailor emerge. She needed to put distance between the revolutionary and the sailor. "Papa's cursed because of *you*, and nothing you can do can bring him back unless you pay your life for his."

Killian ran a hand through his hair, letting out a strangled noise. "My life isn't worth anything anymore."

"I'll let the King decide that."

A whistle pierced the air from far above on the wall, and Wynne jolted. At the top of the wall, lanterns moved like luminescent ants. Silver moonlight reflected off the churning waters of the river as another pierce of a whistle sent a cold shiver through her.

She was running out of time. She needed to capture him now, so she would get the credit. So Papa would get what he needed.

A figure bolted from the shadows, shoving past Wynne and striking Killian, who stumbled back.

Wynne rushed to Killian's side and glared at the sailor. "Leave him alone."

The sailor frowned in annoyance. "I saved your life, and this is how you repay me?"

She scowled.

"We can talk details later, sweetheart, but I'm collecting now." Behind him, Wynne glimpsed the lights on the wall disappear, heard footsteps and clinking armor. He followed her gaze, and his bravado melted with the pinch in his brow. "We need to move."

Her anger flared at the sailor's words. "We?" Wynne laughed. "You're not invited. And you"—she pointed to Killian, rubbing at the welt on his cheekbone—"said you would heal my father."

"He can still be healed..." Killian frowned thoughtfully. "Maybe this is why God crossed our paths twice now... Your journey is starting."

"So why is this sea rat here?"

The sailor laughed. "You can leave. Go back. Go ahead and see what the King does to you for failing to capture a traitor. The guards will trade you in as a conspirator to lessen their own sentences."

Her stomach sank to the floor.

Killian cleared his throat and met her gaze. "There is another way to save your father. God already paid the price for him—and you." He unlatched his bag and produced a silver flask. It was no bigger than the palm of her hand, yet round like an orange.

As soon as she saw it, she snatched it from him. Too light to be worth anything. She unscrewed the cap. "Empty." She tossed the flask to the sailor. "See if you can use this to bargain for your life before the King and the priests."

A muscle in the sailor's jaw twitched. "I imagine it'll be worth more when it's actually full."

Killian nodded, fixing his gaze on Wynne again. "You must go to the well in Armyn, beyond the western border of Paradise. There, you will find God and His Son, the fountain of living water. I'll lead the way for you."

The sailor frowned. "I imagine the King will be more pleased if we brought you back to him. I'd like to be able to go home," he said, "and for that, your life will pay my debt."

Wynne glared at the sailor. "Not just you," she snapped.

The sailor scowled at her. "You're going to make this difficult."

"It would be my pleasure."

The whistle sounded again, this time sending a vibration through her bones. She spun around to see a guard dragon lunging after them. The dragon pounced. The sailor dodged, but not fast enough. He cursed as the creature's claw just missed his arm.

"Watch your head," Killian shouted, throwing his dagger. Instead of bouncing off the dragon's scales, it sank deep in the creature's shoulder. It let out a yelp and leapt away from the sailor. With a twist, it clamped its jaws around the dagger and yanked it out, flinging it away.

The dagger fell at Wynne's feet.

Even tinted red with blood, the blade seemed to glow white in the moonlight. She grasped it, debating briefly about leaving the sailor, before a frustrating sense of guilt grounded her in place. He'd saved her life, after all.

"Hey, dragon," she called. "Want some more?"

She stepped forward, brandishing the dagger, and the dragon turned on her. A spear of fear went through her as she faced the dragon almost as large as Armor.

The dragon lowered itself to pounce, but the sailor was faster. He aimed a kick at the creature's injured shoulder, and it reeled back, growling in pain. When the sailor aimed another kick at the dragon, it scrambled back toward the riverbank.

"Go, now." The voice came from Killian, standing at the edge of the forest. "Find the next town west of here and onward until you reach Armyn." Then he disappeared into the trees.

Scuffling at Wynne's back made her turn around, dagger at the ready.

The sailor glanced back along the river, where the dragon growled, then his shoulders slumped in relief. "We don't have long, but that should keep it away. Are you going to catch the revolutionary or am I?"

"His name's Killian," she grumbled. The sailor frowned, and defensiveness reared in her chest. "He told me. I didn't ask."

"He seems to like you... We could go together," the sailor offered. He looked her up and down. "I'd rather not fight a delicate thing like yourself."

She raised the dagger. "You'd be surprised."

He held out his hand. "Ryder."

The blade slipped from her hands.

It was as if all the breath had been taken from her lungs. No wonder this man reminded her so much of Morgan, with his dark hair and sturdy frame. Before her was none other than Ryder Delmar.

Her mind whirled with a flurry of thoughts. He was a thief, liar, murderer. Morgan's warnings blared in her head like the piercing whistle of the guards.

If you ever have the displeasure of meeting my brother, hide what you hold dear.

But if she was going to drag Killian back to the capital, she would need a strong pair of hands. Armor would be best, but unless she was able to escape the careful view of the watchtower guards tonight, her dragon wouldn't join her for another day at least. Ryder would be a means to an end.

She made up her mind. She took his hand. "Wynne Mayweather."

"A beautiful name to fit your countenance," he said with a wink.

Disgust broiled in her stomach. She yanked her hand back, wiped it on her dress, and snatched the flask from the grass where he'd abandoned it during the fight with the dragon. "Come on."

The way he smirked, probably expecting her to melt at his smile, made her insides churn with distrust. Even though he had a stronger build than Morgan, the glimmer of something darker underneath his light blue gaze made him all the more dangerous.

At least she'd only ever seen the aftermath of his escapades while he'd still been in the capital, even if she'd never glimpsed his face. While Addie bemoaned her brother's near-constant absence, Morgan would never tell her how many disgruntled women came to declare Ryder a scoundrel. Or how the kitchen workers had gingerly picked up the shattered bottles of liquor littering the floor after another one of Ryder's fits. It had been no surprise, then, when he was convicted of murder.

Before he could move, she bowed to the floor and plucked the revolutionary dagger, wiping the blade on the grass and tucking it into her belt. Its glow had dimmed, the only distinction from a normal blade now its white metal.

Wynne steeled her expression and started into the forest. Ryder's footsteps crunched behind her.

"You sure you know where we're going?" he asked, voice teasing.

She didn't bother with a response, just hurried her pace.

They walked quickly, weaving a random pattern through the trees to disguise their path and dampen their scent for any dragon. Soon, they would need to build a fire and dry their clothes, but hopefully they could reach a nearby town by the time they really got hungry. The whistles of the guards pierced the night, keeping her on edge.

After half an hour, her legs burning and her chest heaving, she slowed. "You can take the lead," she offered begrudgingly. She had done her best to keep a good distance between them, and if she walked any slower, he would be right on her heels. A proximity that would only make her stomach roil.

He didn't even pause before turning around in the opposite direction she'd been leading them.

"Where are you going?" She glared at his back.

"This way is west. You've been taking us east, toward the shoreline. Or the cliffs," he shrugged. "Not sure we would have seen them before walking right over the edge."

She scowled. But now that she had paused, and his footsteps were slightly further away, the murmur of the ocean reached her. Her mood soured further that he'd been right. She started after him. Another whistle tore through the night but much further away, and the tightness in her chest loosened.

Before long, they came to a dirt road. A little while later, a wooden sign hammered into the frozen ground signaled a town a few miles away: Kyrn. A small farming town, central enough to see the majority of Paradise's trade before coming into the capital in the harvest months. Now it would be nearly empty.

"The guards are gone," Ryder remarked. The whistles had ceased a while ago, a welcome reprieve.

"Though I doubt we'll be spared from seeing another Armynian," Wynne grumbled, her gaze trailing the stars in the sky and the wisps of clouds now that they were in the clearing of the dirt road.

"Well, you'll just have to defend us until we get there." He held up his hands. "I don't have any weapons," he said with a grin, "unless you count a fishing hook and line." He emptied his pockets.

She nodded as if buying his words, but she only wondered how he'd stowed his dagger so well. If she hadn't glimpsed it in his hand before confronting Killian—and if she was naive enough to trust the charming tilt of his smile—she might have believed him.

They went on a little further, but by that time she could barely feel her legs and her feet were already numb. "Could we stop here?"

Ryder stopped and huffed. "We're never going to catch him at this rate." He smiled, though this time it was decidedly forced. "Should I carry you, Winnie?"

"Go on without me," she snapped, ignoring his offer. "Have fun catching Killian on your own."

He ran a hand through his hair and let out a breath, a gesture so similar to Morgan that she scowled. She barely heard him when he said, "Here is fine." He led the way into the brush before he seemed to find a spot that was acceptable. "I'll get some wood if you can clear more space by cutting the brambles." He spread his arms wide in gesture to the space, but when his eyes met hers, there was a mischievous gleam. "Unless you want to keep warm next to me."

Wynne lifted the dagger, scowling. "I'll start cutting."

He put a hand to his chest, sighing dramatically. "You wound me, Winnie." Sighing, he left the clearing.

She stowed the dagger only when his footsteps were no longer in earshot. He would probably take some time to find the wood, so she set about clearing the thorns while she pondered whether or not to take her chances on her own.

What did Ryder say before?

He needed to bring back the revolutionary to settle a debt. Perhaps the King would accept it, a life for a life. After Ryder killed a man at the port, he'd been conscripted into naval service. That, or face execution. That's what Morgan said when he'd come back from the trial. Even if their sister Addie sang a different tune.

What did Addie see in her brother? Maybe he was sweet behind his flirtatious smirk and capricious demeanor. But sweet didn't mean good.

She shook the thoughts from her head. What she really had to figure out was how soon she could capture Killian and get away from Ryder.

At least Morgan had saved Papa. She could rest easier knowing that he was in good care. She would deal with the downfall of his reputation after his health was secured.

But if she left, it wouldn't be tonight. Now that she wasn't almost running to catch up with Ryder's long strides, her damp skirts turned icy in the winter air, and even the sweat on her scalp made her shiver.

When Ryder returned, he dropped a bundle of sticks and, after some coaxing, sparked a fire. Warmth spread out from her fingers and toes as she unlaced her boots and dried them by the fire.

Now that she sat, the events of the night flashed before her eyes in the dancing flames. Morgan running beside her to corner Killian. His reassurance at the kitchen table. She dug into her pocket, finding Morgan's ring, and pressed her closed fist to her heart. The warmth of his embrace seemed to wrap around her with the crackle of the fire.

Unwanted memories wormed their way in. Fighting Horia, scrambling to the roof, Morgan saving Papa from the flames that engulfed her house.

Morgan's scream echoed in her mind from the dragon's jaws clamping around his leg. It would be infected, as all dragon bites, and those herbs would come at an incredible cost even for the Delmars.

And Papa...

Would he understand why she was gone? If she brought back Killian, Papa would be healed for certain, and if he was made well by an offering on Morgan's part, then at least catching Killian would be enough to pay Morgan back what she would owe.

Resolve steeled in her heart.

"Hungry?"

Her gaze shot to Ryder as he pulled a pouch from his pack and handed it to her.

Her nose wrinkled before she could even register what it was. Dried fish.

But it was enough to make her stomach growl.

He leaned further. "Go ahead, take some. It'll settle your stomach before we can head out at dawn. Armyn is a long way away."

Tentatively, she brought a piece to her lips. Salty. Tough. But it was something. She stared at the fire as she chewed thoughtfully, and she could feel Ryder's gaze fixed on her profile, studying her.

She glared at him.

He looked at her fully now, his lips twitching in a smile as if he was pleased that he'd gotten her attention. "What do you know about the revolutionary?"

"Just his name." She shrugged and took another bite of the jerky, swallowing past the lump in her throat at the lie that had just fled her lips. She hoped Armor's shine wouldn't dull by her small sin, but Ryder was not to be trusted, even with this. "What about you? Haven't you been hunting him?"

"Only since Armyn fell," he started slowly, as if measuring his words. "Our captain was called back to port to hunt down the renegades, and we're to track them down. Killian is only one of a few rumored around the kingdom. He's just the most annoying."

Her skin prickled with anger. "He's spreading his curse to the country."

"It wouldn't be so bad if the people knew their history."

Wynne scowled. Never in all her youth had she glimpsed a scroll of the history of the kingdom. Not unless the priests recited from it to speak on how far the people of Paradise had fallen from the King's grace. What she knew came from Morgan's father's books, and even then, she hardly understood it.

She supposed knowing Paradise's history mattered little if Ryder was so well-versed and yet despicable.

She turned to the fire. She chewed her lip, then let out a breath. Whatever judgment the King doled out, she had to believe that, at the end of this road, there was hope for her father in the next life. The King would accept Papa in his domain, but not so long as Miro reflected the judgment of Papa's sin. But she wouldn't let it come to that.

Either Killian's capture would give her the offering she needed to save Papa's life, or the well water would revive him.

"So why are you trying to catch Killian?" She glanced at Ryder. He responded with a look as if he'd already told her, but she scowled. "You weren't exactly specific before."

"Then let me elaborate," he said, his expression suddenly sober. "I want to catch him for my family... My father is gone, and I need to get back. My family needs me."

His words struck Wynne almost with a sense of amusement as she recalled Morgan's side of the story. Ryder couldn't have run away from Paradise fast enough after his trial—and it was laughable that he would even want to go back. That anyone would even accept him after a man's blood had stained his hands.

"But," he added, a ghost of a smile playing on his lips, "perhaps he might lead us to more revolutionaries and an even bigger reward..."

He went on about the reward but Wynne's mind had snagged on something in replaying the events of the night.

"How did you find me?" Her voice was taut, like a thread stretched too far, ready to snap.

Ryder shrugged, as if her question didn't carry the accusatory tone. "Spotted your dragon chasing Killian by the inn. I got lost, so I wasn't sure what house he was in until the Armynian landed on your roof."

Had he seen Morgan? If he had, Ryder didn't seem to let on. And she bit down on asking; she didn't dare reveal her true connection to Morgan.

"Figured if Killian came to you," he continued, "he would find a way to meet you again. Revolutionaries have a habit of finding the people they're looking for."

"Why do you even want to go back home? What's left for you?" She might have been casting her hand too far here, but he was determined for something. And she didn't want to believe that going back home to serve the King would be a man's main objective. Especially if he was of any relation to Morgan. Or Addie.

Ryder cast her an amused sideways glance. "I think it's best you give up some information, Winnie."

His joking manner cast doubt on his tales. Morgan had said he was a thief. A liar. Should she believe Ryder? Trust him?

No. She had no doubt that even if the revolutionary's dagger was her weapon, Ryder was far more skilled with a fishing line and hook than she would be with a knife.

He seemed to read her expression and nodded, deciding something. "All right," he said, tossing something in the air. She caught the bundle and opened the cloth. A sweet bun with dried fruit. "Finish that. Tomorrow we're up before dawn."

She didn't protest but stared as he got up to the other side of the campfire, closer to the road, and stretched out, facing away from the fire.

While she chewed the bread, she checked her boots. Dry. Slipped them on. After a moment, she pulled Morgan's ring from her pocket, only to hook it back on the chain underneath her dress. She chewed the last piece of the bread thoughtfully, too wired for rest.

In minutes, Ryder surprised her by being fast asleep, his breathing slow and steady, like waves lapping on a sandy shore. Looking up at the dark trees overhead, feeling the crunch of autumn leaves beneath her, she wondered how long it would be before she would see the glimmer of the ocean—or her father—again.

His lungs were on fire.

Morgan fell to his knees, retching from the smoke that he'd inhaled in his dash through Wynne's house. The heat of the fire grew behind him, scorching his back through his clothes, and it took all he had to pull Elwin's ragdoll weight further away from the flames.

Blinking smoky tears from his eyes, Morgan scanned the chaos. The far end of Wynne's yard was consumed by fire, the last of the dead bushes crumbling into ash.

A voice reached his ears over the roaring flames. A guard approached him, while more herded passersby away from the nearby buildings.

Morgan finally stood, though his left leg trembled. Miro came up under his arm, supporting his side. At a glance, he couldn't see Armor, but he knew Wynne had made it over the wall. She should be back soon with Killian.

There was no hiding his face now, so he lifted his chin, and the guard paused, recognition glinting in his eyes.

"Lord Delmar. What business do you have here?" His calculating eyes were fixed on Miro, who shed a few scales as Morgan shifted.

"Spotted the flames and came running." As casually as he could muster, Morgan waved a hand to gesture at the house behind him as two Mandorian dragons spewed water on the flames. Their webbed paws pushed over the rest of the burning structure, exposing the last of the flames to douse.

Smoky tears still spilled from Morgan's eyes, but his vision was sharpening. He spotted two guards by the wall, but they hadn't seem to have found much of a trace.

Good.

"I believe you have more important matters to attend to." The guard eyed him curiously, and Morgan grimaced, knowing what Mother would say if she knew he was among the 'common people' as she put it. She would balk even more if she saw the guards' dragons with their noses to the ground like hunting dogs.

"Anything is important when it involves our citizens."

"We spotted an Armynian dragon. The same white one as this morning. What did you see?" The guard procured a small journal and opened it, looking at Morgan expectantly.

He fought a scowl. He didn't need an interrogation, and he chose the quickest method of shutting one down. "I was attacked. Which one of your men was to blame for letting that Armynian through? It soared right over their heads. They would be responsible for my health, seeing as I was injured defending the residents of this house."

The guard's gaze dropped to Morgan's left leg, the fabric now dotted with blood. His face paled. "I-I'm sure we can reach an understanding, Lord Delmar."

"I'm sure we can," he said, fighting a grimace at his caustic tone. The throbbing in his left leg only flared angrily with each movement as he shifted his weight. "Fortify the defenses. Man the ballistas. It may be back tonight."

Morgan glanced over the guard's shoulder to the other guards with their dragons. One had a revolutionary dagger in his hand while others pointed upward at the wall, and Morgan's heart seized. Could one of them have spotted Wynne?

"Of course, Lord Delmar."

Relief coursed through Morgan. For a while, at least, the questions would be silenced. Perhaps just long enough for Wynne to get back and save her father with the revolutionary's capture. The revolutionary's face flashed fearfully in Morgan's mind, but he dismissed it with a shake of his head.

"Is there anything else you require tonight, my lord?"

Morgan held onto his facade and schooled his expression into neutrality. "Aside from your discretion, I need two of your men to take Mr. Mayweather to the manor."

The guard nodded, eyeing Elwin's prone body and waving a hand. "As you wish."

Two guards knelt, but when Elwin wouldn't stand, breathing shallow and ragged, they hefted him up between them. "They will be received at the manor," said Morgan. "I will summon the priests myself when I arrive."

As soon as they were gone, the guard's gaze shot back to Morgan, and he wrung his hands. "Do you require assistance?"

Morgan shook his head. "I leave the events of tonight to be resolved by your hands."

He started down the cobblestone streets to the manor. It couldn't have been after two in the morning, the silver moon still high in the sky.

His fingers brushed the iron key in his pocket, and he grimaced. If he didn't get back soon to let Orgul out before Mother saw, he would have hell to pay.

When he got to the manor's gate, the whole house was alive with commotion at Elwin's arrival. He caught a glimpse of a servant setting a guest room overlooking the courtyard, and the guards that had carried Elwin trudged down the stairs just as he stepped into the foyer.

Morgan handed them a few coins and sent them on their way. Miro shook free from supporting Morgan's frame and bounded up the steps, surely on his way to check on Elwin as a dusting of flakes followed his trail.

"Should we call them?" a voice said somewhere down the hall. Felipe, Lord Ashton's son. Despite being a few years younger than Morgan, Felipe was a good friend and someone of confidence, though Mother would insist no Ashton was trustworthy.

"Not yet," answered Addie's voice, low and strained but getting ever louder as footsteps echoed. "I will do what I can, but we must not let the word spread beyond these walls. Wynne would not want her father to be disgraced as such, and neither would my mother, as I'm sure she'd blame you..."

Morgan stepped carefully around the rug, leaning one hand against the wall to take pressure off his injured leg. When Addie entered the foyer, he forced a smile at the concern in her eyes. "Morgan, I was just looking for you. What happened to Elwin? What's—ah, you're bleeding!"

She let out a cry as she rushed to his side, abandoning Felipe at the threshold. Her arm went under his, supporting him, and at her steadying presence, he realized he'd been swaying.

His leg was throbbing worse than it had when he was at Wynne's house, and warm blood was seeping into his boot. Addie started to pull him to the stairs, then stopped when he winced.

"I'll fetch some boiled water and rags." She disappeared down the hall.

Morgan stumbled to the sitting parlor, where at least he would only dirty the wood floors.

Felipe followed silently and now stood by the mantle of the fireplace. Sharp brown eyes gleamed under a mop of reddish-blond hair. He studied Morgan with an expression akin to frustration, though Morgan knew it wasn't with him.

"Was it Orgul?" Felipe asked.

Morgan winced. "An Armynian."

Felipe knew of Orgul's fits, but his own dragon was as docile and elegant as Whisper. The pristine white creature settled at Felipe's feet, no larger than Armor, and blinked its red eyes at Morgan lazily.

Felipe grimaced at Morgan's words, then his eyes sparked with some kind of anger. "Are the rumors true?"

"Does it matter?" Morgan let out a mirthless laugh. "The people only believe what they see..."

"But more fall ill every day," Felipe insisted, frowning. "What if we had the solution?"

"Have you seen the sick in your province?" Morgan asked, thinking back on Elwin. He wished it weren't so, but he was more and more convinced it was the same sickness that took Father.

Felipe nodded, running a hand through his unruly red hair. "They're not just sick in body but in mind, too. Do your father's books have anything on the matter?"

Morgan gave him a wry smile. "Your true motives revealed, I see."

Felipe chuckled, rubbing the back of his neck. "Not entirely."

"I'll let you know if I find a cure," he said, though he wished his words didn't sound as hollow as he felt them to be.

Addie returned then with the clean rags and water. "Mother's going to be livid when she sees the spots you left on the rug," she said, flashing a grin. If she had any fear of Mother's wrath, she didn't let on as she sat on the floor before him and set about peeling back the torn fabric.

Her face held the same determination it had when she'd tended his burns this morning, but there was an anger that simmered beneath the surface that unnerved him.

"Tell me what happened," she said stiffly.

He explained the circumstances that led him to the fountain, the chase for the revolutionary, and the fire. By the time he finished, her jerky movement had softened. She wrapped up his leg with the same bandages that marked his arms and sat back on her heels.

"The good news is it was a clean bite and you don't need stitches." She handed the water and rags to a servant and whispered some instructions before finally settling into the chair beside his. Felipe occupied the armchair by the fire, knitting his hands together and watching them.

Morgan shot her a wry grin, dreading her next words. "And the bad news?"

She met his expression with a solemn one. "You know."

His smile fell. Frustration bubbled up in him. "I thought I would have more time."

"You'll have a few days, but we need to get a tonic within the hour to ease the worst of the infection to come."

She stood, but he grasped her hand, and she sat reluctantly, fixing him with an annoyed look.

"Then take a few minutes with me and Felipe, please? I don't want to hear what Mother will say when she wakes up with this racket."

Addie nodded, though her green eyes didn't light up again with mirth as they had this morning. In fact, all excitement seemed to have drained out of her.

Morgan shifted in his chair at something digging into his thigh. He pulled the iron key from his pocket, placing it on the small table between the two parlor chairs they occupied. As he did so, a servant returned with three mugs, which Felipe accepted.

"Hot chocolate?" Felipe smiled as he handed Addie and Morgan their cups. "Good choice."

Addie, still frowning, blushed. Her gaze settled on the key on the table between her and Morgan.

Guilt niggled at Morgan. Orgul had been quite patient when Morgan had chained him up in the cellar earlier in the night. Father hiding his dragon from prying eyes was a Symaran habit, one of the many 'steps' to righteousness, he'd claimed. The chaining of a dragon was a custom abhorred by Paradise but Morgan had little choice.

Morgan would release Orgul, but not right now. He didn't need to add the fear of being roasted to the list of the night's endeavors.

He let out a sigh and grasped her hand, squeezing it. "I will deal with this. Go get some rest." He stood, testing his leg but masking the pain as best he could. It still couldn't quite support his weight, but it would be enough to get him out the door.

"Where are you going?" Addie stood with him.

He glanced out the window, where the stars still winked in the sky. "I need to get the herbs."

"I'll go." Addie yanked her coat from beside the door, moving so fast that Morgan was breathless keeping up with her, grasping the wall against the pain shooting up his leg.

"No," he rasped. "Someone will recognize you and make assumptions. Just leave it be, Addie. It's not your problem—"

"It is when it comes to Wynne, and even more when it comes to you." She buttoned her coat. Her dragon, Whisper, nestled again on her shoulders like a roosting pigeon. "I'm faster than you, anyway, and I should have enough saved for the offering."

She disappeared up the stairs, footsteps thumping on the second floor. Morgan grimaced. Felipe joined him, shouldering his own coat.

Morgan stood by the door as she bounded down the steps. "Addie, please. You were saving that for—"

"Quiet, Morgan." Her eyes flickered to Felipe and back to Morgan. She leaned up, kissed his cheek, and shoved him back a step. "I'll be back within the hour. I promise." And she was out, with a blast of cold air that blew in through the door.

"I'll make sure she doesn't get into trouble," Felipe offered. He flashed Morgan a sheepish smile before following Addie out the door. He figured Felipe would try to help with the costs, and he hoped to rely on Addie's stubborn streak to shy away from monetary assistance.

Morgan scowled, pocketed Orgul's key, and watched her walk down the street until she was out of sight. He turned and froze at a pair of green eyes pinning him in place for the second time today.

"Where is Adelaide?" Mother demanded.

"Going to the Temple." He decided not to tell her about his dragon bite. Why bother when he knew that the outcome would be the same?

"Alone?" Her eyes narrowed.

"Not alone."

Her scowl deepened in distrust. "Those Ashtons are trouble."

"Go ahead and stop him, then." Morgan crossed his arms. "I'm sure there are quite a few nobility who would love to speculate on why Addie and Felipe are out at this hour."

Mother's lips pursed tight, into a thin white line that made her eyes flash like Addie's. "Clean the spots off the rug." Then she left down the hall, though Morgan figured his interrogation wasn't over yet.

Running a hand through his hair, Morgan started up the stairs to the next important task. He entered the guest room, warm with a crackling fire and inviting with the scent of lavender and pine from the western border of Paradise.

A candle by the bedside cast a somber glow over the room. Elwin's breathing was shallow and fast, and his face was a ghostly pallor.

"Where is my redeemer?" Elwin rasped. "My King, my God..." He fell into incoherent mumbling, but his words rang in Morgan's head in a way that made him sick. How arduously had Father strived for redemption only to face the grave in the end?

He left the room and found himself in his study, his fingers roving over the bookshelves for that one book of Father's. He grasped the cracked leather spine, brought the tome to his desk and stared at the cover.

Psalms.

His heart twisted as he flipped through the pages, his fingertips brushing over careful writing in the margins. Father's handwriting, clear and determined, had tried to find meaning in the pages.

Morgan found the song he was looking for and put both hands on the book as if he feared the words would fly off the page.

> *Bless the LORD, O my soul,*
> *And forget not all His benefits:*
> *Who forgives all your iniquities,*
> *Who heals all your diseases,*
> *Who redeems your life from destruction,*
> *Who crowns you with loving kindness and tender mercies,*
> *Who satisfies your mouth with good things...*

The words rang with some kind of truth, but he couldn't make sense of it. What kind of King was this God that would heal and forgive? Why were Father's last words calling out to a God that didn't answer to crippling self-denial?

> *For as the heavens are high above the earth,*
> *So great is His mercy toward those who fear Him;*
> *As far as the east is from the west,*
> *So far has He removed our transgressions from us.*
> *As a father pities His children,*
> *So the LORD pities those who fear Him.*
> *For he knows our frame;*
> *He remembers that we are dust.*
> *As for man, his days are like grass;*
> *As a flower of the field, so he flourishes.*
> *For the wind passes over it,*

And it is gone,
And its place remembers no more.

And before his very eyes, the words became gibberish. Morgan blinked, rubbing his eyes, but the pages were indecipherable.

"Not again." He slammed the book shut, letting out a breath and running his hands through his hair. He stowed the book in his shelf again and started toward Elwin's room when he heard the coughing.

Morgan settled into a plush armchair beside the window and watched the sky turn dark as the moon neared the horizon. Miro was nestled on the opposite side of the room, hidden in the shadows where the firelight didn't reach. Only his yellow eyes blinked back at Morgan.

Elwin had been a good man, tough like the steel he forged. Sharp with his words, cutting anyone down that might threaten his family. They'd gotten along well, at first, as Morgan had been little more than a scholar... Until his family name had become a burden that weighed on Wynne's shoulders as much as his, and Elwin's opinion of him had soured.

His leg still throbbed, and now that he sat, his muscles ached from the events of the night. Wynne... Could she be with the revolutionary now?

She might be heeding Killian's words to find healing...

Or hunting him down to bring him to the Temple.

Hearing Elwin's ragged breaths, Morgan couldn't help but wonder, regardless of what she chose, if she would even make it back in time.

8

Wynne didn't know when she fell asleep, but she woke with a start. She reached for a pillow, but touched cold rock beneath her. The scent of damp earth filled her nostrils as she sucked in a breath.

Then she groaned in remembrance. The rope, the fire, the river, the run through the forest—

"Morning, Winnie."

—and Ryder.

She stifled another groan and forced herself to sit up, blinking the crust from her burning eyes. A frigid breeze whipped the canopy of branches above her, shaking loose the last of the autumn leaves in the pre-dawn stillness. "It's not even light out."

"A hunter's day starts before the guards are up," Ryder answered, and when she sent a sharp glare at him, he grinned cheekily. "Let's go. I hear someone coming down the road."

That jolted her awake. She crawled to meet Ryder crouched at the brush, where he peered out at the shadows moving from down the road. From the capital.

A team of horses was pulling an empty wagon, jostling over every bump on the road and almost tossing its driver from his seat. He grumbled at the animals, his weathered skin accentuating the lines of annoyance in his face. From the musty smell of animal manure as the wagon neared, the man was a farmer, most likely having sold to the market butchers in the capital. Wynne had seen quite a few like him come through the market after the scorched harvest earlier this year.

Ryder stepped forward onto the road, dirt crunching beneath his feet.

The farmer reined his horses to a halt. The man examined Ryder through narrowed eyes. His dragon peeked its head out from the hay in the cart.

"Long live the King," Ryder greeted.

"Long may he reign." The farmer's hold loosened on his reins, though he still eyed Ryder suspiciously. The horses snorted and pawed the ground. "What's the likes of you doing out here?"

Ryder put on a sheepish but charming smile. "My sister and I wanted to visit our mother in Oran. We're worried for her..." He gestured for Wynne to come out, and she stepped forward.

The farmer nodded solemnly as he appraised them, his red beard brushing his brown shirt. "Take advice from an old farmer, boy, and get your mother out of the town. My brother over there's seen some Armynians moving around those parts. Migrating this way. Best not to be in their path, till the King should stop them."

The sky, once a dark midnight, was turning gray. Shadows lightened. The farmer's dragon let out a huff, and the farmer tensed. "Where are your dragons?"

"My sister and I sent them on ahead." Ryder slipped an arm over her shoulders, and she would have shaken him off if it wouldn't have blown Ryder's story. "She was so worried that she couldn't sleep even when we had to stop. They'll be at Oran by now, though I pray they haven't seen any of those revolutionaries yet."

Mention of the revolutionary seemed to stiffen something in the farmer's countenance, and his scowl deepened, eyes flashing. He flicked the reins as if to ready his horses.

Wynne elbowed Ryder and stepped forward once his arm moved from around her shoulders. "We'd have more peace if we could reach our mother faster. Would you take us the last stretch to Kyrn? My brother could help in whatever help you require on your farm today."

"You'd have to go without pay, boy," he said, scowling. "Just sold my best stock."

Ryder stepped forward again, though with a slight hesitation now. Wynne fought the smirk tugging at her lips. No doubt he didn't want to do the work that would be required of him. "That is a fair trade," he said, with barely a grimace.

That seemed to tear down the farmer's defenses greatly, and he moved from the middle of the bench to let them climb up. His dragon blinked blearily at them as Wynne and Ryder mounted the wagon. Ryder sat in the middle, and Wynne squeezed herself at the end, bracing one hand on the splintered ledge and hoping she wouldn't fall off the jostling cart as the farmer's horses broke into a trot.

While they rode, the overcast skies began to drop the first winter's snow. The flakes clung to the vestiges of the red and orange leaves, and covered the horses' prints as they trotted through the forest in a westernly direction, further and further away from the sea she called home.

She wrapped her shawl tighter.

Ryder kept up conversation with the man as they went along, and the farmer seemed to open up more and more. He even offered to take them as far as Oran, but Ryder declined politely. "No need to take you from your duties for so long."

Perhaps it had more to do with the fact that the more they were with him, the more questions he would ask. Or that he would catch wind of their hunt for Killian and try to take the reward for himself.

They reached the edge of Kyrn close to midday—or as much as she could tell in the fuzzy light diffused by the thick snowflakes. The entire town could best be described as a road around which stood some houses, a stable, tavern and inn, and various merchants. More buildings, perhaps shops and markets, were boarded up now, awaiting the warmth of the spring to thaw the deserted trade routes. The rest of the country should have been dotted with barns and silos, but they were invisible now with the cold fog settling over the landscape.

The farmer and Ryder settled on how Ryder could help him clean out the cart for tomorrow's market. Before Ryder set away to do so, he went to Wynne's side where she pressed into the shadow of one of the horses. "I'll get some supplies and secure a horse. Be back here in half an hour with winter clothes for the both of us." He squinted as he glanced behind her. "We can't stay here long."

She opened her mouth to demand an answer, but the jingle of coins quieted her. Ryder held out a pouch. "This should be enough." When she didn't take it, he winked. "You can pay for dinner, Winnie."

She rolled her eyes, took the money, and started down to the brick-faced building that displayed clothing.

The few passersby wore coats already, as did their dragons, which Wynne found puzzling. Armor could dig through ice in the dead of winter without a tremble. Maybe it was something about the dragons out west. When a burly man eyed her with curiosity, Wynne hurried her pace to the store.

The warmth of a cozy fire greeted her when she opened the front door, bell jingling to announce her arrival. The clerk, a petite woman robed in fur, waved her inside, batting the bunched snow from Wynne's skirts.

"Oh, honey, you look like you're just about freezing your tail off." The shopkeeper sat Wynne down before the fire. "What're you doing out here?"

"I'm coming from the capital."

"Where's your dragon, honey?"

Alarm shot through Wynne's system at the shopkeeper's innocent question. She studied Wynne with bright blue eyes. "She's with my mother in Oran," answered Wynne quickly. "We feared for her with the storm. And with the Armynians, too..."

"There are many things to fear now," said the shopkeeper, a sober tone coloring her voice, though her expression remained bright. "At least it's still quiet around here."

"I'm sure," said Wynne slowly, sinking into the chair by the fire.

The woman told her to wait here. Good thing, since now that Wynne was sitting, she thought she might need dragon strength to fight the weariness in her bones.

Still, her mind whirred with worry. Papa's sickness. And Morgan's dragon bite.

Even though the Temple had the healing herbs in abundance, it would be a sacrificial payment even for the Delmars. In normal circumstances, the perpetrator would be put on trial and they would pay for the victim's healing. But the Armynian was long gone, and Wynne was sure Morgan's mother, Diane, would want to keep Morgan's injury a secret, like how she also strived to fracture Morgan and Wynne's engagement.

When the shopkeeper returned, Wynne stood. "I don't have long."

"Neither do I, honey. Come over." She gestured to the bundle of furs she'd brought from the back, laying each one on the counter. "Try these first."

The shopkeeper handed Wynne winter boots made of thick leather. She tried the new pair and took a few tentative steps. Rubber soles made the boots far more flexible than her pair, and the lining was nothing less than deliciously warm fur.

"These are perfect." Wynne joined the shopkeeper again at the counter. "How much?"

The shopkeeper had been examining two coats, and now she handed Wynne the lighter colored one. "Give me your shawl."

Wynne traded her threadbare shawl for the fur coat. It was a thick ermine thing that fell all the way to her calves and made her feel like she was sitting by the fire, sewing, laughing with her parents before everything went awry.

The woman passed a pair of gloves over the counter before Wynne could even thank her. Despite all the layers, none of it restricted her movement too much, and even the gloves felt like an extension of her fingers.

Wynne felt in her skirt pocket, touching the pouch of coins from Ryder. She'd been mentally tallying the items, and a familiar fear had settled on her chest. "How much do I owe you?"

"Is there anything else you need, dear?" The shopkeeper ignored Wynne's question.

"My companion needs a coat and boots." Wynne forced a smile. "I'll pay for it as well, of course."

The woman smiled and ducked into the back. When she returned, her dragon, about the size of Armor, walked at her side. The creature's slender green tail flicked back and forth, finally curling around the woman's wrist like a bracelet. She handed a second coat to Wynne, the large boots, and told her the total.

"Are you sure?" It didn't seem like nearly enough.

The woman's smile brightened. "Of course."

The woman looked over Wynne's shoulder, and Wynne followed her gaze to the wall of white that devoured the light outside.

"Thank you for your help," Wynne said slowly. Guilt swirled in her chest at the woman's generosity. "Is there anything you need?"

"Prayer," she said. The shopkeeper's dragon laid its head on the counter between them. The green-scaled creature examined Wynne with its piercing gaze. "The King is the only one who can keep peace 'round here."

Peace.

The word bounced against Wynne's skull. Had she ever felt peace within the walls of the capital?

She set some amount of money on the counter and rushed from the shop and out into the brewing snowstorm. The woman's trailing words called after her, "May the King watch over you," but she ignored it. She wanted to banish the worry away like she always had, but now she held onto it as she rushed over to the stables, cradling Ryder's coat and boots in her arms.

She reached the stables just as Ryder was leading a horse out. The horse's hooves flashed as the creature stomped, the wind whipping tornadoes of snowflake flurries around them.

"You wouldn't believe me if I told you the kind of interrogation I had to go through to get Tempest," he said under his breath as he put on the coat. "The stablemaster was looking for my dragon." He paused, his eyes roving over her attire and his new boots in her hand. "How much did the shop charge?"

"Check for yourself." Her tone was sharp, but she didn't care. She needed to get as far away from here as possible. Away from the shopkeeper's warm smile that only seemed to be a second away from bringing hot tears to Wynne's eyes.

He opened the money purse and scowled. "Robbery," he grumbled, taking his boots from her outstretched hands. After a quick moment of slipping them on, he tucked the old boots in the horse's saddlebag. "Let's go."

The horse sauntered behind them as Ryder led them out to the center of the street. All the shop windows were blurs in the dim light. Ryder mounted the horse, then reached down for her.

"Wait!" A sharp voice called over the wind and Wynne instinctively froze, drawing her hand back from Ryder and spinning on her heel.

The tension in her chest didn't unfurl as the shopkeeper strode purposefully toward her, determination in the lines of her face. "You overpaid." She held out her hand, the coins winking at Wynne from the woman's palm.

Wynne stepped forward, but a growl from the shopkeeper's dragon froze her in place. The creature had fixed its gaze on Wynne with renewed intensity. The shopkeeper's gaze fell to the white-metal dagger at Wynne's hip, and the lady's brows furrowed in confusion. "Who are you?"

"Nobody." Wynne snatched the coins from the woman's hand, stuffing them into her coat.

"You're one of them." The woman stepped back, her dragon growling at her side. "Hold her here." The shopkeeper's gaze was as hard and unforgiving as ice.

The dragon advanced. Behind Wynne, Ryder's horse stomped its hooves, and Ryder was calling to her. But she would never be able to mount before the green dragon darted at her, either injuring her or the horse or both.

The shopkeeper had disappeared into the flurry of snowflakes, but threatening orange lanterns bobbed further down the street, nearing now.

Wynne drew the dagger and met the dragon's gaze. "I'm not what you think I am," she said, raising her free palm. "I don't want to hurt you."

The dragon lowered its haunches. Green lit the back of its throat only a moment before it pounced.

She scrambled to the left, but not fast enough. Pain stung her shoulder as the dragon's talons swiped across it, slicing the coat sleeve. Its hot breath polluted the air, and fear constricted her throat.

She was backed up against the shop now. The dragon's tail swiped back and forth, and beyond it, Ryder fought with the restless horse.

"Stop it," she snapped at the dragon. "Your master will be judged if you harm me. Would you like your precious King to dole out punishment?"

The orange lights neared. The shopkeeper's voice came shrill and insistent. Wynne was running out of time.

"Come on, Wynne!" Ryder called.

Wynne lunged forward, brushing past the dragon. It swiped a paw at her, catching her skirts, and she tripped. Cold snow dug into her hands, but she scrambled to her feet as the dragon's claws scrabbled on the ground behind her.

The shopkeeper's dragon pounced again, and she struck. The blade sank into flesh and hit bone, but the dragon was too heavy to fling away. The creature slammed into her, pinning her to the ground, and the breath was squeezed from her lungs. Golden light from the shops blurred before her eyes.

Suddenly the weight was gone, and Wynne staggered to her feet, hands trembling now as she gripped the dagger, and swiped at the snow in her eyes.

The green creature was pinned by a silver dragon—Armor. Her dragon let out a roar, blue fire building in her throat, but the shopkeeper's dragon shoved her off and hobbled back toward the ever-nearing orange lights.

Wynne met the electric blue gaze of her silver dragon. "Armor!" She dropped to one knee, releasing the dagger and opening her arms wide to catch her dragon in an embrace.

A purr rumbled through Armor's chest, sending a flash of warmth through Wynne. She wished she could speak with Armor just then, ask her about Papa, about Morgan, but if her dragon was here, then at least they couldn't be in mortal danger.

Visions flashed through her mind. Her house burning. Climbing over the wall and following Wynne's steps without a scent or a trace, a skill only achievable by a person's own dragon. Then darkness and trees and blanketing snow.

Wynne untangled herself from her dragon at the urgency of Ryder's voice. He had dismounted the horse, grasping its reins, and brought it toward them.

"Wynne, we can't stay here."

Armor pawed the ground, shaking her head back down toward the road.

The Temple flashed in her mind.

Wynne shook her head. "I can't go back, Armor. Not yet. This revolutionary will give me a reward that's enough for Papa."

A sudden force slammed into her from behind, but Wynne spun, shedding her coat and spinning back around to glare at the shopkeeper's dragon. "You won't give up, will you?"

The green-scaled creature dripped steaming blood onto the thick fur coat. It turned the snow a sickly pink.

Armor lunged for the opponent, and they went tumbling into the alley.

Wynne snatched her dagger from the snow and shouldered her coat once more.

"Let her go, Wynne. Armor has the upper hand." Ryder was back on the horse, reaching for her. "Get on."

"I'm not leaving her." She started after Armor.

Horse hooves beat against the ground, and she shot a glance over her shoulder as Ryder galloped away. Frustration bubbled up in her, but she felt a glimmer of satisfaction. She was right not to trust him.

"Armor!" she called, squinting into the alley, unable to see past the snow and darkness between the buildings. Blue and green fire flashed; vicious snarls reached her ears.

A weight suddenly wrapped around her waist, and she was swept off her feet as Ryder yanked her on the horse.

"What do you think you're doing?" she snapped at him, squirming in his grip but afraid to slip at this speed. She grasped the horse's mane for balance.

The wind bit her cheeks, and she shivered despite her coat.

A glance back sent a wave of icy fear through her—the green dragon, in hot pursuit. Where was Armor?

"Ryder, turn around!"

"Duck!" Ryder yanked the reins to the right, and the horse dodged a sudden downfall of snow from a breaking branch.

The green dragon leaped, landing on Ryder's back. He let out a curse, pulling something silver from his pack as he shoved the reins into her hands. He sliced down the dragon's back with the dagger. Sparks ricocheted before the metal shattered. The green dragon snapped at Ryder's face.

Wynne yanked the horse to a slower pace and twisted around in the saddle. Grasping the revolutionary's dagger, she stuck it into the creature's side.

It let out a roar but let go, dropping to the snow.

"Go!" Ryder yanked the reins from her hands and started the horse back into a breakneck pace.

They went on, seeming to fly over the snow, until the horse's steps became unsteady, and there was no indication of anything following them for quite some time.

She felt defenseless now, knowing she had left her dagger buried in the dragon's flesh. And she was reminded once again of the reasons she couldn't take Ryder at his word: he'd promised he didn't have a weapon, but he had his dagger. The same dagger, now notched and shattered, that he tucked back into his pack.

They rode on in silence. Wynne picked up Armor's footsteps behind them, and relief flooded her.

Now that there was some space between them and their pursuers, Ryder slowed the horse. The horse's trot was steady, but Wynne still couldn't stop shaking. Armor trotted beside them now.

"She's beautiful," he said, voice humble for the first time since she'd started the journey with him. But a glance behind her told her that his expression was somber and serious.

"I'm no saint," she grumbled.

"Better than me."

9

MORGAN STARTED FROM A dreamless sleep at a sudden pressure to his shoulder, shaking him awake. "Get up, quickly."

Mother.

He wiped the sleep from his eyes, squinting at the sunlight streaming through the window. Dawn. He sat upright, letting out a groan.

Orgul.

Now Morgan would really feel Orgul's frustration, and without the derangement to blame.

He glanced over at Elwin. Still sleeping, but not as pale as last night. And his expression was one of peace, not torment. Good. That was one thing dealt with.

"Get changed. You look filthy." Mother pressed a clean white rag into his hands. "The Prince is here to see you."

Alarm seized Morgan as he stood, then pain shot up his leg and he gasped. "D-did he say why?"

"No." Mother scowled as she eyed his injury. "But I hope you covered your tracks from last night."

Morgan opened his mouth to say something, but Mother lifted a hand. "Don't tell me what you did. The less I know, the less I have to lie. Go deal with it." She pushed Morgan out of the room and closed the door behind them both.

"Where's Addie?" Morgan glanced over at his sister's bedroom door, ajar. If she wasn't here, she must've been down stealing some pastries from the cook. "Does she know the Prince is here?"

Mother's expression tightened, her eyes full of meaning. "No."

Now fear crashed over Morgan like an icy bath. "Where is she?"

His words seemed to yank her from some faraway place her mind had retreated to. "All the servants are out searching. Lord Ashton is also looking for his son," she said stiffly. "I will tend to Elwin now. Go to the Prince; he is in your study. We will speak later."

Morgan changed quickly in his room, wetting his hair to slick down the dark curls and scrubbing at the ash and grime coating his face. Just a glimpse of his reflection in the mirror and he let out another groan. Dark purple colored the skin beneath his eyes, and a miserable gray pallor cast over his face even after he scrubbed the soot away.

He checked his leg. The bandages were still white, but the dull throb would soon become a roaring ache if he didn't get the herbs from the Temple.

Once he found Addie, he would have to get some himself and repay her with the savings he'd set aside for a new life in Mandor. A life away from the Prince and the council and the judgment.

It was torture enough to have to meet with Prince Tannin for the council, but worse to have him enter Morgan's own home.

The last time the Prince had come through the doors of the manor was to pass condolences for Father's death ten years ago.

Morgan had been shocked as Mother changed from a grieving wife to a cold-faced noble as the Prince announced they were still to look over the city.

Morgan dried his hair and let out a breath. He would deal with the Prince, whatever he wanted, and then he would find Addie. He had to.

And free Orgul—but Morgan didn't hear his dragon bellowing in the cellar, so he had time. At least, for now.

Steeling his expression into a mask of disinterest, Morgan strode into his study. Bookshelves lined the walls on either side, and at the far end, below a tall window, was his desk. His peppermint candles were lit, and Morgan fought a frown.

And there, with his boots on the desk, leaning so far back in Morgan's chair that he thought the man might tumble back and go through the window, was Prince Tannin.

Morgan remained standing, biting down frustration. As precious gifts from Wynne, he didn't burn the candles without reason, but it seemed the Prince wanted to take a flame to his life and watch it burn. He bowed slightly. "How may I be of service?"

The Prince scoffed, his eyes flashing with anger. "Don't play at hospitality." The Prince swung his feet off the desk, boots stomping on the ground as he leaned forward. "If it were up to me, Delmar, I'd have you buried with your father, but the King favors you more than you deserve."

He tossed a bundle of papers on Morgan's desk. All of Morgan's other documents had been swept to the side in a haphazard pile.

"The King wants you to do a formal inquiry. You are hereby decreed to investigate, hunt, and retrieve the revolutionary. And everyone that is found with him."

Morgan couldn't fight the frown that tugged his lips downward at the onslaught of the King's request. He knew the Prince didn't care for him or his family, but he'd never guessed the Prince would want him dead. Or that the King would somehow stay Tannin's hand—and make Morgan into something of a bounty hunter.

What would the King's favor get him?

His leg throbbed from the dragon bite. He could use the favor for healing, spare his family the money for the herbs.

Could this blessing be what he needed to keep Orgul in check?

Perhaps it would even be enough to free his family from the Prince's council altogether.

"It is imperative that you and your dragon do so together." The Prince smirked, eyes flicking over Morgan's shoulder to the space where Orgul normally occupied.

The iron key weighed heavily in Morgan's pocket. "Is that all?" He fought the urge to shift under the Prince's gaze, which fixed intently on him like a snake looking to strike its prey.

"Not quite." The Prince grinned, sending a shiver of apprehension down Morgan's spine. He reached into his blazer and removed a white scroll.

The door opened.

Morgan turned and his brows drew together in confusion. "Felipe?"

Felipe came to his side and lowered his voice so only Morgan could hear. "It's Addie."

The tone of his voice and the white pallor to his face sent a wave of fear through Morgan. He didn't wait to be excused but started moving toward the door to the study. "Tell me more," he whispered to Felipe.

"Stay, Delmar," called the Prince. "I'm sure I can be of service." He knit his hands together, planting his elbows on Morgan's desk. His eyes gleamed with rapt attention. "What is the problem, Lord Ashton?"

Felipe shot Morgan a worried glance but obeyed the Prince. "Adelaide is being held by the Temple," he said, measuring his words. "Her penalty is under investigation, but it would be best if Morgan could come and clear it up."

A penalty. What could Addie have done?

Morgan's stomach sank. He had the sneaking suspicion he was to blame. She'd gone to the Temple on his behalf, for his healing.

A sudden patter of footsteps past the study caught Morgan's attention, and he spotted Mother's form flying down the corridor. He didn't ask for permission; he just went after her.

"Mother," he called.

She didn't seem to have heard him as she rushed down the steps to the foyer, where her dragon belched out streams of smoke as it paced. Morgan's heart leapt in his throat as he followed her. He caught her arm just as she reached for the door, ignoring her dragon's warning growl.

"Mother, wait."

Her face was tight with fear, and tendrils of her silver-brown hair had slipped from her usual immaculate bun. "I need to go, Morgan." Her eyes were bright with tears. "I must see her."

"I'm sure all is well." The smooth voice stopped Morgan cold, and he turned. The Prince strolled down the last steps of the staircase. He offered Mother what might have been a reassuring smile, but Morgan only got the impression of a snake flashing its fangs.

"I must see for myself, Your Highness." Mother's eyes sparked. Though her expression was neutral, Morgan could see the gears grinding behind her eyes, the absolute fury radiating from the slight downward curve of her mouth as she faced the Prince.

Prince Tannin nodded solemnly, though Morgan saw straight through the facade. "Of course, Diane. May the King weigh in her favor."

Mother scowled and spun on her heel. She flung open the door and disappeared down the walkway to the street. Morgan had reached the door when the Prince's voice caught him around the throat.

"We're not finished, Delmar," he said coolly.

The fire of hatred in the Prince's eyes flashed in Morgan's mind, and he froze, his eyes pinned on the open door, the bright blue sky and freedom.

Felipe cast Morgan a glance over his shoulder before he left in Mother's wake, his dragon almost dragging its paws. The door clicked shut behind them like the bars of a prison cell.

Silence suffocated the foyer, and it was all Morgan could do to turn back to the Prince, who had turned to inspect Father's portrait overlooking the entrance.

"Your father was a brilliant man," Prince Tannin said, "for being Symaran." His voice had lost the charm in speaking with Mother, now cold and derisive.

Defensiveness coiled in Morgan's gut, but he couldn't leave until the Prince had finished whatever he'd come for. "He taught me everything I know, Your Highness," he answered stiffly.

"Tell me, Morgan,"—the Prince reached up, touching the golden frame of the portrait—"did your father miss Symara?"

"Not after he came to Paradise." Father didn't miss the desert or scorching sun, but even so, he had still locked his dragon in the cellar as was the desert custom.

The Prince turned, his green eyes fixing on Morgan, a mocking smile distorting his features. "Do you take after your father's sins?"

Morgan scowled to hide his rising worry. His heart pounded in his ears, and the ground even seemed to shake beneath him. But then the vase before the portrait rattled and—the ground *was* trembling.

The rhythmic thumps grew into roars below the manor. Icy fear of recognition shot through Morgan at the telltale stomps.

"We do have one more order of business, Delmar," the Prince said quietly, grinning. Reaching into his coat, he removed a scroll. The same one from the study.

The Prince unfurled the scroll and spoke.

Bow before your serpent King.
Confess the guilt that you have wrought.
Or chains will brand your mortal skin.
And sin will bind your heart.

The words made the air feel heavy. As the Prince finished, the paper glowed white, making his face take on a ghoulish quality.

"I wonder, Morgan," he said, "which side are you on?"

Dread clamped down on Morgan's throat. "I'm sure you know the answer, Your Highness," he said slowly, measuring his words.

The scroll flashed brighter, a beam of light emanating from it.

"How are your burns?" asked the Prince, the amused tone of his voice all the more unnerving.

Morgan licked his lips. "Healing."

Another beam of light shot from the scroll. The light became substantial, thin chains, white like snow, that dropped to the ground. The glow faded, but the gleam in the Prince's eyes only brightened. "Need a hand, Delmar?"

No, Morgan wouldn't let him get the satisfaction of putting on the chains. He would do that himself.

As he crouched to grasp one chain, it shifted. He yanked his hand back as the second chain reared one end like a cobra about to strike. They circled him, wrapping around his ankles before moving apart again.

One snake-chain lashed forward to Morgan's knee. He kicked the creature, sending the chain flying back. Then another shot toward him, and it wrapped around his wrist. The silver chain of that snake wound around his arm to the elbow with a flash of heat, charring the sleeve of his shirt to ribbons.

Then another snake gripped his right arm and bound him. The chains tightened, flush to his skin, like fire. Then the metal darkened to black.

Morgan grimaced. His fingers itched to rip off the chains, but as he did, they tightened further and flashed white, a rattling sound filling the air.

The roars from the cellar shook the ground.

"Give Orgul my regards," said the Prince. As he spoke, the roars were cut short. Silence. Tannin smiled. "I will have my man find you when he is ready to depart on the hunt."

10

Wynne and Ryder lapsed into silence as the horse carried them further and further from Kyrn.

The hazy sunlight that had so markedly defined the day seemed to be snuffed like candlelight. Pines swayed, dropping their heavy loads whenever she or Ryder dared to trespass too close. She wasn't even sure if they were following the road.

She had almost convinced herself he was leading them in the wrong direction when she spotted something. Ahead, between a fallen pine and a natural ravine, a thin path led to a tiny cottage. Its orange light just barely reached them, and when Ryder led them to it, she could almost cry with relief.

She didn't wait for him to dismount from the horse but scrambled off as soon as he slowed enough. She knocked on the door, her breath coming out in clouds of crystallized air.

Another knock. No answer.

Ryder went to the window, wiped the condensation, and peered inside. He made a sound like a groan of aggravation. "How are we going to get in?"

Wynne's stomach growled, and she let out a frustrated sigh. "Do me a favor," she said.

"What?"

"Don't steal anything." She dug her fingers into her hair, removing a pin that held her curls away from her face. She could feel Ryder's curious gaze as she went to the door and removed her gloves. After a moment of fumbling with her trembling hands, it opened.

The blessed warmth did away with any reservations she had of entering a stranger's house. She sank down in a plush armchair by the fire, while Ryder sat on the edge of a rocking chair. Armor came in, dragging dirt and mud, before settling at her feet, her piercing blue eyes trained on Ryder. But she wasn't growling. Just observing, like she had Morgan when they'd first met.

"We'll stay here during the day and head out tomorrow before dawn," he said. "The sun will melt our footsteps before the guards can catch us. Killian should meet us again at some point along the way."

"You're not in charge." Wynne shot him a look.

He smirked. "I think having saved your life twice now—"

"Once, the river—"

"—and with the angry mob at Kyrn," he added, and she snapped her mouth shut. His grin widened. "Having saved your life twice now, I'll take the lead."

She started to protest, but he ignored her. Ryder grasped a flower pot and went outside.

Her stinging shoulder drew her attention, and she slipped off her coat. A shallow cut, no longer than a sewing needle, grazed her skin. At least it had been the creature's claws and not its venomous teeth. She could handle a small cut.

At last, Ryder returned with the flower pot full of snow. He set it before the fire and stirred the embers.

Ryder peeled back the threadbare tatters of his torn sleeve. Red claw marks scored the flesh of his left shoulder. Scabs had formed over the cuts from the wrestle at the riverbank, but holes cut into his flesh where the shopkeeper's dragon had almost stolen him off the horse.

He tore off the loose shreds of fabric that was his left sleeve, revealing spiderwebbing scars that crisscrossed his arm. Some were jagged, maybe knife wounds, but many followed the parallel gashes of dragon claws.

Wynne's mind flashed back to Morgan's burns. Burns were one thing—defiance—but the scars cut deep. Papa had a few dragon scars from his youth, and when he'd drunk himself into a stupor he often clawed at them as if they seared his very conscience.

At the thought of Papa, fear twisted in her stomach. "So what's your amazing plan to catch the revolutionary?" she asked, fighting the bitterness welling up in her chest.

He looked up at her and offered another stupid smirk. "If we meet him by the river, Jessie will help me catch him. If she's in the mood."

"Jessie?"

"That would be my dragon. Don't worry, Wynne, I'm all yours." Ryder smiled, but now it was more of a grimace.

"Don't change the subject," she snapped. This time, Armor did growl. "Why do you have to be like that? All charm and lies? Why can't you just be like—"

She cut off. Ryder's eyebrows shot up. "Like who? Like my brother?"

All humor had left his expression.

She pursed her lips together.

"I'm not surprised you've heard of my escapades, Wynne." He wadded up some snow before placing it on his shoulder. "But there is more than one side to every story. You can't know the inner workings of my family well enough to see there is more pride in my brother than in my little finger."

She scowled. "Liar."

She knew her Morgan. To the untrained eye, the set of his shoulders and the hard line of his jaw would be arrogant, but she knew the weight that made those shoulders tremble and the worry that clawed at his throat. She knew him before the burden of the council forced him to harden his heart to all but a few that wouldn't see his 'weaknesses' and target the chink in his armor. Weaknesses that she rather thought were noble.

Qualities that Ryder didn't possess.

Ryder shrugged. "You need something from me, and I from you. I could try to find Killian on my own, but it seems he's laying something aside for you. Though I doubt you can bring him back to Paradise with your little gecko here."

Armor whipped her tail against the floorboards, but he didn't flinch.

Wynne was silent. He was wrong—of course she and Armor could get Killian on their own. But then, what would stop him from taking Killian from her? From stealing the credit for the reward she needed?

"So," he went on, "I think you can suspend your distrust of me for the moment until we drag him back to get both of our rewards." He shrugged, then winced at his shoulder. "If you can't, then I guess we can part ways now."

Wynne studied him for a moment, and she could see through the hard set of his frown to the worry simmering beneath the surface.

He needed her. He was serving a prison sentence on a ship. Years already, but how many remained? And all this, for what? If he was guilty, he would never be free. Ever.

She got up, snatching the shreds of his sleeve from before the fire, and tore it into strips. He protested, but she shut him up with a hand in the air. "If you want me to help you, you better keep your mouth shut. Armor is watching you."

Ryder's surprise turned into a grin. "I expect nothing less from your loyal companion."

Wynne tended Ryder's wound in silence. His face was turned to the fire, and Wynne couldn't help but see the same worry in the tilt of his head and the stoop of his shoulders as with Morgan.

How was Morgan? She hadn't even had a second to think about him or how she could reach out to him to let him know what she was doing...and where she was going. Armyn. To the same place where the revolutionaries first betrayed their kingdom. And now Paradise thought she was in league with Killian—and running from the shopkeeper's dragon in Kyrn didn't help.

Her heart warmed at remembering the plans they'd made—the boat passage to Mandor. If Papa's health was restored quickly, they could all go—and better now, since they would escape the chaos on the mainland with the revolutionaries.

"Stay put a minute," she said, pressing a hand on Ryder's shoulder.

"I was only getting more comfortable. The way you have me leaning over, I'm almost falling off the couch."

"We don't want to get blood on anything here. The owner might come back soon, and they'd notice the difference."

Ryder sighed. "They're not coming back. Didn't you see the cabinets? The beds? They're stripped bare. These people fled from something. Probably from Armynians."

"But they left the fire going—"

"To deter suspicions. They're probably on the way to the port to get to Mandor. It's the only option for some of them now."

Aside from Armyn, Mandor was Paradise's greatest ally. Citizens passed freely across the border to the island kingdom. Meanwhile,

Symara would never let a Paridisian through to its sandy dunes. They would shoot a Paradisian on sight of his dragon.

"The people in the capital aren't leaving," Wynne protested. There may be a sense of unease, but not fear. Not fleeing. As long as their dragons were by their side, there was no fear. As long as the King and his Prince reigned.

"You left." He met her gaze, and she glanced back to his shoulder.

"Do you have that fishing hook? I don't have any needles."

Ryder let out a chuckle. "Sure, Winnie." He pressed a silver hook into her hand.

It was small, curved, but sharp. Sharp enough to serve her purpose. "Do you have any liquor?"

He handed her a small flask, and she bit back a comment. It was what she needed. "This is going to hurt."

"They say love is pain."

Armor let out a low growl, and Ryder lifted his good arm in surrender. "Maybe it's best if you leave the stitches for a professional."

"Mama was, so let me." She went to the kitchen, found a shallow bowl. Poured the contents of Ryder's flask. "You can have it back now." She held out the empty flask as she returned to his side.

Ryder frowned. "It's okay. I don't need it anymore."

"I can keep this as clean as possible, Ryder, but that doesn't mean it won't hurt."

"Just get started." He turned his face toward the fire again, back stiffening. "I'd like to sleep the rest of the day if you don't mind."

By the time she was done, Ryder still hadn't spoken beyond the grunt he gave when the hook first penetrated his skin. She moved back to her chair, then dropped her head in her hands. It was one thing for Mama to have told her the steps, quite another for her to do them.

Before she knew it, she heard rustling and lifted her head. "Ryder, you should—"

But he was on his feet, taking the bowl and rags outside. He returned a few moments later, then stretched out on the rocking chair, his expression more peaceful than it had been earlier.

She moved to one of the empty bedrooms, curling up on the tick mattress as Armor nestled at her feet, and slept.

Morgan finally spotted Mother on the steps of the Temple, bright sunlight broadcasting her presence as it refracted off Mother's dragon's scales. Elya was the mirror image of Orgul, only with ice blue eyes to Orgul's amber. And, of course, without the derangement spells.

Elya towered over a priest, and with a groan, Morgan recognized Eli's stubborn frame. Vendors and passersby in the square quieted as Morgan passed, whispers and glances shared as they must've speculated on the nature of the Delmar family's newest spectacle.

At least Orgul had been content to nurse his injured paw in the manor after Morgan had released him. Morgan didn't need more attention.

"—will let me in this instant, sniveling fool." Mother thrust a finger in Eli's face. "Anias will listen to reason."

Eli scowled. He looked small and pathetic without his dragon, and as Mother spoke, he backed further and further toward the entrance of the Temple. One of the doors was cracked open. "You have spoken your piece, Lady Delmar. The rest must be said before trial—"

"Trial?" Morgan's voice boomed as he reached the top of the Temple steps. Eli's gaze snapped to him.

The smirk that graced the priest's features sent a wave of hot anger through Morgan. "What trial? Addie is innocent, whatever you want to accuse her of."

Eli lifted his chin. "Enlighten me, Lord Delmar. Did Adelaide set out for the Temple before dawn to seek healing?"

All the anger fled Morgan's frame, replaced by cold fear. "That is private information," he snapped. "What's spoken in the confessions should not be repeated, or do you make a habit of—" Hot fire flared up his arms as the chains glowed, and Morgan was scorched to silence.

Eli's gaze fell to the bindings, his eyes alight with glee. "Try again, Delmar."

Morgan pulled down the cuffs of his coat sleeves, humiliation warming his face even further.

"She did go to seek healing," he spat, jaw clenched. He sensed Mother beside him, but he couldn't look at her. Wouldn't. He didn't need her judgment.

He was fulfilling all her expectations of him now.

"She was found behind the veil," Eli said.

Mother gasped. Morgan fought to steel his expression.

"Having entered the archives. She carried a bundle of herbs for someone important, she said." His gaze flashed as he looked at Morgan. As if in response, the dull ache in his leg flared to throbbing. "Diane explained that young Adelaide is going through a difficult time, missing her brother and all, and to have mercy."

"We can pay the debt." Morgan now dared a glance at Mother, and she looked hopeful, eyes bright with expectation. "How much?"

"That will be determined by the King," Eli said, "in trial. For now, Delmar, all you can do is try to gain favor. And stealing from the priests is not a good start." Eli waved a ringless hand, and Morgan's face flushed.

The Prince said that Morgan was in the King's favor, but he doubted it was the kind of favor he wished for, if it so stoked the Prince's ire. He'd have to find another way.

Morgan cast a disparaging look at Eli before storming from the steps of the Temple. He could hear Mother's voice, distant, over the drumming of his heart in his ears.

He was on the steps of the manor when Mother's hand gripped his arm.

"Morgan."

His shoulders tensed at the fearful tone in her voice, but he didn't turn to face her.

"What are you going to do?"

"What I can," he snapped. "And I can get started if you would just let go."

Her fingers released their hold on his arm. "This is your fault," she all but hissed.

"My fault?"

"If you hadn't left the manor to do King only knows what, then Addie never would have—"

"Addie would have done what she wanted." Morgan spun to face Mother. She was a few steps below, and he towered over her.

Her careful composure had snapped, and she pressed her hand to her forehead. "She is all too much like your father. Stephan was too outspoken..."

"And the better for it," he answered.

"Don't you think I know that?" She was shaking, face red from anger. "I've been trying to protect her—"

"Like you protected me?" Morgan almost felt accomplished when Mother flinched at his words. "Sending me into the council in your place?"

"That was not my doing, Morgan." She met his gaze now, her eyes wide and imploring. For the first time in years, he actually recognized her. His anger dimmed to a simmer.

Mother looked to the floor, smoothing her skirts. When she glanced back up, she had schooled her features, the lines of desperation in her face masked by cool indifference. "It was the King's decision, and you need to accept it. We can't lose her, too."

"Like you've lost Ryder."

Now Morgan understood his place in the family. Always called to hold up the sky but never valued. Mother couldn't stand to lose the two children she actually cherished. Morgan ran a hand through his hair, yanking at the ends so his head hurt. "Thank you, Mother, for such words of encouragement."

"Not Ryder." Mother gave him a look full of meaning, and all at once, Morgan understood.

His mind spun. "Father? But that was a sickness—" He cut himself off. He had hardly believed it as a child, and even less now that he heard of Wynne's father's plight.

"There is only one disease that kills the soul as well as the body." Mother's voice was soft, but it shattered the morning's quiet song. All Morgan could hear was his heart pounding in his chest. "And the revolutionaries are not to blame."

She reached forward, brushing his arm where the chains had already left bruises. "Be careful, Morgan."

Then she dropped her hand to her side and stepped around him. The front door closed with a click, and by the time Morgan collected himself enough to enter, she was gone.

He sank to his knees in the foyer, head spinning.

His fingernails were still gray with soot, the creases of his palms stained black. And if he looked beyond his fingers, he could see the stain his own blood left on Father's rug, brilliant blue marred by specks of brown. It was humble dirt below a lofty sky, never able to reach the sapphire heights of heaven. Never able to escape this suffocating fire and brimstone.

II

Wynne's dreams were full of light. Of Morgan's smile and his gaze that warmed when it landed on her. Then Morgan with the stiff collar, slicked hair, and cold blue eyes when he was walking out of the Temple.

Wynne woke to the glare of moonlight reflecting off the snow. A blue sheen fell over the frozen landscape, making the place seem so much more serene compared to the churn of emotions that abounded in her heart.

The little sleep she'd gotten after helping Ryder tend his wound brought no rest, only a deep pit of emptiness.

She draped an arm off the bed, brushing her fingertips against Armor's back. Only the rise and fall of Armor's chest, her quiet breaths, broke the silence. The fire in the other room crackled and sparked, though little warmth reached her in the bedroom.

Armor stilled and raised her head to gaze at Ryder's form moving in the darkness beyond the frosted windows. Wynne might have thought it was an intruder at first, but the white blaze of his shirt looked like a beacon in the moonlight.

Her dragon didn't growl, didn't stir, just as when she'd first met Morgan.

Even that first day, Morgan had come to her defense. He stood between her and the lying vendor, who glared at her as if she was nothing better than a sailor, and paid the difference for the fabric. She thought he'd done it because he recognized her from the tailor shop after one of Addie's fittings, but then he asked about her. Like he actually cared about someone so far below his family's station.

Maybe the rigid son of Lady Delmar was more than he let on.

From the beginning, she was surprised that a Delmar would pay attention to her. But it was also surprising to see him down at the guard barracks, training in blood and sweat between his hours of study in history. But he was so much more humble and kind than she ever thought just by looking at his older brother.

When Morgan had approached Papa to court her, Papa had accepted. Until Ryder's trial. Then all it took was for Papa to hear the Delmar name and he'd just shut the notion down entirely, raw from Mama's betrayal. It was then that any praise he'd given her became scorching judgment.

Just like Clara, he'd said. *Just like your mother.*

The door opened, and a draft of cold wind made Wynne wish for the fire as she sat up. Ryder crept into the cottage. She stepped into the main room, and he glanced her way as he shook wet clumps of snow from his boots.

"Couldn't sleep?" He set a few logs on the fire, nudged the dwindling embers with a poker. "That makes two." The skin under his eyes was dark.

The scars on his arm rippled as he adjusted the fire, like grotesque snakes winding up his arm.

"What happened? To get so many..."

"Scars?" Ryder stretched and shrugged, a snared rabbit dangling on his fishing line. "You tell me, Wynne. What do you think?"

He went to the small kitchen, where he laid the rabbit across the counter and pulled out his knife. The long blade was a jagged stump from where it had shattered against the green dragon's scales earlier.

He worked quietly, efficiently, but for once, Wynne couldn't imagine the careful fingers of this sailor to have been the same to order his dragon to kill another for a debt unpaid.

"We're all sinners." Ryder pushed down on the handle of his knife. Cartilage cracked. "To the bone. Is your dragon the only one to feel the effects of your mistakes?"

He met her gaze, and she looked away. She shivered as she remembered nightmares and overwhelming fear, before she could rush to the Temple with her offering for whatever sin she'd committed.

"Armor is well-behaved." Ryder skewered chunks of meat. He tossed one in the air, and Armor caught it, licking her chops as she laid back down again. Her purr reverberated through the floorboards. "Has an appetite, but not insatiable."

He crossed the room and put the meat over the fire. The scent made Wynne's mouth water. Armor had fallen back to sleep, snoring softly at Wynne's feet.

Curiosity burned in her chest. To ask about his past. What had happened that day at the port.

But if she asked, and he answered, would he demand honesty in return?

She pursed her lips. It was best to remain silent, until they dragged the revolutionary back to the King's scales.

He held out a rabbit leg. "Here, take it. I can hear your stomach growling."

"Thank you." She devoured it in moments, and Armor swallowed the bone. Ryder handed her another, and when she was done with that, he stood, wiping the grease from his palms on his pants. "That should be enough to get us to King's Pass."

Wynne froze, her gaze shooting to the impenetrable darkness outside. "Today?"

"We'll have a few stops." He tossed her his flask, heavy with water. "Drink up. We can fill it again when we cross the river."

She donned her boots while Ryder snuffed the fire with snow. If his wounds still hurt, he gave no indication, but shouldered his supplies and walked to the door.

Outside, the horse was tied to a branch. Ryder brought something out of his bag when he approached the creature.

A carrot. Wynne had to smile at that.

On the run and Ryder still thought of the horse. Even though it was probably stolen.

Ryder mounted, and Wynne swung up in front of him.

Stars twinkled above, and the steady clip-clop of the hooves crunching through powdery snow tempted her to close her eyes again. She was almost asleep when Ryder spoke.

"You must really love your father to go to such lengths for him." Ryder sighed, his chest dropping with his breath.

Wynne blinked. How could she *not* have gone for Papa? She was suddenly reminded of Diane's expression when Morgan introduced her, the look of pure disdain and contempt. Not to *her*, but to her son.

"What else would I do? He's my father."

Ryder stiffened. "That doesn't always mean much."

Tense silence grew between them, and when he took another breath, Wynne wondered if he might just tell the truth. "My freedom isn't the only reason I'm here." He shifted in the saddle as if to lean back and create more space between them. "My sister, too."

Wynne fought the urge to roll her eyes. What kind of lie would he tell now to gain her sympathy? "Sister?"

"She's young, fourteen," he said, running a hand through his hair. "But she's troubled. She needs someone to look out for her—"

"And you're the man for the job? The convicted criminal?"

"It's your turn to answer some questions, Winnie." He chuckled, but the laugh was flat and airy.

Wynne clamped her mouth shut.

"What else did you hear of me?" His voice was low, and the sudden change in his tone to serious made her want to turn around and see his expression.

She took a breath. "That you're a murderer. Killed a merchant at the port. And that's why you're on the ship."

"Do you believe it?"

"Are you confessing?" When Ryder didn't answer, she sucked in another breath.

Ryder cleared his throat, but the sudden flash of a swinging lantern caused Wynne to speak up.

"Is that Killian?" she whispered.

He shushed her, slowing the horse so the clomp of hooves through snow was barely a whisper.

As they neared, the swinging orange orb split into two lanterns suspended on either side of a bridge. Icy water babbled below, eastward, to dump out in the ocean miles away. It seemed they'd managed to follow the path without nearing the bank, but the sudden curve of the river to the south, cutting off their access to the mountains, was enough to force their hand to cross it.

The haze became sharper and distinct, with a third, yellow-orange orb between the two posts marking the bridge's beginning. A man stood on the bridge, breath coming out in large white puffs that caught the moonlight like a spray of silver mist. His distinctive dragonscale coat rippled when he raised a hand to them.

Ryder pulled the horse right up to the edge of the bridge. "Just wait," he whispered to her, "we need—"

"Go around behind him," she snapped. "I'll distract him. Wait for my signal."

Without waiting for a response, she scrambled off the horse and stomped toward Killian. She raised the flask. "This well," she snapped, "where is it?"

Just to the left Ryder dismounted and held the horse's reins tight, penning Killian in. Killian's eyes darted to Ryder.

She waved the silver flask. "Well?"

Killian faced her again, placing his lantern on the walled edge of the stone bridge. "Beyond King's Pass, in the Armynian temple, there you will find the well of living water." His face was gaunt in the moonlight, and he looked scarily resigned. "The journey ahead is hard, and going back is worse. You have started on a path that will reveal the heart of your dragons and yourselves." He let out a sigh. "I know because I've walked it, too."

Armor pressed against her side, and Wynne's hand reflexively went to stroke her silver nose.

"What would you say if you could see the hold they have on you? How big will she get before you lose control? Before your defense becomes your prison?"

Anger flared up in her chest. "Is that why you killed yours?"

Killian's expression fell. "Are you still so lost?" His eyes went skyward. "Why couldn't You have made it easier?"

The sun climbed on the horizon, turning the sky a dusky pink. Ryder stepped behind Killian, rocks crunching underfoot, but Killian's gaze was still fixed on the sky as if searching for answers above.

Beside Wynne, Armor crouched, her tail lashing, head low. A growl rumbled in her throat.

Wynne patted Armor's flank. "Now."

Armor pounced. White light flashed. With the raise of Killian's arm, a shield formed, sending Armor flying back with as much speed as she had lunged forward. Armor sailed back down the bridge behind Wynne, tumbling back into the brush.

"Armor!" Wynne started after her, her mind flooded with darkness and thorns and anger so fierce it scared her.

"Wait!" The tension in Ryder's voice made her spin around. He was fighting the horse that had begun to yank against the reins. "Come on, Wynne, we almost got him."

Killian pulled something out of his coat, and Ryder brandished his broken dagger, though the horse's jerky movements made it fall from his hands.

But Killian didn't have a weapon. Another white scroll, not unlike the scrolls from the archives in the Temple. "You will need this." He tossed it at Wynne's feet, and she snatched it up.

A hideous roar drowned out the rest of his words, and Ryder was thrown backward by the horse's panicked movements. Tempest barreled past the revolutionary and almost ran Wynne over in his mad dash across the stones.

A large blue head arched over the bridge. Ryder's face went white. "Jessie, wait," Ryder ordered, waving his arms to get her attention.

"Ryder," Wynne snapped, panic coiling in her gut, "why is your serpent here?"

Any response he might have given was lost to an enraged roar.

Wynne leapt back when the blue dragon's gargantuan paw slapped the bricks, her webbed fingers splaying almost as wide as she was tall. She slammed another paw down, choking off the revolutionary from running down the bridge toward Ryder.

Large scars wrapped around her neck, and though the chains were missing, Wynne could guess all too well where Ryder had fastened them around her neck in true Symaran fashion.

"Just hold him there." His voice was firm as he spoke to his dragon, but he grasped his dagger from the ground and readied a strike. Would he really deliver a blow?

Jessie snarled defiantly, baring her teeth at his words.

"Jessie, enough." He flexed his grip on the dagger. A growl emanated from the creature's throat as her gills flared, and Wynne froze. Would his dragon really harm him?

Jessie snapped her jaws down at Ryder. Ryder dodged and Killian sidestepped, his hand flashing with a small, glowing knife. His lips seemed to move as if he were praying. He slung the knife, hitting one of the dragon's great black eyes. She let out an angry roar, rising up on her hind legs, body towering over the bridge.

Swallowing a shriek, Wynne bolted across the bridge. Her feet stumbled onto the hard earth a moment before the dragon's paws came crashing down.

The bridge's structure crumbled, stones falling into the river overflowing with snowmelt. Jessie struggled against the current, but the churning muddy water thrust her away and out of sight.

On the opposite shore, Armor paced, tail whipping like a lion stalking its prey. She crept to the river's edge but jumped back at any surge of water.

"Come on!" Ryder shouted for Armor to come over, but she continued to pace.

"She can't swim. Maybe if we—"

A few hundred yards down the stream, Killian crawled onto their side of the shore. Ryder started after him, but Killian dashed off into the forest ahead of them. A few minutes later, Ryder came back to her.

Ryder adjusted his pack and shed the coat, slinging it over one arm. "Come on, Wynne. We should move."

She stole a glance back. "But—"

"She'll be fine. She'll find a way across. She found her way to you in the first place, right?"

"Fine, but you carry this." She handed him Killian's scroll.

Wynne sent a wave to her dragon, hoping it came across as an apology, and started after Ryder.

They trekked through the snow, the flask jingling at Wynne's hip with every step. The sun rose steadily to their right, making the snow slushy, wet, and miserable.

Her head started to throb with the same kind of ache when she'd worn herself thin trying to finish an order at the shop, and it lingered even after she drank from the flask and accepted some stale bread from Ryder. She didn't understand what Killian had said. But wasn't there some truth in his words?

How many more nobles were scorched?

How many sailors had scars that ran inches deep?

Even though Armor had maintained her sheen in the past few years, she had almost doubled in size in the last six months. That was Wynne's doing for sure. She'd been swiping from the tailor shop's earnings to cover the payments that Papa drank away.

It was wrong, but it was worse to get thrown out of her home. To face ridicule for her absolute lack of decorum compared to Morgan's smooth transition into nobility.

Wynne paused, leaning against a tree to wipe her brow. The coat, with the warming noon sun, was enough to drench her in sweat. When she knew Ryder was far enough ahead to be just out of sight, she inspected her skirt pockets.

The revolutionary's dagger was gone, and Ryder had the scroll, but she had pocketed the shopkeeper's refund. She counted the money with quiet movements, shuffling the coins from one pocket to another, and sighed. It wasn't much, but it could be enough to save her from another unwilling sacrifice. Morgan had entrusted her with his ring twice now, and she wouldn't part with it again.

"Wynne, hurry up."

She pressed a hand over her bodice where the ring lay against her skin.

For a moment, eclipsed by the trees ahead, he almost sounded like Morgan. The thought hurt, then rankled, so she stuffed her hands in her pockets and trudged on.

12

AFTER HOURS OF TURNING over in his bed, Morgan finally found fragile rest in an armchair in the sitting room. His dreams were plagued with the hateful look in the Prince's green eyes as they flashed and the sick smile that tipped the corners of his mouth when Orgul's roars had silenced.

The same sick smile that was plastered on the high priest's face on that day when he'd first got Orgul from the Temple at twelve years old.

Morgan had been about to enter the sanctuary when Father's hand dropped on his shoulder.

"Are you ready for this, Morgan?" The concerned note in Father's tone made Morgan frown.

"Of course I am," he answered. He had done all the cleansing rituals to pass through the veil, and he certainly didn't need Father to remind him. He lifted his arms, his animal-fur cloak rustling with the movement as if to prove his point, and raised a brow.

"Of course." Father smiled sheepishly, though it didn't quite reach his eyes. He removed his hand from Morgan's shoulder.

Morgan couldn't wait any longer and passed through the veil. He was almost shaking with anticipation as he crossed the sanctuary and bowed to High Priest Anias.

His eyes roved over the large silver scales, the golden accents, before settling back on Anias when he cleared his throat.

"You must remain still while your dragon approaches," he said, voice grating as if Morgan had already messed up. Hot defensiveness prickled across Morgan's skin, but he tamped it down and nodded, forcing a smile.

The high priest set down a bundle of silver cloth at Morgan's feet. It opened like a blossom, a writhing coil of black scales nestled in the center. The snake lifted its head, amber eyes glinting, before flicking its tongue in the air.

"What's its name?" Morgan breathed, unable to tear his gaze away from the creature that would be his. A very reflection of his soul.

"Orgul. He's been waiting for you."

Morgan knelt before the snake, and it reared back as if startled by his sudden movement.

Hisssss.

"Stand up," the high priest chided. "Let him approach."

Morgan heard Father's sharp intake of breath as the snake slid toward him, curling, hissing. Smooth black scales brushed around the hem of his pants, sending a sudden wave of apprehension through him.

Searing pain shot up his leg, and Morgan lurched back. Orgul slid to the floor with a hiss, and Morgan fixed a glare on the creature as his hand went to his ankle. Two red pinpricks dotted his skin.

"Well done." The high priest grinned.

Morgan blinked. Well done? He shot a glance at Father, who grimaced.

"Now, watch."

The high priest's voice drew Morgan's gaze to Orgul.

Even before his very eyes, Orgul's scales rippled like the tumultuous waves of the ocean. Limbs grew, horns sprouted, and the black snake morphed into a dragon the size of a housecat. Whatever thread of trepidation had tripped him up snapped, and Morgan knelt before his dragon, his jaw dropping.

Awe gripped him, and he held out his hand, palm down. "Come here."

Pain seared the back of Morgan's hand, and he stumbled back. Tiny claw marks scored his knuckles, and his dragon let out a hiss of warning.

His eyes blinked open, and he gasped, hands gripping the chair as if he was still lurching backward from that first interaction with Orgul. He shook his head to clear the dregs of his dream—nightmare—and touched his temple where his heartbeat pounded in his skull.

A knock at the door sent a ripple of pain through his head.

Footsteps sounded, and Morgan stood. "Let me." He dismissed the servant and rolled his stiff shoulders as he entered the foyer where morning tendrils of light illuminated every stain on the rug.

If it was bad news again, he would rather face it himself. Swiping a hand through his hair and adjusting his shirt sleeves, he steeled his expression and opened the door.

The Armynian captain.

Morgan looked him up and down. His uniform had been replaced by a worn leather jacket over a black shirt and pants. Only the fancy gold pins on his jacket showed his achievements in Armyn's armed forces, even a medal from Symara. His dragon, a red-scaled winged creature, looked sullen, dragging its paws as it trudged up the walkway to the captain's side.

"Lord Morgan Delmar." The captain crossed his arms.

"Captain Corl Vander," Morgan answered dryly.

"Prince Tannin insisted I join you to catch the revolutionary and bring him in," he said, frowning as if he was as displeased with the idea as Morgan was.

Morgan scowled. Not only did the Prince detest that the King favored Morgan, but now he seemed to actively contribute to make Morgan fail. Of course the Armynian would do everything in his power to keep the revolutionary from Paradise's grasp.

But Morgan wouldn't be defeated easily. His heart twisted at the thought of Addie trembling in the cold dungeons.

"We'll leave in an hour," the captain said. "Be ready."

Morgan didn't care to reply. He closed the door and pressed his forehead to the cool wood.

He loathed the idea of traveling with Corl, but he had no choice. Morgan would just have to make sure he brought back the revolutionary. That would be more than enough payment for Addie's freedom.

His mind echoed with Wynne's voice, the memories of their last words, and the terrible weight she bore.

Orgul's footsteps shook the floor as he came up beside Morgan and rested his tail across Morgan's feet. He couldn't help the wry chuckle that left him. "Armor's rubbing off on you, huh?"

"Morgan." A soft voice from behind made him turn. Mother pulled her shawl tight around her shoulders. "Are you sure you want to do this?"

The hunch of her frame and the redness of her eyes aged her at least a decade, and she looked as if she hadn't slept the night before either.

"You know better than most that I have no choice, Mother." He lifted his arm, his sleeve falling to show the glint of metal. The chains. "Promise me you'll do what you can for Elwin. You know what to do." He reached forward, pressing a hand to her shoulder. "We'll get Addie back."

Then he dropped his arm and left to busy himself with the preparations to leave.

He was ready within the hour and met Corl in front of the manor with two horses from the stables. Morgan mounted and took the lead.

"We'll stop by Kyrn first," said Corl. "There's rumors of the revolutionary being sighted there."

As soon as they passed through the fortress walls and were out overlooking the countryside, Morgan felt a shift in his heart. The two people he was responsible for, Elwin and Addie, were barricaded in the city, and he would be powerless to help them until he returned.

The quiet countryside opened before Morgan as he followed the captain down the road westward. Orange and red leaves encroached on either side of the path as the misty Armynian mountains grew larger on the horizon.

Orgul trudged silently behind Morgan. Ruby, the captain's dragon, drifted overhead for short spurts, then fluttered to the ground whenever her tattered wings couldn't hold her weight, even though she was no bigger than Armor.

Just as the forest closed around them, Morgan spotted a wooden sign. Then he heard the bustle of the town, the clop of horse hooves, and the murmur of voices. As they went, snow slushed underneath their horses' hooves and they eventually dismounted as they entered Kyrn, while Corl directed Ruby to stay at the edges of the forest to avoid suspicion from the townsfolk.

Morgan debated about revealing Captain Vander's heritage anyway but decided against it. The Prince would just send someone else that was even more of a nuisance, and by that time, the revolutionary could be long gone.

Morgan dismounted without waiting for Corl, and the captain seemed plenty content to turn his own horse in the direction of the stables.

His boots sank into the mushy ground, wet from the snowmelt. A glint caught his eye, and he crouched down.

A silver scale.

Confusion mingled in his chest. Could this be Wynne? A glance over his shoulder told him that Corl was in the stables, but this scale was right in front of a shop.

He could find out about the revolutionary after. First, Wynne.

He entered the brick-faced shop. The establishment, with chairs before a fireplace and racks of fur and leather clothing along the opposite wall, was altogether cozy and welcoming—a stark contrast to the expression on the shopkeeper's face when her eyes fell on him.

"What do you want?" Her eyes flashed, and a green dragon at her side let out a low growl. It cradled its leg against its chest, a white bandage wrapped around the limb. "Show me your dragon."

Wordlessly, Morgan stepped aside, and Orgul ducked into the shop. The woman's shoulders relaxed, and she waved Morgan further in. "How can I help you, sir?" she tittered, red creeping up her neck in embarrassment.

"I'm here on the King's errand."

The woman's expression sobered. "What does the King need?"

Morgan cringed inwardly at her reverent tone. If only she knew the truth of the King she really served. "I'm tracking anything to do with the revolutionary. Have you seen him?"

"Those blasted revolutionaries," she grumbled. "I've seen two come through here. One was two days ago, and the second one was a woman! She attacked my dragon."

The dragon let out an exaggerated whimper when Morgan's eyes turned to the creature.

"We found her weapon in the woods a little further west."

"Could you show it to me?"

The woman motioned for Morgan to come to the counter, then unwrapped a leather bundle. A small white dagger glowed faintly in the light, and recognition struck Morgan as the same weapon that he'd held in his hands at the council meeting. A few more silver scales were nestled beside the dagger.

Morgan forced his expression to remain neutral and met the shopkeeper's gaze. "What did this revolutionary look like?"

"Blonde hair and blue eyes." The woman scowled. "Young, too."

Wynne.

Now Morgan was convinced. But if she had hurt this woman's dragon, she must have had a reason to. He asked and the shopkeeper went through her tale.

"...and her companion, a sailor mind you, stole Juon's horse right from the stables!"

Morgan froze. "A companion?"

The woman nodded, frowning. "I didn't get a good look at him. You'll have to ask Juon and his men over there. They're talking with your man right now." She gestured across the street, where Corl stood with a few men.

"Thank you." He bowed and left the shop, Orgul on his heels. He crossed the street quickly and joined the men.

Corl was speaking, looking a bit lost in thought. "The revolutionary is leading people somewhere, Juon," said Corl, "possibly gathering them..."

"Treason, no doubt," said Juon, leaning against the wall of the stables.

Juon's eyes flickered to Morgan as he approached, distrust in his gaze. His sandy dragon curled up on the front in front of him. It wore a coat over its back, and its yellow eyes glinted as it surveyed the town. A few more people exited and entered shops with the same dragon coat. Not metal, like the priests' adornment, but leather and strong.

The town of Kyrn was lively now, though a foot of snow still buried half the town. Some dragons breathed flames to melt the flakes, while others stood at each end of town as if on guard.

"Tell Delmar what you told me, Juon," said the captain. "What did the sailor look like?"

"I told you all I know, Captain Vander," Juon snapped. "What will telling another do?"

"You can't refuse an order from the King," countered Corl.

Juon frowned. "The sailor was like any other. Same outfit, same vulgar talk"—Juon glanced at Morgan—"and he looked like, well, like you."

"If you didn't want to help, you should have said so," Morgan said, frustration prickling. It was one thing to give a false description, quite another to give such a brazen lie. "Which way did the woman and the sailor go?"

"West."

Corl and Morgan mounted their horses, then started down the street of Kyrn. Orgul and Ruby trotted behind them.

"We must continue until we find them," said the captain as soon as they had crossed the edge of the town. "If they are going all the way to Armyn, it may be impossible to find them among the crevices and cracks of the mountains. If the King is with us, we will find that they are in Oran preparing to go through the pass."

"We're not here for them," Morgan snapped, fear for Wynne curdling in his stomach. "We're here for the revolutionary."

The bright spot over the clouds, sinking now toward the horizon, told Morgan they were closer to noon, which meant they still had daylight to catch up.

Morgan let his horse fall behind the captain and his dragon. He couldn't see any footprints beyond the brown mush that the horse and dragon churned up in front of him, but Corl seemed to have a way of knowing.

Suddenly, Ruby darted in front of Corl, and he pulled his horse to a stop. Morgan made it to the captain's side and caught a glimpse of Ruby, nose in the air, before she shot off the path in a northern direction.

"Come on." Corl spurred his horse, and Morgan shot after him.

Wynne. If she was there, he would make sure she could go free.

A musky stench reached Morgan just as he spotted its source—horse manure. But it was overshadowed by a small cabin, its chimney spewing clouds of smoke. The captain knocked on the door.

No answer.

Corl broke the door handle with a solid kick.

Morgan shoved past the captain to get inside, freezing at the threshold.

Everywhere he looked he saw evidence of Wynne and another traveling together. The couch was marked by where one had slept, and from Corl's observation in the second room, another had taken the cot. Remnants of coals, bootprints crisscrossing the cabin, and a single silver dragon scale.

"Check for footprints out back, Delmar." Corl's voice yanked him from his thoughts.

Morgan trudged outside, his mind whirling, only to be disturbed further—the axe hastily thrown aside, the remnants of the innards of some creature buried under snow but not deep enough to stop the snow from turning pink as it melted. A few kicks with his boot revealed a wooden bowl and a fishing hook.

No, Wynne was not alone. She might trust the person she had found to be a companion, but could he?

His heart ached.

"Come look at this, Delmar."

Morgan groaned in frustration and kicked the wooden bowl. It skittered across the ground and hit a tree. He spun on his heel.

At the front of the house, Corl was crouched before some marks in the snow.

Morgan glanced at the markings. "Those are Orgul's prints."

"There is another set." He gestured to the left, where another set of footprints clearly did lead in a westernly direction. "We must be close."

"If the woman or the sailor have dragons, then they can't be with the revolutionary," Morgan offered. "We should look for bootprints, not dragons."

Corl shot him a scathing look. "I know how to hunt revolutionaries, Delmar. Where there is one, unsavory sorts of people follow, looking for false hope." He straightened and stood. "I wouldn't like to see what kind of woman travels with a sailor on the heels of the revolutionary."

Morgan scowled. "You are not the judge of the woman's character," he said, defensiveness rising in him. "She could be a good woman in difficult circumstances."

"Not so difficult that she can't keep warm." The captain met Morgan's scowl with a glare.

"Let's keep going." Morgan turned and went to his horse. He didn't wait for Corl to mount before he and Orgul set off westward.

Anything Corl might have said was cut off at the sound of clomping horse hooves through the forest. Then a horse burst out of the brush, wild-eyed and foaming at the mouth. Morgan scrambled off his horse to grasp the reins. The horse's mane was tangled and knotted with twigs in its mad dash.

He looked it up and down as recognition struck him. "The stolen horse. Why would it be coming back like this?" Morgan shot a look in the direction the horse came from—the very way they were headed—and worry speared him.

Corl dismounted and stood at Morgan's side. "It might be able to show us what spooked it. Ruby, go ahead and scout the area."

The red dragon bounded forward, flitting upward into the trees, and Morgan wondered if Corl knew just how much more the Prince would loathe him for ordering his dragon about as if it were a base creature of the earth and not a gift of a King.

The horse resisted, but Corl gripped its reins with both hands and strode forward. Morgan was left to lead both of their horses after the captain. His mind spun. Was Wynne all right? Had she fallen from the horse? Could the unnamed sailor have betrayed her?

The trees opened up to a churning, muddy river. But the bridge to cross it was gone. Two lonely lanterns on this bank and the pile of stones were the only remnants. Corl was standing beside Ruby, turning slowly in a circle. The stolen horse had been tied to one of the lantern posts, and it fought against the reins with a few tugs.

"I suppose they wouldn't need the horse if we can't get across," Corl said, actually appearing impressed. He looked at Ruby. "Go up and down the bank. See if you can find someone with a boat to take us over."

Cold fear struck Morgan. Corl had taken only the morning to follow the path that Wynne had traversed over two nights. And now there was no doubt that they were hot on Wynne's heels to catch the revolutionary.

Corl stood with the horse, who suddenly began to buck and try to pull free. Morgan glanced around in time to catch a flash of silver by the trees before a mid-sized dragon shot out of the bushes.

Armor.

And she was headed straight for him.

"Stop!" Morgan hissed, raising a hand to halt Armor's path. Her electric eyes only brightened as she all but leaped to him and nestled into his side. "Armor," he said, shoving her, "you need to go—"

149

"I see we have an uninvited guest."

The captain's voice sent a spear of ice through Morgan, and he stopped trying to push Armor away. She plopped down at his feet contentedly.

Morgan clenched his jaw so hard he could feel the throbbing pounding of his head throughout his entire skull. Stupid. He'd all but told the captain of his connection to Wynne—or at least that he knew someone they were tracking. Conflict of interest. If they'd been on the same playing field before, the captain now had the upper hand.

"It listens to you." Corl looked between Armor and him, as if reaching the same conclusion Morgan had settled on moments ago. Morgan hoped he was wrong. "It will join us. No doubt it will lead us to the woman or the sailor. It must have tracked the horse by their scent."

"What about the revolutionary?" Morgan asked, trying to throw him off. "We can't detour."

The captain smiled, looking back at Armor, who perked up at the mention of the man. "I have little doubt this dragon will take us to both."

Ruby returned. Corl stepped to his dragon's side. "Is there any way across?"

The dragon chirped back eastward.

Morgan followed the dragon's direction with his gaze and froze. At the edge of the river, a few hundred yards down, he spotted a blue figure. The dragon was huge, with iridescent scales that glistened in the sunlight. It turned its head to gaze at them, one eye swollen shut.

The captain said something else, but Morgan was hardly listening past the rush of his heartbeat pounding through his ears.

Jessie.

And if Jessie was here, that meant that the sailor with Wynne was no one other than his own brother.

Morgan reeled back a step, unable to hide his reaction at the gargantuan dragon shrinking in the distance. Cold fear settled in his gut. If Wynne was already in danger of judgment by being associated with the revolutionary, now her very life was on the line.

13

WYNNE AND RYDER ENTERED Oran at the base of the mountains by the time the sun hung between the two mountain peaks on either side. The last of the snow had long since melted, and Wynne's boots were almost dry as they staggered through the foliage crushed into the mud.

Ryder's breakneck pace was exhausting, even if it did increase their odds of catching Killian before anyone else.

She leaned against a tree, switching her weight from foot to foot. Both throbbed and ached, and she would do anything to just take a rest. Or to have him walk so far away that she would be able to escape his company and catch Killian on her own.

She didn't need him or Armor. Killian would listen to reason.

"Keep moving." Ryder's voice shot back at her through the trees. "Am I going to have to drag you?"

Wynne scowled but pushed off the tree and stumbled after him.

The farmlands they had crossed around Kyrn gradually became hills and rocky slopes the closer they got to the mountains at the edge of Armyn. Cold wind whipped about them, seeming to push them back the way they came. But Wynne persisted.

A shape grew on the horizon, first a speck and then growing to large buildings belching smoke. A mining town, Oran was at least twice the size of Kyrn, with many main streets spiderwebbing out from the center square. A fountain sprinkled water, reminding Wynne of that fateful night not so long ago.

A glance over her shoulder showed the fortress walls of Paradise as a speck of gray on the horizon—dwindling now with the coming dusk that could snuff out Papa's life with it. Her mood soured further.

She had to run to keep up with Ryder as he entered the tavern across the square.

Few people graced the greasy tables and even fewer dragons looked up as they entered. Ryder made a beeline for the shadowed booth at the far corner and made an order with the innkeeper.

While he was out, Wynne could finally sit with the thoughts she'd been stewing in during the whole last leg of their trip.

She needed to finish this on her own.

She was going to catch Killian and bring him back herself. And she didn't need Ryder.

"Eat up."

Wynne jumped when Ryder dropped a plate in front of her. She scowled at him, annoyed at the light tone of his voice. But the enticing aroma of the stew made her stomach growl with a fierceness that surprised her. She ate quickly, both from the exertion of the morning and since it'd probably be the last hot meal she could get on her own. The warmth settled in her belly, but it didn't ease the chill in her bones.

She cast her gaze to the door over Ryder's shoulder. "How are we going to find Killian if he's in the city somewhere?"

"Same way we did last time. He'll find you, Winnie."

"Will you stop calling me that?" Her voice came out sharper than she intended, catching the glances of a few people. She hunched her shoulders, lowering her voice. "Let's wait."

"Let's see about a little light reading." Ryder flashed her a grin as he dug into his pack and pulled out Killian's scroll. He cleared his throat and started reading as if telling a bedtime story to an eager five-year-old. She let out a huff and dropped her head into her hands.

For everyone has sinned;

"Oh, wow," she grumbled, her voice muffled against her hands, "thank you for that brilliant insight."

we all fall short of God's glorious standard.

"I don't need to hear of how you're a terrible person, Ryder," she said. "That's well established by any metric."

When Ryder didn't go on, she lifted her head. His eyes were glued to the scroll, but her gaze was drawn to the foreign expression on his face. Concern knit the space between his eyebrows, his lips curled down into a frown.

"What? No more dramatic reading?"

Ryder's gaze flicked to hers, and he cleared his throat.

Yet God, in his grace, freely makes us right in his sight.

"For free?" She scoffed. "Sure, that—"

He did this through Christ Jesus when he freed us from the penalty for our sins. For God presented Jesus as the sacrifice for sin. People are made right with God when they believe that Jesus sacrificed his life, shedding his blood.

She scowled at the words. This is what the revolutionary really believed? This Jesus was God's son? If this God had really given his son for her, what would He ask for in return? She didn't want to know.

By the time she looked back at Ryder, he had regained his composure—even a little smirk to his expression. He stored the scroll.

"There are rooms available. We could get one for the day," he offered.

She shot him a glare.

He lifted his hands innocently. "We can take turns resting up before dark. I know we've gone a long way, and we still have to get through King's Pass."

She shivered again at mention of the King's Pass. The one carved by fang and scale by the King of Paradise thousands of years ago when the first human became his mouthpiece. At least, that's what she'd been told. Maybe the scrolls of the archives said something different.

The pass was wide enough for two carts, with exposed, jagged cliffs arching up on either side that sent down showers of rocks at any loud disturbance. Many said that to go through the King's Pass was to walk in silent reverence of the kingdom of Paradise, for even the slightest sound could set off a rockslide that would take days to clear.

"I'll go first," she offered, feigning a yawn.

Ryder nodded. "At your service, Winnie." He shot her a wink, which she ignored, and went to find the innkeeper.

She pushed her empty bowl away. Over the clinking glasses by the kitchen, she heard Ryder's voice and that of the innkeeper's.

A commotion by the fountain caught her eye. A man snapped at his obsidian black dragon. She had seen quite a few of those in this region of Paradise, and each time, she thought it looked more and more like Orgul.

The man lifted a hand to pull back his hood, revealing black wristbands that wound up to his elbows. Wynne grimaced. Though she hadn't worn them, Wynne knew the bands well—had seen enough of the scars that branded those who couldn't pay their offerings or penance.

The hooded man at the fountain paused when another figure barked something at him.

The black dragon turned, and Wynne gasped.

Orgul. His amber gaze pinned on her.

A moment later, the hooded figure turned. Morgan.

His face went white. His lips mouthed the echo of the last warning he'd given her: *Run.*

She froze. His name burned on the tip of her tongue, itching to fill the chasm that had somehow formed between them. But the pain in his eyes and the concern that knit his brow was enough to stagger her.

His lips moved as if he were saying something else, but her attention was stolen when she caught sight of Armor traipsing alongside a red Armynian dragon. But her dragon hadn't seemed to have spotted her yet. Morgan turned back to the figure with him, and pointed down the street in the opposite direction of the tavern.

She had to go. Now.

It was the only chance she had to catch Killian.

A glance around the tavern revealed a back exit, and she caught sight of Ryder following the inn owner upstairs.

She had just stepped outside when the first gust of wind almost knocked her off her feet. Dark clouds bloomed on the horizon, beyond the mountain pass, sending a burst of air through the narrow ravine.

She cast one glance back to the tavern to see Ryder, frozen, at a window, his face twisted in anger before he disappeared. Quickening her step, she moved out of the alley, pushing against the crowds toward her freedom and Papa's healing.

Wynne was gone.

One second, he spotted Wynne at the tavern window, and then her face vanished. Armor perked up, tail lashing, her nose to the sky. West, directly toward King's Pass.

Morgan crouched beside the silver-scaled dragon. Her blue eyes trained on him. "Armor, listen to me, you need to take us back toward the entrance of the city. I know you want to see Wynne, but turn around—"

"Has she caught something, Delmar?"

The captain's voice made Morgan freeze. He turned and stood. 'No' was on the tip of his tongue, but the shackles around his arms tightened. "Ask the dragon if you must, Corl." Then he stepped aside.

Corl knelt down to Armor's level. "You know where your master is, don't you?"

Armor's tail lashed. Her teeth flashed as if she would take a bite out of his face.

Since crossing the river, they had to leave Morgan's horses in Kyrn. They could pick them up on the way back. As Morgan's leg throbbed the more they walked, both Orgul and Armor tensed as if they sensed his pain. And his current distaste with the captain's breakneck pace after Wynne and the revolutionary.

And Ryder, though he was nowhere to be seen at least.

"Now, be reasonable." Corl flicked her nose. Armor growled, but lowered her haunches and sat. "You want your girl, or sailor; I want the revolutionary. They're together."

Corl looked at Morgan expectantly.

Morgan met Armor's gaze, hoping she might obey. "Lead the way."

She darted down the street directly opposite in the direction of the tavern and the King's Pass. Relief flooded Morgan. The captain and his dragon started after Armor, but Orgul remained at Morgan's side.

"Let's go find her," he said to his dragon. "Go around and see if you can spot her."

He entered the tavern. A few patrons glanced up at him, but then went back to their business. He glanced around, but Wynne was nowhere.

She couldn't have exited the front, but maybe there was another exit? He caught a glimpse of a back door and pushed through it, and he started at a brisk pace toward the King's Pass. If the revolutionary was set to go there, Wynne would not be far behind.

His mind churned as he walked. Something in him hoped to see Wynne, make sure she was all right, but as the moments passed and sun dipped below the peaks, Morgan found himself praying she really wasn't ahead. Would she turn him away? What lies might Ryder have told her?

Morgan's eyes went skyward to the dregs of the sunset dripping down to where the stars twinkled. Over the tops of the trees, the stars glittered green, like the eyes of the serpent King.

At the base of the path, towering walls of stone rose up on either side of them, naked spots where recent landslides had stripped the mountainside. The King's Pass.

"Stay here," he said to Orgul. "Don't let anyone through."

Orgul obeyed, settling in a corner of the path, his sandpaper skin a dark shadow against the brush and rocks.

Morgan walked on. Just before a bend in the path, the hush of whispers reached Morgan's ears, and he crept forward, low, until he could see around the corner.

A man had his back to Morgan as he spoke with a shorter figure, a woman.

"Why can't you just come back?" The woman was saying, voice taut with agitation. "I don't need this well or your God."

"I will go," he responded, and Morgan recognized the voice. Killian. "But not now, not with you. You must go on." He glanced over his shoulder, eyes locking directly on Morgan as his expression tightened. "It seems my time is up."

The woman looked over, squinting, letting Morgan finally catch a glimpse of her face.

Wynne.

Wynne started at the figure stepping around the bend. Morgan's shocked face greeted her, but she couldn't hide the surge of relief she felt at seeing him. Her face broke into a smile.

She shoved past the revolutionary and wrapped her arms around Morgan before he could say another word. He enveloped her in a hug, his heartbeat strong against hers.

When she broke away, he held her close, his grip tight around her shoulders. His breath tickled her ear, voice low and strained. "Wynne, it's not safe here for you."

His words struck fear into her heart, but her fingers tightened around his arms. "It is if you're with me," she said. "What are you doing here? How's Papa?"

"He's alive. And I'm fi—" His words cut off in a hiss and white chains flashed around his arms. "Could be better," he finished with a grimace. Morgan squeezed her shoulders tight. "Listen to me, Wynne. The King sent me after the revolutionary. I know you aren't with him." His gaze shot over her to Killian. "But I can't guarantee your safety."

"What are you talking about?" Wynne stepped back.

"Your father is stable, but I don't know how long he'll hold. As soon as I get back, I'll speak with the priests on how to cover his sin." Morgan stepped forward, but not closer to her. To Killian. "But I need to take the revolutionary. Alone."

"You can't do that!" Wynne grasped Morgan's arm, but a look of pain made her let go. "I'm sorry, Morgan. I have to bring him back. The King may even forgive my father's curse."

Morgan stared at her for a moment before he pulled an envelope from his pocket. "Wynne, you can't be seen here. Until I clear your name, you can't be in Paradise either. Take these."

She took the envelope, looking up at him. "These?"

He smiled sadly. "Our papers. Take them."

"What about you?" Her heart was beating out of her chest. She couldn't just let him go. Alone. "Can't I come back with you? You can explain things to whoever is with you. I can see Papa—"

"No." Morgan's expression was grave, urgent. "Go, Wynne. You're not safe here. I'll be all right."

He pushed her away, face contorting in pain. That's when she saw the bands weaving up his arms, glowing white-hot.

Before she could speak, an arm clamped around her middle, and she was pressed against a sturdy frame. "Let me go—"

"Shut it, sweetheart." A cold blade pressed against her neck, but she didn't need to look to know who it was.

Ryder.

"What are you doing?" she hissed, but his blade dug a bit deeper, stinging, and she silenced.

She'd known better than to trust Ryder, and this moment was just another boulder to the mountain of reasons she'd ignored. She'd hoped she could use him, but now it was clear that it was the other way around.

"Chains suit you, Morgan." Ryder's voice had a harsh tone to it, a sneer that Wynne had never heard before.

"Just following in your footsteps." Morgan's dark blue eyes were stormy as they fixed on Ryder. His hand gripped the hilt of his sword, and the turn of his frown made her insides twist. "Let her go. She's got nothing to do with this."

"Oh, but she does. You're going to let me take the revolutionary back to Paradise," he said, "and I'll let Winnie live."

The use of her unwelcome nickname grated, but she forced herself to stay still. Morgan's eyes flickered to her, concern etched in the lines of his face, before the wall over his emotions came down again.

"You can't take another life and expect to be forgiven." Morgan stepped closer to Killian, who had bowed his head as if in fervent prayer. As Morgan neared, the revolutionary looked up, and Wynne saw the sorrow in his eyes—not at her, but at Ryder.

How could this man have compassion for Ryder when he was holding a knife to her throat?

"Go ahead, Morgan," Ryder snapped. "Say how much better you are than your murdering brother. Your Wynne"—Ryder's grip tightened around her, squeezing air from her lungs in a gasp—"will love to hear who you really are."

Morgan's gaze flitted back to her. "I'm afraid she's already well aware of my shortcomings," he said with a grimace.

"Of course she is." Ryder laughed. "Wouldn't you like to know how we kept warm in the snowstorm? Your Wynne—"

"Enough!" Wynne's voice echoed in the pass, silencing Ryder and drawing Morgan's tormented gaze to her. "He's lying. Take Killian. Papa needs to be healed—"

"Shut up." Ryder's voice was dangerous as he whispered in her ear. "You don't want to interfere now, Wynne."

"Let her go, Ryder!" Morgan's agitated shout cut over whatever response she might have given. At his words, a rumbling began. Pebbles tumbled down the sheer cliff faces on either side.

"Not until you give up the revolutionary," Ryder said. "Forgive me if I don't take you at your word, Morgan."

"And forgive me if I don't see beyond your actions," Morgan countered. Bigger rocks followed the pebbles down the cliffs, and Wynne struggled in Ryder's vice-like grip.

"Will you both just stop it?" Wynne's voice was shrill to her own ears even as she cut over them. "We need to get out of here—"

Her voice was drowned out by a loud rumbling. The pebbles trembled at her feet as bigger rocks hit the ground. Then rocks the size of her own head.

Ryder yanked her back just as an avalanche of rocks came tumbling down.

The last thing Wynne got to see was Morgan's arms going up as the first boulder slammed into him.

Lost

Look out,
you who walk,
reign over your soul
the serpents stalk;
My path is narrow,
straight and true,
and on its stones
crooked hearts are made new

14

"Morgan!" Wynne gasped, struggling against Ryder's grip with renewed force as he dragged her backward. Her voice didn't echo back to her down the pass, but it died in the wind and the icy drizzle of rain that pelted her skin.

"Be quiet, or you'll send the rest of the mountain down on us," Ryder snapped, one of his hands clamping over her mouth.

Rage fizzled through her blood. She couldn't leave Morgan. She wouldn't.

She dug her nails into the flesh at the back of his hand, but his grip didn't waver. A string of curses dimly reached her over the rhythm of her pounding heart.

The mountain pass dropped off into the pine forest, and Ryder's grip on her fell away. She tumbled to the ground, scraping her hands, but the stinging only fueled her anger.

She turned on him.

Her mind flashed with the image of Morgan stumbling back against the first rock, and her fury intensified. "You killed him." Ryder stepped closer, and she flinched. "Leave," she hissed.

With that, she spun on her heel, sobs wracking her frame as she stumbled back into the path. Rocks crunched under her feet, the sound of her footsteps lonely in the cavernous pass. Dark tendrils of night filled the sky, casting the ravine in darkness that reflected her very soul.

She fell to the ground at the rock pile stretching far above her. "Morgan!" she called.

No answer.

"Morgan!" she screamed again. Her voice cracked, but it echoed back to her. The mountains were silent, as if mocking her grief.

Her fingers dug out the chain under her bodice, winding tight around Morgan's signet ring. Her engagement ring.

This was her fault.

She could have stopped all of this from happening, if only she had waited. If she'd accepted Morgan's help to give an offering on Papa's behalf, she wouldn't have had to go after the revolutionary. And he wouldn't have come after her. Her own pride killed Morgan, and now it would kill Papa, too.

She cried until her tears didn't come. The damp ground sapped the heat from her bones, and she slumped against the rocks, curling into herself.

Blood at her neck from where Ryder's blade had nicked her was sticky now, but she didn't care to clean it.

Her hopes were gone. Maybe she'd never had any to begin with.

Maybe she deserved this for being all too much like Mama. So determined to get what she wanted that she didn't care who she wounded.

And now Morgan was her casualty.

In the blur of her swollen eyes, she spotted a shadow in the darkness. A figure, pacing. Then, the figure neared, and she recognized the stark white shirt and the dark mop of curls.

"Murderer!" she shouted.

Now the rocks trembled, as if the mountain was preparing to send another rockslide on her right then and there.

Her engagement ring—Morgan's signet ring and position of power—was hot in her hands. "Why don't you go and take what you deserve?" Snapping the chain, she flung the ring in his direction, where it clinked and rolled along the rocks and grass.

Ryder, a dark blur in the moonlight, stilled. His arm went up, and he seemed to run a hand through his hair, tugging at the ends.

He strode forward, and she tensed as his footsteps crunched. But he stopped, stooped to the ground, and picked up the ring. He froze as if he was going to say something to her, but turned wordlessly and walked into the darkness of the forest.

15

WHEN THE FIRST ROCK hit Morgan, he stumbled back, bracing himself for the rockslide. But nothing came. He cracked an eye open, and his jaw dropped.

The revolutionary had stepped in front of him, his arms spread wide as he murmured, "God, my hope and my shield..." A white shield, like a glass bubble, had arched overhead as the rockslide fell over them. The boulders swallowed the hazy sunlight, but white illuminated the revolutionary's determined expression.

The rumbling ceased as the rocks settled over them. It was impossible to tell how deep they were buried.

"God did this?" Morgan gasped. He got to his feet, wincing as his leg throbbed from the dragon bite, and touched the shield. Though luminescent and clear, it was firm and cold like metal.

The revolutionary nodded.

The shield that saved his life, that gave him precious moments of breath, struck something deep inside. Anger welled in his gut. What kind of God was this that saved his life on a whim but let his father die?

The revolutionary opened his mouth to say more, but Morgan beat him to it.

"My father died calling out to your God!" Morgan said. "Where was He when Father was desperate for hope? He did everything he could to follow some stupid rules!"

Father had died under the weight of sin, and Morgan wondered if that end felt something like he did now, suffocated under the threat of the rockslide without hope for escape.

"I don't know about your father," said the revolutionary. "But what about you? Who do you look to for redemption?"

Morgan scowled. The expected answer was the King, the one who held the scales of the Temple in balance. But the chains on his arms warmed at just the thought of speaking a lie. He couldn't claim to put his hopes in the King when that same King had bound him. "No one," he said finally.

The shield around them flickered, and rocks crunched as they pressed in.

"Not yourself?"

No. By his own strength, he would never calm Orgul's fiery spells. Or be free of the council's influence. Or breathe freely without the crushing weight of guilt that fell over him in the darkness of midnight when comfort and sleep eluded him.

The revolutionary sighed. "I'll go with you back to Paradise," he said.

"Why?" Morgan studied him. "You could release the shield, leave me here, and go on your way. You don't have to face the King's scales."

"I must."

"You're going to your death."

"I know where I'm going," he answered.

"The King won't let you into heaven." Morgan eyed the revolutionary.

"Good thing heaven is not his domain."

At last, the wave of a hand from the revolutionary expanded the shield like a tunnel, pushing the rocks back. Morgan led the way, letting out a breath only when he finally moved out from under the boulders.

As soon as the revolutionary was out, he dropped his arm and the tunnel collapsed. "Thank you," he said, eyes skyward.

A shadow shifted and suddenly the revolutionary was on the ground, pinned beneath Orgul's paws on his chest. Orgul snarled, blowing smoke in the revolutionary's face.

"Be nice," Morgan chided. Orgul let out a huff but eased back enough to let the revolutionary take a gasping breath.

Beside Morgan, Armor tried to climb over the wall of rocks, but after falling for the fourth time and narrowly missing a falling boulder, she seemed resigned to settle at Morgan's feet.

If Armor was here, Wynne was still alive.

Relief washed over him at sight of the silver creature, and he knelt before Armor. Her blue eyes shone just like Wynne's, sparking with fire and determination.

"If you're wanting to go after her," he said under his breath, "someone should be coming to clear the rocks soon enough."

Armor let out a long sigh and dropped her head, staring out at the bend in the path from where help would come.

How would Wynne be faring on the other side of King's Pass? Hopefully in the chaos of the rockslide, she would have escaped Ryder's grasp, far off into the rocky terrain where any sort of cave could hide her. And somehow, Morgan would come back to get her. Clear her name. They would miss the ship to get to Mandor, but at least she would be safe.

Gravel crunched, and two figures came around the bend: the captain and his dragon. His eyebrows arched in surprise and then he scowled, no doubt frustrated at how Morgan had avoided him earlier.

"I caught the revolutionary." Morgan gestured to Orgul, and he stepped back, letting the revolutionary stand.

"Killian," he offered dryly, brushing the dirt from his clothes.

"Let's get him out of here. Now," said the captain, ignoring Killian's introduction. "Men are coming to clear the path. We can't have the word spread that we caught the revolutionary. Take his coat."

Morgan stepped to Killian's side and got his dragonscale coat. The material was surprisingly light, rippling across his fingers. Where it touched his sleeve, the chains on his skin burned, and he tossed it to the captain. "You carry it. Killian can walk with me."

More footsteps sounded beyond the path, along with voices shouting, checking for any injured. Corl gingerly stowed the dragonscale coat in his pack. Two guards rounded the bend and stopped short at Captain Corl and his dragon.

"An Armynian!" one guard shouted, drawing his sword. As he lifted a hand, his arms glinted with new chains, and Morgan tugged the cuffs of his sleeves down lower.

"Captain Vander is with me." Morgan stepped forward, and the guards rounded on him.

The older guard, hand on the hilt of his sword, frowned in confusion when he spied Orgul. "And who are you?"

"Lord Delmar, councilor to the Prince. We're on an errand for the King. Long may he live." Morgan fought a grimace at his own words.

"And long may he reign," answered the guard, bowing in respect. "How may we—"

"What kind of errand?" the hotheaded guard asked, his sword still pointed at Corl, who shot Morgan an annoyed glance. They needed to get moving.

"He is awaiting our report on the outer cities of Paradise," Morgan continued. "I'll make sure the King hears of how you aided in his cause." Morgan nodded to the older guard, whose chains were dull with rust. "We need horses to get back to the capital."

"At your service." The older guard bowed again, then all but yanked his companion down the pass. "That's enough out of you..."

Morgan started after them, Orgul pushing Killian forward and Captain Corl falling at the back with his dragon.

At the edge of town, the guards had secured two horses and ignored Morgan's request for a third for Corl. Despite that, Corl mounted one horse and Morgan took the second one, and they set off.

Corl pushed the group like a team of hunting dogs down the road toward the capital. They followed the river's twists and bends. When the current dumped into the ocean, they would cross at the main bridge to the capital.

Since Armor had stayed behind at King's Pass, only two dragons flanked the revolutionary. Ruby nipped at the revolutionary's heels so he stumbled forward. If Killian so much as thought of running, he would lose an arm to a serpent.

Between the sharp pain in his forearm every time he made a fist and throbbing in his left leg from the dragon bite he'd suffered three days ago, Morgan could just about collapse. And he would at the moment—if it didn't mean he'd be sliding off a moving horse.

"Keep moving, Delmar." Corl's voice drifted back from the head of the party. "If you want any hope of finishing the mission," said Corl, "we need to get the revolutionary back before we're stopped."

Morgan straightened. "Stopped?"

"There are some of my people who would. Rumors of sightings often take wing."

Corl gave Morgan a meaningful look, and Morgan understood. Armynians. They had been rumored to be making their way through Paradise, and Corl had mentioned it at the council meeting. But why would the Armynians want the revolutionary? Weren't they working together?

After speaking with Killian, Morgan wasn't sure if that was entirely true. But he was too exhausted to investigate further.

Shadows danced before his tired eyes, and he could almost see wings flapping in the branches of overhanging trees.

Leaves rustled with the evening wind and crunched beneath both horse hooves and dragon paws. The path was edged on either side by bushes and brambles, but once they got to the riverbank, the forest cover would open up, and they would be within the eyes and protection of the capital defenses.

And it would be best if Morgan was the first to be spotted by the watchtowers and not the Armynian. "I'm taking the lead." Morgan flicked the horse's reins.

He went to the front, overtaking Ruby, who fluttered her wings at his approach.

The pace quickened further now, and the rustling of leaves and snapping of branches only grew louder. Or maybe it was his imagination. But even that was not enough to keep him entirely awake. How much had he even slept in the last few days? Not nearly enough.

Morgan was shaking himself to attention when he heard the whisper of voices behind him.

"Where is your scroll?" The captain's voice, hard and suspicious.

No response.

"Your dagger?"

"Gone," came the terse reply from Killian.

"Just summon another one," the captain hissed. "Stop wasting time."

"You know it doesn't work like that. And I have time. What about you, Vander? What are you in such a hurry for?"

"Getting you on your knees before the King would be the highlight of my life," snapped the captain. "So you better watch your mouth if you don't want a worse punishment than death."

"I'll take my punishment over your chains."

The captain huffed and whispered something else, but Morgan couldn't hear. Maybe he was dreaming the whole thing. Movement in the trees stole his attention, and a pair of serpentine red eyes met his. They winked out, and only darkness blinked at him now. The hairs on the back of his neck stood on end.

He glanced behind him. Corl rode at the back of the pack. Ruby and Orgul stood on either side of the revolutionary, but where Orgul's gaze was trained on Killian's every movement, Ruby's eyes flicked up to the trees.

Morgan turned his attention to the front, where a clearing opened up a few hundred feet away. The stomping of feet seemed to echo through the forest, and even up ahead. He put a hand on his sword and quickened his horse's pace, mind whirling with the potential for an upcoming attack.

They were only a few yards from breaking into the clearing, and Morgan could see the fortress walls of the capital over the river, when a sudden motion made him reel backward.

Dragon claws swiped the air where his head had been.

"We're under attack!" Morgan shouted, drawing his sword. His horse skittered forward, shaking its head in fear. "Orgul, get the revolutionary out of the forest."

He certainly wasn't going to trust Corl to go up against his people to defend the interests of the King of Paradise. He glanced back to see Corl with his sword drawn, but Ruby flew up into the trees and disappeared.

"Move!" Corl shouted at the revolutionary.

Killian stumbled forward as another dragon swooped down. Orgul shot a burst of amber flames, setting the trees ablaze.

Morgan broke through the tree cover and dismounted, letting his horse run for the river. He would be a still target, but he wouldn't have to worry about falling off a moving horse with his feet planted on the ground. The revolutionary stumbled out after Morgan, and Corl came blazing through on his horse, sword raised as he faced the forest.

"Get him back to the capital," shouted Corl. "I'll hold them off."

A third dragon burst from the trees, but a red blur rammed into it midair. Ruby tangled with the other dragon, clawing at its hide and sinking her teeth into its leg. The dragon let out a roar.

The dragon untangled from Ruby and shot down to the forest, where more eyes blinked out at them.

Morgan grasped Killian by the arm and started dragging him down to the river. His eyes were wide with fear, though a certain look of sorrow also came over his features. "Enough of this!" Killian shouted. "You are going down the wrong path!"

The only response was four more Armynian dragons swooping out of the trees, four figures after them. Morgan's skin prickled with apprehension. They were outnumbered, humans and dragons alike.

Morgan's gaze shot to Corl, holding his sword steady at what Morgan would have guessed were his comrades. But not so by the look of aggravation on his face. Corl shot a fierce look at Morgan. "Go!"

Morgan turned to Killian, whom he still gripped by the arm. "Can you swim?"

Killian frowned.

"If you don't go, I'm going to have to make Orgul drag you, and that won't be fun."

Killian's face was that of stoic determination, and Morgan wondered if the revolutionary actually wanted to see the King. He must have had some idea of the bloody fate that awaited him.

"Watch out!" Corl's voice sounded from up the hill.

Morgan turned in time to see three Armynian dragons swooping for Killian. He shoved Killian to the ground and drew his word, bracing to take the leftmost dragon.

Boom.

The air shook with a sudden wind as a net soared over Morgan's head and trapped the first dragon. A wave of relief sagged Morgan's shoulders as the shouts of guards behind him reached his ears. Reinforcements.

The gates opened and guards stormed out. Ballistas fired, downing dragons with nets or stunning them with a solid blow. Corl knocked out another Armynian man.

The tides had turned. Now the Armynians retreated to the forest as the Paradisian guards crossed the river and reached Morgan and the revolutionary. The guards took Killian and one brought Morgan's horse back to him. He mounted, but waited for Corl and his dragon to approach.

He nodded at Corl. The captain had earned his begrudging respect and a flicker of trust. He hadn't taken Killian but actively tried to help Morgan get him back to the capital. Pink dawned on the horizon ahead, chasing away the dregs of night and the adrenaline coursing through Morgan's system.

He noticed the guard beside him, awaiting orders.

"Take the revolutionary to the Temple with the men, and hold him until I arrive," said Morgan. The guard nodded and obeyed. Morgan looked to Corl, whose face was marred with a streak of blood where a blade or claw must have nicked him. "Get some rest, and we'll speak with the Prince later."

The revolutionary went with the guards, four dragons now on every corner, as he was escorted through the gates. Captain Corl followed them.

Morgan waited until they were out of sight before he urged his horse forward. Exhaustion made his seat on his horse precarious, but the empty streets shot a sudden bite of fear into Morgan. Eyes blinked out from shutters, some from the rooftops, and even a few in the alleys. Morgan heard the whispers even as he strode further into the city.

A single light illuminated the manor. A guard rushed to open it as Morgan neared, and by the time Morgan reached the front stoop, half a dozen servants received him as he slipped off the horse. The moment his feet touched the ground, searing pain shot up his leg and his vision dimmed.

Arms went up around his shoulders as the ground swayed beneath him. A sharp voice cut through the air, "Go deal with the horse," Mother barked, "and fetch a priest."

She continued to spew orders at the servants, but the words were drowned out by the pounding in Morgan's ears. Mother's arms slipped and the ground came up to meet him. Black flashed before him with the slither of scales.

Darkness fluttered around the edges of Morgan's visions as he felt a soft surface beneath him. The pull of sleep was overwhelming, enhanced now by whatever warm potion someone pressed to his lips. The bitter liquid sank in his gut before nightmares finally claimed him.

His dreams were accosted by visions of snapping jaws, unbreakable shackles, and Wynne. Sometimes smiling, eyes alight like waves glittering on the shore, sometimes dark and moody like rumbling thunderclouds on the edge of the pier.

When, at last, he woke up and stared into a pair of serpentine orange eyes, he could still feel the pressure of crocodilian jaws clamped around his neck.

Orgul blinked at him and left the room.

Morgan turned his head to follow the scaly creature. The curtains he usually kept closed had been drawn, the pale morning light catching dust motes floating in the air.

His head pounded, and even as he blinked into consciousness, he felt the unmistakable pull to the depths of slumber. Sleep claimed him once more.

Wynne awoke to the glitter of gold. She squinted against the sunlight red against her eyelids, swiping at the salt and grime on her face from where her tears had left tracks. Pain pierced her as she remembered Morgan, the landslide, and grief squeezed her heart like a snake trying to suffocate her.

She was struck with regret and self-loathing so strong it forced the air from her lungs. Why hadn't she listened to him? Why hadn't she trusted him to have given an offering for Papa's life? With a payment from Morgan, that would have been enough to heal Papa.

This was her fault.

Morgan was gone, and soon, Papa would be, too.

She missed Armor's comforting presence, her silver tail wrapped around her ankles. Grounding her when she thought she would dissipate into thin air. She tried to reach Armor, but her connection felt tenuous, like a frayed string stretched too far.

So she had no comfort, only her aching back where a rock dug into her spine and the dry grit of dirt on her tongue that made her realize she was still here. Alive.

When Morgan was not.

She forced her eyes open and sat up, clutching at her pounding head.

Her stomach let out a fierce growl, and she groaned. "Quiet."

She stood and grasped the wall for support as her world swayed.

But then she froze.

She was not where she had been before. She was at least a hundred feet from the rockslide, and large boulders had been moved. But the pile of rocks was still insurmountable.

Unsurvivable.

She forced her gaze to study her surroundings and spotted a fire farther down the path, the direction that Ryder had dragged her yesterday. The embers glowed faintly in the morning light, above which a small creature roasted.

Her stomach growled with a vengeance, and she found herself at the fire, removing a chunk of meat and putting it to her lips. It had to have been some kind of small game, and it was cooked to the point of dryness, as if someone had forgotten it on the fire, but just the smell of it made her stomach cramp with hunger. She dropped the morsel of meat.

With a swift movement, she kicked her heel against the ground, spraying dirt over the embers and the roasting meat. She scowled.

She knew who'd left this.

And Ryder would not get a hold on manipulating her again.

She beat the dirt from her skirts and started down the King's Pass. Her flask hung at her hip, jingling with each step. It was a quiet reminder of her final chance: the well of living water.

She didn't care for Killian's God or Son or whatever. But if their water could bring life where the King couldn't, she would take it.

16

MORGAN WOKE TO THE golden glow of sunlight. He turned his head away from the window, and gathered the will to tear himself from the comfort of the blankets.

He'd caught the revolutionary, but he wasn't done yet. Not until Addie was free.

He sat up, rubbing his eyes. How long had he been out?

He shifted his legs over the edge of the bed and almost gasped. His wounded leg, which had throbbed and ached since the Armynian dragon had bitten him days ago, was healed. Where teeth marks had once punctured his skin, now the flesh was knit back together, slightly swollen but as if from a few bug bites and nothing more.

Someone must have paid for the herbs from the priests.

The Prince wouldn't have given it out freely, even if Morgan had completed the task of bringing the revolutionary back.

Morgan tested his weight. His legs held, though pain lingered. He took a deep breath. Even though his headache had subsided, the dull throbbing in his bones remained.

Clothes, folded neatly at the foot of the bed, greeted him. When he reached for them, cool metal registered on his skin—the chains—and he groaned.

He dressed in what little peace he could, soreness in every movement of his fingers and breath in his lungs.

A quiet knock sounded.

"Come in."

The hinges squeaked as the door opened, but silence filled the air, and Morgan lifted his gaze. Shock registered over his frame when he spotted Mother.

She eclipsed the doorframe, clutching her arms around her middle. Worry carved the lines of her face, and her thin lips were white as she pressed them together.

"Are...are you hungry?" Her voice was steady, though her frame looked as broken as when she'd told him that Father had gone on to eternity—though what eternity, he didn't know.

It took him a moment to register her question. "No." He cringed at the sharpness in his tone. "Thank you," he added softly.

She took a tentative step into the room. "Are you well?" Her eyes dropped to his neck, where he knew dark bruises exposed the difficulty of his journey chasing after the revolutionary.

Killian, his mind corrected. *He has a name, you know*. He shook the nagging thought away and stood.

"I will be when I free Addie. What news is there for Elwin?"

Mother grimaced, and Morgan's heart beat twice as fast. "He's been moved to the Temple for final mediation." Her gaze fell to the floor.

Fear cinched Morgan's throat. "Since when?"

"Right before you arrived. Wait, Morgan, you must rest—" She raised her hands to block him, as at her words he had crossed the room.

He ignored her last comment. Elwin might still have time—though not much. Fierce anger coiled in his chest like a serpent ready to strike. "Why didn't you do anything?"

If Elwin was dead, on his count, would Wynne ever forgive him?

"Why didn't you get a priest?" Morgan glared at Mother. "Why didn't you pay an offering?"

"I did try."

Dread seized Morgan around the throat while self-loathing at his own words seeped into him. "Did they weigh your offering?"

Mother hesitated. "I–I'm not certain."

"I'll weigh it myself." He snatched his coat, but Mother wouldn't move. Her green eyes seemed to penetrate his facade. Her brow furrowed in concern.

"Morgan, you are not well."

"I can walk. I can breathe. I am well enough to go get my sister—"

"The Prince sent notice that she will be facing trial today." Mother passed him a white document with elegant lettering.

Morgan ran a hand through his hair and tugged at the ends, frustration and anger and fear tangling in his chest so he wasn't sure which one would win. "How could you let this happen?" he snapped.

Anger, then.

Hurt flickered across Mother's features before she steeled her emotions. Beyond Mother, her dragon, Elya, let out a growl of warning.

"I did all I could." Her lips twitched into a frown.

"It wasn't enough." Fire seethed in his belly, but his words tasted bitter.

"Nothing will ever be enough." Mother's voice was soft and cold, though her eyes flashed. "I am not like your father. I am no saint, but I can't see you make the same mistakes that I did."

Morgan let out a bark of laughter. Sometimes he'd considered how much better it would have been if Father were still here. But the venom of his own thoughts poisoned him, and he winced.

What kind of person was he becoming?

Morgan tore his gaze away, went to the water basin, and washed his face. He couldn't mistake the bruises crawling up his neck, the dark purple under his eyes. Or the glint in his eyes that made him look wild. He splashed water on his face again, but the expression remained.

Mother was watching him in the reflection of the mirror.

"Your anger doesn't serve you... Don't let it ruin your heart like it has hardened mine." With that, her vulnerability was hidden behind her mask of indifference, and she left.

By noon, Wynne reached the border of Paradise and Armyn with little spectacle.

She'd managed the pangs of hunger by snagging some berries. But with all the rough terrain she'd had to navigate, climbing over boulders and through thick brush, she was starving. All the while, she'd been hoping Armor would be coming on her heels. She caught glimpses of running through the barren fields, the forest, as Armor crossed Paradise to reach her. Hopefully she would reach Wynne within a few hours.

She also had an unexpected and unwelcome shadow on her heels.

Ryder had been trailing within at least a hundred feet as she continued her trek to Armyn. She could hear his footsteps over the wet pine needles whenever she paused to catch her breath or give her aching muscles a rest. She could sense his wariness in the set of his shoulders, but she was glad he didn't approach.

His footsteps ceased when she did as she stopped at the edge of the clearing to the gates. Sentry posts guarded the narrow entrance to the kingdom of Armyn, but not a soul stirred. Abandoned.

She crept forward, her boots barely crunching over the gravel, and went to the gate.

The thick metal frame was bent and marked where dragon claws had scored the gates and torn through into Paradise. Fire scorched the ground, and a few blades lay scattered in the snow. A battle had occurred here.

But she didn't think she wanted to know the outcome.

When she turned, she spotted Ryder in the clearing. He went to the sentry houses—tall, narrow buildings built into the border wall. Firelight flickered out of one of the houses as Ryder peered in, all but ignoring her.

The look of concern on his face sent a wave of fear through her.

"What is it?" She broke the silence between them and stepped forward, but he held up a hand in warning.

Her hand fell to the dagger at her side.

At last, he straightened and faced her. "They're gone."

She frowned, tasting bile as her stomach twisted. The guards were dead. Taken down by the Armynians. The way the doors twisted outward, like a can being turned inside out, made her think the force had been overwhelming.

But why hadn't she spotted any more Armynians since Horia? Where were they hiding?

She dared a peek into the second sentry house. No bodies there.

She frowned. If all the guards were in the first sentry post, then this had been a calculated attack. Hidden, so anyone who came across it might not immediately recognize the reality of the events that had occurred here. But just brazen enough to leave a message that the border of Paradise had been breached.

But she needed to keep going, find the cure for Papa.

Before she left, she entered the sentry tower and searched the pantry. The trek up to the capital of Armyn, at least a couple of miles up and westward, would be difficult to undergo on berries alone.

At last, with a makeshift pack slung over her shoulder, she stepped through the gates into Armyn. Ryder was nowhere to be seen.

Where lush pine trees populated the western Paradisian rise of the mountains, the Armynian side was barren. Gray ash plumed into the air as she stirred it. Even her footsteps were muffled.

Since entering Armyn, the ground had sloped upward, and now as Wynne looked back, she saw the border wall, the desolate winter fields beyond, and just a glimmer on the horizon that would have been the sea and the capital.

She kept going, and the higher she went, the wetter the ground became. Ash and dirt became a kind of sludge. Little green shoots of new growth barely peeked through the carnage that blew through less than a week ago.

Wynne had seen the fire that ravaged the mountains, the sparks that seemed to fly from the hills as Armynians fled into Symara and Paradise. Silence settled over her like a blanket of snow.

Where were the Armynians? They couldn't all have perished... Maybe those that survived the fire chose to hide themselves in the infinite expanse of caves carved by rain and ravines. And Wynne could hardly blame them. After all, if Paradise had been the country to face a disgraceful rebellion, Wynne would've preferred to hide her face than spy the looks of judgment from neighboring kingdoms.

But something was definitely wrong now.

She hadn't studied maps like Morgan, but she imagined she would've reached a city by now. Or some kind of landmark. Killian said to go to the Armynian temple. Large outcroppings of rocks and cliffs made the path treacherous.

She stopped in her tracks. What she thought had been the charred trunks of trees or strange rock formations was actually a home. A shell of what it might have been, scorched to its foundation.

Beside it, another. And another.

A city. In ashes.

She stepped forward further into the ruins. The heels of her boots clicked against stones, too straight and level to be an accident. She kicked at the sludge with her boot until she caught a glimpse of cobblestones.

What could've caused all this? Wynne felt tears prick her eyes.

She stepped forward. Something crunched under her boot, and when she stepped back, the ivory gleam of bones peeked out of the ash.

Digging her fingers into the bricks of one structure, she hauled herself higher. Then a little bit more. She reached as high as she could go, about fifteen feet up, and finally spotted what she couldn't see over the remnants of the buildings.

Seeing the ruins of the city had brought ice to her veins, but what shocked her like a blast of icy water was the white marble stones of the Temple scattered. The Armynian temple had fallen.

17

By the time she reached the steps of the Armynian temple, the hair on Wynne's arms stood on end.

The great double oak doors of the Temple were ajar, one off its hinges, deep grooves marking where a large dragon must have clawed his way inside. The steps were broken and uneven.

The realization hit her with a wave of dread.

This was not the work of the revolutionaries.

No, the Temple had been destroyed by Armyn's own people.

And now the Armynians were in Paradise, having torn through the border wall. How much longer until the same fate befell Paradise?

She let out a shuddering breath, steeled her shoulders, and started up the broken steps to the Temple.

The sanctuary was in shambles. The veil between the foyer and the scales lay on the floor in charred scraps stained with mud and ash. Beyond, Wynne couldn't help but marvel at the remnant of the splendor she had never glimpsed in her life.

Morning rays cut through the cracks along the domed ceiling, which still rained down dust at the softest breeze. A large hole dug straight down into the heart of the marble flooring. At the very end, where Wynne could only imagine the glorious carving that had once been there, sat a grotesque carcass of a snake.

His body, as wide as the largest tree trunk in Paradise, was covered in blue-gray scales, slashed in some places where a knife must have cut his hide. His head rested on one end of the massive scale, white eyes glaring at them, almost alive, if it wouldn't have been that his head was severed from his body. Two large fangs cut grooves into the slick marble, as if the scuffle had ended and someone had dragged the body to the scales.

On the other side, pristine and silver, sat the other scale plate.

It was only when Wynne saw the body of an older man laid out before the scales that she recognized the creature before her. The King of Armyn had been killed. And the Prince had perished with him.

A sudden rustle made Wynne jerk back. Her heartbeat drummed in her ears. She spun toward the sound and spotted Ryder at the edge of the sanctuary.

Metal clanged against the floor as Ryder threw his blade down. He stepped forward, palms up. He worried his bottom lip with his teeth, a gesture she recognized from Morgan when he was deciding what to say. She scowled and shoved down tears.

"Wynne, I—"

"Can't listen, can you?" She strode forward and snatched the dagger from the marble, inspecting the shattered blade.

"I'm sorry," he blurted.

She scoffed, the fiery anger in her belly fueling her words. "Sorry? You?"

He swallowed, his throat bobbing. "I'm a wretched man," he said, "and I deserve every horrible punishment."

"And you're about to get one now if you don't leave, Ryder." She raised the dagger. The scab at her throat pulled when she swallowed, a reminder of the dangerous man who stood before her.

But the Ryder ten yards away was not the man who'd taken her hostage. His shoulders, usually tall and set with some kind of arrogance, were stooped with shame. His callused hands, the ones that clamped her mouth so she wouldn't scream, were shaking.

The expression in his dark blue eyes, so often that of guardedness, was laid bare. Regret. Fear.

The hilt of the dagger felt slick in her palm. Wynne lowered the weapon and tossed it into the hole in the ground.

It clattered when it hit bottom a few seconds later, echoing below the Temple as if revealing a cavernous area.

Relief flickered across Ryder's features, and he stepped forward. "Wynne, I don't deserve forgiveness, but I need to believe that there's something more."

She tensed when he reached into his coat. Something glowed in his clenched fist.

Killian's scroll.

The light bounced off the lines of Ryder's face, making him look all the more serious.

She scoffed. "So you're one of them, now?"

"I need to try," he said. "If God can't help me, no one can. Maybe He can help you...and Morgan," he added the latter as if to himself, his words a quiet breeze over the all-too-stagnant air of the sanctuary.

"I don't need another ruler over my life," she snapped. "This God isn't any different than the King."

Ryder opened his mouth as if to protest but snapped it shut. "I—I don't know...but I need to find out."

"Do it on your own." With that, she turned on her heel.

She had nothing to do immediately, so she went to inspect the hole at the center of the temple. A strong scent of moist earth reached her, and she stole a glance at Ryder as he inspected the jeweled carvings on the walls.

She didn't like being so close to him. He walked carefully, as if trying not to scare a caged animal, and his gentleness aggravated her to no end. She turned from the sanctuary and went into the Temple archives.

Shelves lined each side of the room, where scrolls and books and papers weighed down the wooden shelves. Further down, she knew the curtains led to the confession rooms, where the priests took a person's words of repentance and presented it before the King on their behalf.

She didn't step any further down the archives, however, as the smell of rotting flesh assaulted her senses. She was just about to reenter the sanctuary when she heard Ryder's voice.

"...I don't know where to go, God, but if You can, please show me..."

Anger bubbled in Wynne at the vulnerability in his voice. He didn't deserve to beg for forgiveness when he'd killed Morgan. He deserved punishment.

She pushed through the curtain to give him a piece of her mind and froze.

Ryder was gone. The only sign that he had been there were the footprints by the well. She rushed to the edge, dropping to her knees as she leaned over the darkness. "Ryder?"

There was nowhere he could've gone—but down. But the well was dry—wasn't it? Or was it some kind of hidden passage?

But the dagger had fallen for a few seconds. She would have heard Ryder below.

She squinted into the darkness. Even with the broken sunlight filtering in overhead, the bottom looked dark, and it was impossible for her to believe he could've gone down without her hearing it.

Wynne got up and walked to the front of the Temple. No other set of footsteps appeared beyond her own, but maybe he'd run quickly enough—and silently enough—to make it outside?

She squinted against the sunlight when she looked out over the city ruins.

Then she spotted silver. Armor bounded to the bottom of the steps.

"You came!" Wynne couldn't help but smile. She dropped to her knees, wrapping Armor in a hug.

A second later, she drew back. "You're bigger."

And so she was.

Where Armor had only reached Wynne's hips back in Kyrn, now, as Wynne stood, she balked. Armor's blue eyes were level with hers.

Where she would have felt elated at the newfound prestige that would have come with a larger dragon, she only felt a sense of dread.

Killian's words echoed in her mind.

What would you say if you could see the hold they have on you? How big will she get before you lose control?

Before your defense becomes your prison?

Armor growled as if sensing the turn of her thoughts, and Wynne shook them from her head. She brushed a hand over Armor's snout. "Come on, girl. Let's save Papa."

She started back into the sanctuary, Armor's claws striking the marble behind her as she followed. Her dragon let out a growl as they entered the sanctuary. Wynne went to the hole. "Over here."

But Armor didn't move. Her gaze was fixed on the dead King and the Prince. Her body tensed, the silver scales rippling with the force of her muscles beneath.

"It's all right, girl."

Red flashed in Wynne's mind, a flash of anger. Wynne shook her head to clear the feeling. "Snap out of it. What's going on with you?"

The anger pressed in on Wynne again, stronger and deeper than before. And a vision filled her mind: Mama's golden hair tussled by the breeze, a radiant smile on her face when she was helping Wynne with her own unruly mane. Not that Wynne had known it would be the last time her mother's careful fingers would wind her hair into a semblance of propriety.

Wynne scowled, swallowing the sting of betrayal. "I know you're upset, but that was uncalled f—"

Another image seared her mind. And she saw herself as Armor saw her—leaning away from the dragon, hesitation in her eyes. A barrier that hadn't been there before. And her dragon's overwhelming sense of betrayal. She shook the vision free as Armor took the first step toward her, a low growl in her throat.

Icy fear shot through her, and she raised her hands. "Armor, this isn't you."

The elation she felt melted under the scorching heat of Armor's glare.

She stepped back as Armor growled.

Wynne reacted the same moment Armor pounced. Her fingers wrapped around the flask at her hip, and she nailed Armor across the snout and ducked. Armor sailed over her, scraping against the marble as she clawed to a stop. Barely maintaining her balance, Wynne straightened.

"Stop!" she shouted. "What's gotten into you?"

Armor adjusted her stance to pounce again, kneading her paws against the marble. She leapt forward again, but when Wynne ducked, searing heat went up her calf. Armor flicked her tail back, blood dripping from the silver scales. Wynne bit her lip to keep from crying out.

Armor circled.

Wynne tightened her grip around the flask. "Don't do it, Armor. I don't want to hurt you—"

Armor pounced. Wynne dodged. Too slow.

Her dragon swept her feet out from under her. They went tumbling over the hole's edge. Armor clawed at her shoulder, her jaws snapping inches from Wynne's neck. Wynne squeezed her eyes shut, bracing for the ground.

Cold water enveloped her. Her eyelids went red with whatever light shone on her face, and she blinked her eyes open.

Instead of Armor wrestling with her in the water, a shadowy figure held Wynne's arms pinned to her side. The sunlight cut through the water like a sword, seeming to tear into Armor's flesh, leaving bright red spots of exposed meat.

Bright blue eyes glared at her as the wraith-like figure screeched. "Give it up!" the creature seethed, convulsing and hissing. "You'll never make it... Come back and maybe you'll get mercy for Papa—"

"No!" In a burst of bubbles, Wynne released her breath and pulled the wraith's claws off her arms.

She started paddling toward the surface, the circle of light. The wraith cut through the water, its silhouette eclipsing the rays. Where the sunlight touched the creature's silver head, gold hair sprouted. Its limbs grew and paled, though spotted and disgusting...and when it inched closer, the sunlight dimmed. The wraith looked like...her.

"Stop this." The wraith extended a hand. "Be who you know you are."

As it spoke, the last of the wisps of darkness disappeared to reveal an elegant dress. Jewels adorned her neck and hands.

"No!" Wynne's head pounded as the last of her breath escaped her. Water flooded her lungs, dark spots clouding her vision.

The last thing she saw was a crown glittering atop the wraith's head before her consciousness slipped to the depths.

Morgan stood stiffly at the edge of the sanctuary, squinting at the figures that entered through the veil. Light flickered as the fabric parted and met again, but it didn't pierce the darkness that infiltrated the Temple.

First Mother. Then the council. Captain Vander.

Mother fell in line beside Morgan. Lord Ashton kept by the veil, while Lord Soam and Corl stood opposite to Morgan.

Soam shot a smug look at Morgan and Mother, but if Mother noticed, she didn't let on.

Morgan didn't think he was hiding his frustration at all. It was bad enough that Addie was on trial—worse that everyone would be witness to his family's humiliation. Again.

The most he got was an unreadable glance from Corl. Morgan had met him inside the sanctuary after pushing past the High Priest earlier, but no one would let them speak to the Prince. Despite all his efforts, Addie would still have to face trial.

Captain Corl didn't look fazed by the beauty in the space, his eyes solely fixed on the gold grate in the center of the room. His dragon paced behind him, wings fluttering.

Felipe Ashton crossed the room and stood beside Morgan. Even though his gaze was fixed on the scales and the High Priest, when he spoke, Morgan knew it was to him. "Adelaide will go free today," he said.

"How do you know?" Morgan felt the coins in his pocket. He knew Mother brought more, but it may not be enough anyway. The standards of the scales were fickle and unjust beyond reason.

Felipe's eyes glinted with determination. "I have something to trade. The King has often asked my father for it."

Morgan frowned. Best friend or not, he couldn't stand if he owed Felipe a sum he wouldn't ever be able to repay. Mother surely wouldn't allow it. "I should hope it won't come to that," he answered.

"I hope for many things," Felipe said, "but mercy is not one of them."

Morgan's stomach twisted.

"It is a rare quality in this kingdom," Felipe went on, eyes darkening as the priests balanced the two scale plates with weights and set the scales. "They're starting."

A chill went down Morgan's spine. Witnesses, the Prince said. That was what the council members were for. Morgan ventured it served more as a reminder of what would happen if they spoke blasphemy against the King.

He'd seen a High Trial before. And Ryder had barely escaped with his life weighed against the scales.

Morgan crossed the room as the curtains behind the scales parted. Addie entered, hands at her sides, walking stiffly before the rotund form of High Priest Anias.

He was unremarkable from the other priests, with the white-gold robes and dangling emeralds, only he wore the most expensive and decadent of the offerings around his neck each year.

Morgan jolted. Around Anias's neck, hanging almost so it would have blended into the folds of his white robes if Morgan hadn't seen it all the years of his life, was Father's family crest. A falcon cast in silver.

Realization almost took the breath from his lungs. His dragon bite had been cured, but he never questioned at what cost. His gaze shot to Mother, but her eyes were fixed on Addie with a determination he was only beginning to understand.

The high priest led Addie to stand by the scales; then he raised a hand, and the whispers of the council hushed. Eli came in behind Anias and held a small bundle in his hands. Morgan thought he looked smug.

"Greetings, blessed. We come today before the scales to weigh the case of Adelaide Delmar. She stole a parcel of healing herbs from the Temple stores." Anias lifted a bundle. "We may hear her defense or repentance once the scales speak their piece."

Addie stepped up onto one plate, and it sank to the floor with her weight. Whisper went to the other side. Despite Whisper's bird-like size, the scales balanced.

The high priest placed the herbs on Whisper's plate, and Addie yelped as her scale shot up a few feet.

Morgan's breath caught in his throat. A great imbalance. A huge debt.

"You may speak your defense, Adelaide," Anias said solemnly.

Addie straightened, though her hands shook as she clasped them in front of her. "I did take these herbs," she said, "for my brother's injuries after a house fire."

"Why didn't you go to the priests or the Temple for healing?" the high priest asked. Addie hesitated. She glanced at Morgan.

He nodded, and she took a breath. "Morgan didn't want the priests to know."

High Priest Anias frowned. "Was he injured in sin?"

Morgan felt Eli's glance move to him.

"No," said Addie.

"Did it involve a revolutionary?" Eli interjected.

Addie fumbled, looking like she wanted to take the words back all over again. Morgan felt the stares turn his way. At last, Addie nodded.

"You must speak," prompted Anias.

"Yes." Then she pursed her lips shut.

Eli looked like he wanted Anias to keep going, keep drilling, but the Prince looked bored. "Morgan is not on trial here," he snapped at Eli.

"But his dragon—the burns—" Eli hissed.

"Morgan brought the revolutionary back," answered the Prince, flashing a look of annoyance at Morgan, as if reminding Morgan how much he'd wished for him to fail. "What more do you have to say, Eli?"

Eli was silenced.

The high priest looked to Addie. "What payment will you find to appease your sin? Will anyone step forward to pay your debt?"

Morgan stepped forward. He procured a small purse from his pocket.

Eli snatched them and went to the plate where Addie stood. One by one he placed the coins by Addie's feet. Slowly, ever so slowly, the plate drew downward. The purse emptied.

But it was not enough.

At least a foot of difference sat between the two plates. Morgan's pulse ricocheted in his skull as he met Mother's gaze.

She stepped forward, procuring a second purse.

Eli snatched that as well, though now with a malicious glint of glee in his eyes, and dumped the purse unceremoniously on the scales. Addie's feet were covered in gold coins, but the plates didn't move.

"The King demands a tribute of greater worth," said the Prince. "Money is not sufficient. What else do you have to offer?"

Mother froze and Morgan tensed, his mind whirring as terror suddenly cinched around his throat.

Mother spoke first. "Take my life." She let out a breath. "The years that she would pay, take them from me. Don't chain her."

The Prince frowned. "What part of your life does the King not already own?" He waved a hand dismissively. "That's not enough."

Mother blanched. Morgan stepped forward, but a hand stopped him.

"Take mine," said Felipe, stepping forward.

"Felipe," Lord Ashton snapped, throwing his son a firm look. His brows were pinched with worry.

The Prince glanced between Lord Ashton and Felipe, an amused look on his face. "Come forward," he said, and Morgan could have sworn he saw a victorious expression cross the Prince's features.

Morgan's heart drummed in his ears so loud he couldn't even hear the Prince recite the words that had bound Morgan a few days ago, but the result was the same. Felipe was stoic as the animated chains snaked up his wrists to his elbows and seared his skin with a hiss of burning fabric.

At the moment the chains darkened on Felipe's arms, the scales balanced, and the tension uncoiled in Morgan's chest.

The payment had been enough.

Addie let out a cry when her plate dropped.

"You are forgiven," said the high priest. He cleared the coins and gestured for Whisper to move. The gold dragon hopped off the plates, and Addie was once again on the ground.

Addie rushed to Felipe's side and crushed him in a hug. Whisper leapt to Orgul and hid behind the bigger dragon. After a few moments, Addie suddenly pulled away, swiping at her tears with her sleeve. "I'm sorry," she said, stifling a laugh, "you're all dirty now—"

Felipe smiled, though Morgan caught the sudden tension to his frame. Morgan felt the same, now that he saw Addie up close and could spy the grime and filth that clung to her.

"Let's go, Adelaide." Mother gripped Addie's shoulder.

Addie frowned, but Morgan interjected before she could protest. "Go check on Elwin for me, please?"

He gave Addie a look that hopefully conveyed his worry for Elwin and not his apprehension at having her stay.

A trial before the priests was tame compared to the King.

Addie and Mother left, and Felipe was once again at his side, his features drawn in apprehension. Guilt clawed at Morgan's insides at seeing his friend bound, but he was stopped from speaking by the beginning of the second trial.

The curtains beyond the scales opened a second time, and the Prince entered, followed by the revolutionary. It was with a bitter reluctance that Morgan recognized Killian's expression was like that of Ryder's before his judgment.

Anias made the revolutionary stand on the scales, which fell to the floor at his weight. Killian raised his chin in noble defiance.

The high priest held out the revolutionary's dragonscale coat. "This man is to be tried before the King. He is charged with the murder of his dragon."

Anias gestured, and Eli went to the center of the sanctuary, where a golden lid hid a drain. At one point, when Paradise was first founded, the drain would catch the blood of animals sacrificed to appease the King. Paradise didn't sacrifice animals to cover people's sins anymore, so history had been covered up by a gilded golden circle. As if there was beauty to be found in having another pay for the price of one's sins.

With great effort, Eli lifted the golden cover and pulled it aside. Wisps of smoke poured out, curling around the spectators' ankles, before two green orbs of light cut through the fog.

The King emerged with the grace and ferocity of a panther—first the large flat head, flicking pink tongue, and stunning verdant scales over his long, slender body. Eyes gleamed with the same fierce intelligence as they had before, only now the

King seemed larger as he circled around the scales and lowered his face before the revolutionary.

Now Prince Tannin stepped forward. His green eyes flashed as he faced the revolutionary. "You, Killian, have put yourself at war with me and Paradise." The King hissed at the last word.

Killian did not even acknowledge the Prince.

"How will you defend yourself?" Tannin shouted. "There is no longer a way for me to help you, to save you from the fires of damnation. What will you do now that you will perish with the rest of the revolutionaries?" The snake took on a softer hiss as Tannin spoke, purring, taunting. "Speak."

The King flicked his tongue across Killian's face.

Killian flinched, but his voice didn't tremble as he spoke, loud and resounding, in the air of the sanctuary.

"Your Temple and your Paradise are a mockery. You can't save me. That's already been done, but not by you."

"Liar," said Tannin. "Can your precious God pay the price for your soul?"

Anias threw the dragonscale coat on the scales—and instead of shooting down to reveal Killian's guilt, the plate remained motionless. Murmurs arose around the council.

Morgan was almost breathless.

The King hissed. He lifted his tail and pressed down on the scale opposite the revolutionary.

The scales didn't move. Killian remained on the ground.

Killian was right. He owed nothing to the King, not even his life.

Eli rushed forward. With the hooked pole, he removed the dragonskin from the opposite plate. Put it on the scales again.

Nothing.

A furious hiss emerged from the King's mouth, and in a flash, his tail smacked the revolutionary. Killian flew through the air, hit the wall, and crumpled.

"Ssstand," said Tannin, now in tandem with the King.

Killian groaned and sat up, one arm bent at the wrong angle. "You may deceive many, but not for much longer. Your reign over this world is coming to an end, as it has long ago—"

"Blassssphemy!" shouted Tannin. The snake reared back, coiled as if to strike.

But it wasn't the King who moved.

With a rustle of scales, Orgul pressed forward. Then Elya, Mother's dragon. Then the other council members lost their companions as they marched forward and formed a ring around the revolutionary. Dread twisted Morgan's gut.

"Let's ssssee if your God will help you now," said Tannin.

All at once, each dragon let out a burst of fire. Colored flames licked the revolutionary's clothes and hair. Morgan almost looked away, but he would've missed what happened next.

Wherever the red or black flames touched Killian, white glowed on his skin. His elbow moved back into place. His leg unbent from the crooked break. His skin healed.

Beside Killian, a figure appeared. If Killian was white, this figure was radiant. It helped Killian to stand.

Then both figures were gone.

Not even Killian's clothes—or ash—remained.

Morgan felt like he was going to be sick. Beside him, a few nobles exchanged perturbed glances as their dragons went back to their sides.

It was one thing to serve the unseen King, quite another to face his wrath.

But the wretched King didn't immediately go back to his hole. Instead, he stared at Tannin. The bright green faded from Tannin's eyes, replaced instead by a brown the same color as his son's eyes.

You are disappointing.

Morgan almost jumped at the reptilian voice that rumbled in his head. One glance at Felipe showed he had heard it, too.

Tannin tensed. "My lord, in what way have I failed? I captured numerous rebels—"

Not fast enough.

"They've only been around for a week—"

Fool! This move is recent, but his kind have come before, and worms greater than you have squashed them in a day! You are not fit to stand by my side, Tannin.

Tannin blanched, but his face hardened like steel. "My lord, reconsider. I have been with you since my youth, followed your ways, made sacrifices—"

Not enough. Or you would throw yourself on these scales at my mercy.

Tannin didn't move. His hate-filled gaze fell on Morgan, and Morgan was reminded of the Prince's threat in his study before he set out to catch Killian.

It is time to select from the next generation. The green eyes swept over the room, pausing on Morgan, who fought the urge to cringe. *One who wouldn't hesitate to destroy anything in their path to accomplish their will.*

Tannin snapped back to the King, steeling his shoulders. "My lord—"

You were wise when I picked you, knowledgeable over the four kingdoms and a heart to please. Accept your fate, and make room for my next mouthpiece.

18

THE FIRST THING THAT registered when Wynne opened her eyes was a delicious lungful of air and soft grass beneath her cheek. Then she gasped, sat upright. She scrambled to her feet, her skirts twisting around her ankles as her muscles tensed for another impact from her dragon's sturdy frame.

Nothing. No movement. Only a white brick path and green grass. Beside her, a fountain babbled. But while her eyes took in the unfamiliar world around her, her mind spun with the images that danced before her vision every time she blinked. Dread coiled in her stomach.

Armor had attacked her. Attacked. Not just growled when Wynne was doing something out of line, as she had precious few times before, but had sliced the air with her talons as if to sink through Wynne's flesh.

If the penalty for harming someone with your dragon was death, what kind of penalty was there if she was attacked by her own?

This was all Killian's fault. God's fault.

She needed to talk to Armor. Fix whatever had broken between them when she'd walked into the Armynian temple.

She gingerly placed weight on her injured leg and gasped. Giving no care to propriety, she yanked up the hem of her skirts to her knee. Her skin was unmarked by Armor's claws.

Healed.

Wynne rubbed her eyes, but the vision didn't diminish. Her legs trembled, and she sat on the edge of the fountain.

"You made quite an entrance, Winnie."

She froze at the familiar teasing voice, pinching her eyes shut for a moment. Of course, the whole God and repentance thing had been an act. She steeled her shoulders and turned to the voice.

Ryder stood on the other side of the fountain, munching on some kind of red fruit. "Hungry?" He grinned.

Her stomach growled, and she crossed her arms around her waist and frowned. "Where are we?"

He shrugged, and she scowled.

"I'm all right with a little ambiguity," he said, smiling. "What about you?"

She let out a long breath. She couldn't talk to him right now. Couldn't look at him. When he smiled, he looked like Morgan, and it sent a sharp pain through her chest.

"You hit your head there?" Ryder laughed. The resemblance between the brothers evaporated, and Wynne's mood soured further.

"I think you might have hit yours," she snapped.

"Probably."

She grumbled but didn't respond. Instead, she looked again at her surroundings.

The brick path stretched beyond the courtyard to...the Temple? It was like the one in Paradise, but far whiter, almost blinding, and taller than the highest wall of the capital.

A gurgled roar broke the silence and Wynne jumped to her feet. Water gushed out of the fountain's pool. Armor's jaws were snapping, pushing against the surface of the water as if it were a glass that would not break at her strength. Wynne grimaced as the silver head finally disappeared beneath the surface.

She felt Ryder's gaze on her, but she didn't look at him. It was enough that she was humiliated by her dragon, worse that Ryder had witnessed it.

To his credit, at least he didn't throw another teasing comment her way. Instead, he started toward the other side of the courtyard, to the base of the Temple steps.

Wynne stayed at the fountain. Sunlight kissed her face, but the light only felt glaring. Like Diane Delmar's scrutinizing gaze, penetrating through her exterior to see who she was within. The courtyard's stillness was almost expectant, and she had the distinct feeling of being watched.

With that, she decided. It was better she was in the Temple, out of the sight of whatever unseen entity seemed to study her.

She hurried to meet Ryder, and as she neared the grand doors, muffled music reached her.

"Do you hear that?" She glanced at Ryder, who nodded. She still hated him, but talking to him filled the uneasy emptiness of the courtyard.

"Look at this." He ran his hand down the grooves of the pillars. Wynne squinted at them, but she couldn't make out any letters of the foreign language.

Ryder started first into the Temple, and Wynne trudged behind him.

Candles lit either side of the stone walls, but tall windows above let light stream in like water. She couldn't shake the feeling of familiarity, as if she were walking through the Temple in Paradise, but instead of dread and shame, she only felt a lightening of her heart, encouragement. And it frustrated her.

At last, the music grew, and Wynne could make out clang of cymbals and the melodies of harps and strings.

The hallway opened up to a large sanctuary and a veil that shimmered, dividing the space. As soon as they entered the room, the music dimmed and sounded even further away. Wynne's heart sank. She'd never heard the priests play anything but funeral songs, and this had been rather...lovely.

She hung at the back while Ryder stepped forward into the sanctuary.

"Hey, I'm here." Ryder's voice echoed as he spoke over the music. He spread his arms out, throwing his gaze up to look at the ceiling. "What do I do now?"

Wynne scoffed. "You'll be waiting here until you die before you get an answer," she said. "This God doesn't exist. If He did, you would see Him."

If Ryder heard her, he didn't let on. He dropped his arms to his side and fixed his gaze on the veil. He gripped Killian's scroll tightly in one hand. "Your scroll says You paid for me. That You gave Your life, Your Son's life, as the sacrifice for my sin. For a murderer like me. Why?"

Electricity seemed to crackle in the air, and even Wynne held her breath. Though, she hoped God wouldn't answer.

That He really was just a delusion of the revolutionaries and a figment of Killian's imagination.

Or, if He answered, that His voice was like the slithering hiss of the King of Paradise. It would be easier to ignore Him that way.

Tense minutes passed.

Wynne let out a huff, annoyed with herself for expecting anything.

"I'm going to fill the flask at the fountain." She unclipped it from her belt. "I don't want to know what kind of rules your precious God wants to crush us with now. Gods and Kings don't do that. They don't just care about someone like us unless we have something to offer."

Ryder didn't answer, though his expression was one of wistfulness, like he was clutching a thread of some invisible hope. Something had shifted in him, and Wynne didn't think she liked it.

"You're wrong, Wynne."

She scoffed. "Sure."

She had only taken a few steps when Ryder's voice echoed in the large sanctuary. *"Can we boast that we have done anything to be accepted by God? No...our acquittal is not based on obeying the law. It is based on faith."*

The words hung in the air, and Wynne glared at Ryder as he was reading the scroll. His knuckles were almost as white as the parchment.

"Well, I'm here, God, in faith...even though I know I'm beyond even Your redemption—"

Condemnation is not for you, Ryder Delmar.

Ryder staggered back, and Wynne's gaze shot to him, then to the veil. The voice had rumbled as if from beyond the veil and above her at the same time. All around, like the steady drum of a heartbeat. Light from the windows above blazed like fire. The music hushed in reverence, and Wynne felt for all the world like a spotlight had fallen on her and not Ryder.

Ryder's hands clenched into fists and unclenched. "I deserve it."

The payment for sin is death, but My path brings life. You have knocked, and I will answer. I am not like the false serpent king, who pays in greed and judgment. Follow My Son, walk His ways, and find redemption.

Ryder stepped back. Something like a kind of peace seemed to radiate from his face, and it ignited a fury in Wynne.

She stormed forward and jabbed a finger at the veil. "That's it? Are you going to give me the same flowery speech as him? I don't need your 'words of wisdom;' I need the well of healing water!"

Soon it will be your father's time to be weighed, before he passes into eternity, but what will bring him life beyond?

Fear wrenched her gut. The blazing light softened, but it still burned her skin and set her insides aflame with anger. "You're saying Papa's going to die? He can't!" She gripped the flask with trembling hands. "Your water, Your path, is supposed to bring life—or are You just a liar?"

Try to save your life, and you will lose it. But if you give up your life for My sake, you will save it. Your father's time comes to an end, but his life is not yet lost.

"What do you want me to do?" Wynne flung the flask against the veil, and it bounced to the floor with a resounding clang. "What else do I need to do? I can't do anything else except die!"

Her hands shook as if with the memory of all the sleepless nights she'd worked.

She couldn't throw herself on the scales for Papa; her life wasn't worth enough to bring him back. She wasn't good enough to save him, not even to save herself. Her fingernails cut crescent moons into her palms, her heartbeat thudding so loud in her ears she almost didn't make out the voice's words.

Fear not, dear child, for I have paid the price for sin.

"All of it?" she snapped.

She would never be able to pay it back, hard as she tried. She could barely ever pay off her own penance to the King. And now that she'd been so rude to this God, He wouldn't help her either. Her body tensed as she waited, waited, for the angry blow from God's mouth.

You are loved, Wynne. Your path is not finished, nor will you walk it alone.

Tears pricked her eyes as heat pulsed over her. Not of scorching judgment, but of enveloping love.

Like she was once again five years old, sitting at Papa's feet while he told her embellished tales of his glory days in the army. Nestled in his arms by the crackling fire, as if no threat could come near her while she was wrapped in his arms. His sword defended her from any enemy.

The image of Papa's sword, shattered when she'd brought it up against the Armynian dragon, pressed on her mind.

The rush of warmth and peace turned ice cold down her back. Papa was dying. And his steel, no matter how expertly forged, had shattered against a dragon's hide.

You will find life for you and your father. But you must go, now.

The light faded as if a candle had just been snuffed out. Darkness fell over the Temple so Wynne could only see the flash of the silver flask. The sudden abandonment of the warmth made her tremble, and she felt like she was back at the Temple in Paradise before the veil, waiting to hear the verdict of the unforgiving King.

And the memory of what she'd felt dimmed. She wiped her tears with her sleeve.

Could this God really be any better than the King? her thoughts hissed.

This God had scales, too...but He said He paid the price. That all she needed to do was find His Son.

But what would God demand in return?

This time, the thought struck her with fear. God hadn't said it was free. He hadn't said it would be easy, or comfortable, or fair.

Wynne turned away from the veil, but Ryder wasn't in the sanctuary anymore. She picked up the flask and stopped at the fluttering curtain that would normally hold the priests' archives. What would God's temple hold?

She pushed through the curtain. Shelves neatly lined with scrolls—and a few leather-bound books. Dust covered every surface, but smudges and fingerprints revealed that she was not the first one to come by this Temple.

Which one would hold the answers?

Wynne reached for one thick scroll on the second shelf. But when her fingers grasped it firmly, it didn't move. It was as if the paper scroll was made of lead. She reached for another. Nothing. Then the leather book. It warmed at her touch, and it lifted easily from the table.

Maybe it had instructions for how to make shields like the revolutionary. Or maybe it had a map to find this man, this Jesus, the Son of God.

When she went outside, she found Ryder standing on the Temple steps.

"I'm impressed He didn't strike you with lightning," he said, shooting her a grin.

She rolled her eyes to the blue sky, hoping her frustration hid her disturbance at her conversation with God. "He still might."

"Hopefully he'll wait until I get home," he said, and her gaze shot to him expectantly.

He let out a breath. "I'm taking Morgan's place." He ran a hand through his hair, the gold and red ring glinting in the light.

She opened her mouth and closed it again. Her eyes narrowed, and she studied him, the determined set to his shoulders. "You'll be ridiculed," she said.

"Yes."

"Tried for Morgan's death," she pressed.

"Yes." He didn't flinch, his unwavering gaze looking all too much like Morgan when he'd told her to run back in Oran. "I will face the consequences. If that is the death of me, so be it."

Wynne thought she would have liked that, but faced with the sudden vulnerability in his gaze again unnerved her. Guilt wound up her throat.

"Don't look so worried, Winnie," he said, grinning, though his smile didn't quite reach his eyes.

She steeled her expression and crossed her arms. "How are you getting back?"

The courtyard on all sides was closed off with iron gates. It was too high to climb over the walls. She wouldn't go back in the Temple... So that just left the fountain. Maybe it would spit them back out where they had come in. It would be better than trying to get back home from here.

She went to the fountain and peered into the water. Beneath the reflection of the cloudless sky, she caught the shimmer of blue and green like the ocean depths. Maybe it was a mirage, but it was something to go with.

Wynne wrapped the book up in cloth and tucked it into her pocket—only to brush against parchment. Her papers. She pulled them out. Dry and clean, as the moment when Morgan had pressed them into her hands in King's Pass. She fought back the tears and shoved the envelope back in her pocket. She would save Papa, and then...well, then she'd work out the rest.

She clipped the flask, now full of water from the fountain, to her belt.

She nodded to Ryder. "You first."

He chuckled and stepped in. He had just gotten his two feet on the solid bottom when he sank through the water like a stone.

She rushed to the side of the fountain and peered down. Darkness gaped at her, air bubbles coming to the surface. With a hand, she reached into the water, her fingers brushing the smooth, slippery bottom of the fountain.

He was gone.

The water hadn't killed her the first time she'd gone through it, so hopefully it wouldn't do so now.

She stepped in, and nothing happened. She stomped her feet a little, groaning at the water that now soaked the bottom of her skirts.

"What now?" she grumbled. "Do I have to say the revolutionary's magic words?"

She dug in her pocket for the book from the Temple and sat at the edge of the fountain, her feet still in the water.

The pages were thin but sturdy enough for her to flip through them briskly. She turned to one page and balked.

Gibberish stared up at her.

She flipped to another page. More gibberish.

Why couldn't she read it?

Wasn't this book the same as one of Killian's scrolls? Ryder had been able to read the one he'd been given, but why couldn't she?

Fear gripped her chest. If she couldn't make it through the well, she would never make it home to Papa in time.

She was cutting it close as it was already.

She hung her head. Letting out a breath, she swallowed a little bit of her pride and spoke.

"If you're really there, God, now would be a good time to help a girl out."

No sooner had she spoken the words than the ground went out from beneath her, and she sank into the water's embrace. Bubbles flew from her nose, up toward the white sky—only to suddenly turn back toward her feet. She spun and kicked and swam to the light.

A gush of water like a geyser threw her out onto solid ground. Not marble like the Armynian temple—but grass. She scrambled to her feet.

Far beyond—though certainly much closer than if she'd been in Oran—stood the fortress walls of the capital of Paradise on the edge of the ocean. Grass rustled around her. The hustle and bustle of a town reached Wynne's ears, and she turned. Kyrn.

She spotted her book on the grass in front of her, and she snatched it up and gasped. Words. Real words, not symbols, greeted her. She snapped the book shot and tucked it away, worried that if she looked at it too long it would go back to being gibberish again.

Now to get home. To find Papa.

She turned toward the capital and froze when a pair of blue serpentine eyes fixed on her.

Armor.

19

Morgan swiped a hand across his eyes when the words blurred again and let out a groan. At least this time the words hadn't become gibberish; more than likely the headache pulsing in his skull was to blame.

His mind spun with the events of the trial. And Mother's words from a few days ago: *There is only one disease that kills the soul as well as the body. And the revolutionaries are not to blame.*

Killian had been weighed. And he had been found without sin.

But no one was free of sin, of guilt, no matter that Elwin thought Morgan had the money to cover his wrongs. Maybe so...but what was it that caused Orgul to lose his mind and turn on him if not his own sin?

A sudden gust of wind swept across his desk. He squinted into the darkness, the smoke rising from his candle like an incense offering to the King.

The peppermint scent suddenly made him nauseous.

Rap tap.

He turned to the open window. The capital of Paradise slumbered below, shutters closed to the world and the chaos outside the warmth of their homes. But how many shuttered the windows to hide their burns?

Rap tap.

The sound came again, quieter, and he froze. A shuffle, fabric rustling. Then a small voice: "Morgan?"

Addie.

Morgan ran a hand through his wild hair, trying to smooth it down. "Come in."

The door cracked open and Addie entered. He straightened further. "What are you doing up?"

She hesitated at the door. "Couldn't sleep."

The breeze behind Morgan from his open window blew across the room, and Addie shivered. Morgan waved her in, pulling out his reading chair from beside the bookshelves, and she sank into it.

Her eyes went over the map and the book laid out on the desk, but she remained silent, her lips pursed. Worry struck Morgan with another gust of wind from the window. It blew over Addie, but her mouth only pulled down into a frown.

No interrogation.

No teasing complaints about the cold.

He closed the window. "What's wrong?"

She sighed. "I keep having nightmares...about the dungeon... I heard him in the darkness, the King..."

She trailed off, and Morgan bit his lip to keep from filling the silence. His gut twisted at the thought of the King and the Prince, but he couldn't plant that seed of bitterness in Addie. He wouldn't bring this darkness upon her if it was under his control.

He sighed. "I hear he can be rather pleasant."

She lifted her gaze, eyes flashing. "He's good, Morgan. He's the King." But even as she spoke, she grimaced as if some stench had reached her, and she suddenly looked so much older than her fourteen years.

Morgan cleared his throat and stood, retrieving his map to spread it out before her. "I've been studying Father's maps," he said, trying a casual tone. "Here's Symara, its capital...and Mandor and its five islands. Do you remember the mangoes?" He caught her gaze.

She huffed. "Mm-hmm."

"There's a small island here—rocks, really—where our ships stop on the way to Mandor and back. Neutral waters, you can call them, though I doubt any water is neutral that has a Mandorian dragon below the surface."

Addie's mouth turned up in a half-smile, but she quickly covered it down with a frown again. "I like Mandorian dragons," she said defensively. "They're good, Morgan."

He sighed, running a hand through his hair. He was saying all the wrong things.

"You're good, too, Morgan." Her fingers brushed across the chains on his forearms, her features twisted with remorse. "Your good outweighs your bad, just like mine."

Morgan looked away.

Even Father, for all his piety and careful obedience, had been weighed and found to be balanced. Father had paid for that balance, if not in money then in deeds. But what if that balance between a man and his dragon wasn't enough? How would Morgan find salvation when he was still stumbling in the dark?

"Does it really work that way?" Morgan spoke before he could hold back the words, and Addie leaned away from him.

"The King says it does, so it does," she said. "If the scales are even, that's what matters."

But what would someone have to pay to even the scales? Felipe wore chains because of Addie's imbalance. And Morgan still had his, though he had no inkling of why. The Prince had bound him in service to find the revolutionary. He had succeeded, so the chains should've broken.

But what if the only payment for his sin was in his death?

"She's going to be all right," said Addie.

Even though she didn't say, he knew who she was talking about. He'd told Addie of finding Wynne in the King's pass and how her future still hung in the balance.

How her future was in the hands of a killer. But he wouldn't pick a fight over Ryder's conviction today.

His mind filled with fears of what Ryder could be doing to Wynne. What anger would have possessed him when he didn't get the revolutionary? Did he take it out on Wynne? Was she on her way back?

The questions had plagued his mind until he couldn't breathe. But a small voice had spoken to him.

Be still. Will worry add one day to your life?

The words had caught him by surprise, but he had been alone. They'd brought an inexplicable peace over his heart, and it almost seemed as if the chains weighing him down had lightened. Then he'd poured himself over Father's book, but he only had more and more questions.

"She's just scared, you know," Addie said quietly, tracing the lines of the Mandorian isles. "Not of you, of course, but this." She waved a hand aimlessly about.

Morgan nodded, though he had to force himself to swallow the desperation that wound around his throat.

When he'd planned to leave with Wynne, they'd bargained on bringing Elwin and convincing Addie. Though convincing may have had to be more like trickery. He'd thought Mother would be fine on her own, but now he knew there was no place for his family within the walls of Paradise. He needed to find a way to include everyone.

"Sit with me, Morgan," Addie said. He sat on the footstool beside her, and she grasped his hand. She yawned. "Tell me about your wedding plans again."

Morgan chuckled. "You've heard them already. And you've had a very strong opinion on some things."

"Can you fault me? I love Wynne—and she deserves the best."

"And this won't be?"

"Go on," she said, yawning again. "You always sound so happy when you talk about it. I miss that."

Morgan let out a breath. "All right."

So he began.

The day would be at the start of spring, right when everyone would have forgotten about the winter and the ports opened again. He'd have a dress made for her, and not by her skilled hand, even if she insisted on saving the money. She would sample the food from all corners of the kingdom to pick for the feast.

"She doesn't like cherries," mused Addie, eyes closed.

"Or nuts," added Morgan. "So I'll order them all," he said, laughing.

Addie blinked open one eye. "To torment her?"

"To ensure she wouldn't get one."

She waved for him to go on.

Even if Mother insisted, it would be closed to all but those closest to them. No council members. No nobility. Just Wynne's friends from the shop, and if Morgan had to make an exception for nobility, it would be for Felipe.

And then they would move to the countryside. Some quiet town where their temple was small and forgiving and their priests didn't care who you were. A temple without a King. Somewhere where he could search Father's books in peace and try to decipher what secret hope they held within their pages.

But no matter what, he wouldn't go back to see the Temple in the capital of Paradise. No, after today, he would never step foot on its marble floor. He didn't say that last part out loud, but even if he had, no one would have heard him.

Addie was asleep. She didn't even start when he placed a hand on her shoulder.

The pink of dawn bloomed on the horizon through his window. The sunlight glanced off the silver emblem decorating the note he'd received last night.

A summons. Private, in the priest confession room. Morgan could only speculate what he would have to suffer.

He doubted the Prince would be so benevolent as to remove his chains.

He had half a mind to shackle Orgul in the manor, but then discarded the idea when doing so might risk a worse punishment. Instead, Morgan folded his map and tucked it in his coat, along with a purse of coins.

Pressing a kiss to Addie's forehead, he ran a hand through his hair and left the room, closing the door with a soft click.

The water closed over Ryder's head with a rush of bubbles and the tug of a current. He'd told himself he would be fine, that the panic that cinched around his throat wouldn't be as bad if he expected it, but it wasn't so.

He blinked his eyes open as the current shifted down and the bubbles started flying past his feet toward a circle of light. Ryder swam toward it, and the white light became blue sky as he breached the surface of the water.

A fountain.

He stumbled as the ground came up beneath him and he was suddenly knee-deep in a fountain filled with coins.

A few people nearby pulled back at his sudden appearance, throwing him both looks of confusion and disgust, but he didn't care. His gaze was fixed on the unforgiving face of the Temple glaring down at him.

He was in the capital, the Temple square, and people had gathered. Their faces were turned expectantly toward the Temple doors.

But then a voice cut over the crowd.

"Get out of here!"

"Traitor!"

Ryder froze, feeling at once like the ire of the people was on him, but he was wrong.

A sudden whoosh and an Armynian dragon shot into the air, a human on its back as it soared over the edge of the city.

Ryder's gaze shot back to the Temple, where sick men and women walking up the marble steps were hurriedly pushed to the shadows by priests and attendants.

Ryder stood on the edge of the fountain to get a clearer view above the crowd. A few people were already standing on the fountain's edge, but they stepped down in fear when the Temple doors opened. Ryder didn't care. The priests could reprimand him, but they didn't hold power over him anymore.

Only God.

High Priest Anias came out, but if it wasn't for his ornamental robes—with royal blue instead of white—he would have been unrecognizable. Dark bags colored underneath his eyes, and the scowl on his face seemed to have taken a severe downward turn. His dragon emerged behind him in regal glory, and all around the square, voices hushed.

"Thank you for your loyalty, people of Paradise, even in this trying time. Many renegade Armynians have come to breed rebellion, but those of you who stand here today believe in the strength of your dragons and your King."

Murmurs of approval rippled through the crowd.

"Many of us have seen the sick—been affected by the poison of revolutionary words. Be calm," he said to those on the steps. "The King will judge you in time, and should your actions or offerings outweigh the grievance of what the revolutionary has done to you, then you will be healed.

"Some of you have brought trouble on us with interrogations and unfaithfulness," he went on, "but those who hear the truth know why we keep the rebels outside of the great walls of this city.

"We must remain unified to reality: when our King gave us dragons, we were given a gift. We should not expect them to be ruled by our standards, but by the King. Those of you who accuse your companions speak only falsehood. Instead, ask yourselves: what have you done to deserve wrath?

"Those of you who come to us with the tales of rebellion, we thank you. You protect the capital from the people who only wish to tear it down—"

A voice cut over the priest. "What about the other cities? Will they be left defenseless from this plague?"

The High Priest scowled. "They have their own priests and gatherings. The King works across leagues. You cannot escape judgment, same as you cannot outrun your shadow."

Ryder stiffened as he recalled his judgment at his trial.

Green flashed in Ryder's mind, the serpentine eyes of the King. He could still feel the brush of silk as he passed through the veil of the Temple, and all the breath fled his lungs as he was thrust back into one of the worst days of his life.

The domed ceiling of clear marble had reflected his own stunned face back to him, still dotted with some of the victim's blood. Dark oak floors were icy even through his boots, and veins of gold ran down the floor to pool in the center of the room in a gold oval.

The oval cover had been moved to reveal a gaping hole, and whispers seemed to fill the air even though neither Morgan nor Mother or any of the council dared to speak.

At the far end of the room, the silver scales sat in perfect balance. Ryder had been shoved into the sanctuary from a passage. He held himself straight. He had spoken carefully, clearly, and when he had finished speaking the truth—his innocence—the chains that bound him had snapped.

But it hadn't been enough to spare him the scales. He had to face punishment...someone did.

After all, it couldn't be said that a dragon killed their own person.

A sudden cheer from the crowd shook Ryder from his thoughts. The High Priest raised his arms now before the people in the square, just like the Prince had when he called forth the King.

"—and so you must take heart in justice of the scales, in the blood and sweat that you have shed for your King. Take up your prayers, take up your armor, and we will have victory!"

"Long live the King!" someone shouted.

The High Priest bowed. "And long may he reign."

Ryder flinched and turned, mind whirling. For a moment, he thought he caught a glimpse of Morgan, but then the crowds moved and Ryder was sure he had dreamt it.

Ryder swung over the edge of the fountain, his clothes dripping into a cold puddle of water that formed beneath him. The sea breeze chilled the air, but he had to go. He couldn't waste time. The crowd around him pressed closer, but he shoved against them.

He started toward the manor.

As he wove through the streets, a few sailors glanced his way. Some faces he recognized as those who traveled with him on the ships he'd been assigned over the last two years. They shot him derisive looks as he passed, and Ryder steeled his shoulders.

He had been awful to his fellow sailors. Not only had he wanted to get free as soon as possible, but he knew that liberty was impossible as a scapegoat. In his bitterness, he had snapped at anyone who might have had to work with him, and he had drowned his sorrows in whatever he could when the ships docked in Mandor or a city further south of Paradise. He'd always avoided entering the capital by making sure he had a splitting hangover... but in Killian's scroll, he had found hope.

A chance for the future.

A chance to pay for what he'd done but also find grace and life.

When Wynne had thrown the ring at him in King's Pass, he'd been ashamed, broken. All of his efforts had been self-motivated, and that had resulted in wounding Wynne and killing his own brother. He may not have killed the man whose death he'd been convicted of, but he definitely deserved a punishment worse than death.

But now, if he could, he would take Morgan's place on the King's council. He had to make something right, at least.

He found the manor exactly where he remembered, but he paused at the edge of the walkway leading up to the front door. Should he even go to the front door? Or sneak in through the back?

He sighed. He was a stranger here. He should give Mother the chance to turn him away if she so decided. At least this time she would have to face him.

He knocked on the front door. Footsteps sounded and the door swung open.

"Hello, Mother."

She balked at him, her eyes wide. But what struck him first was the dark purple under her eyes and the quivering of her hands.

He swallowed. "I'm here to take Morgan's place." The ring was hot around his finger. "I've been running long enough."

Mother reached forward, her fingertips just brushing the curve of his jaw. Then stinging pain seared his face as her palm struck his cheek.

He stumbled back a step. "Mother!"

"What are you doing here, Ryder?" She hissed, her face twisted with urgency. "You're going to get us all killed."

"I won't let that happen," he said, dropping his hand from his face. "Please, Mother, I know Morgan is... I need to do what I should have done in the first place."

Mother's eyes fixed on movement over his shoulder. She grasped the cuff of his sleeve and tugged him inside, casting a glance outside before closing the door. She whirled on him. "You need to go, Ryder. Addie won't agree to leave if she knows you're here. And they would never let you in..."

She stormed down the hall, and he followed her into her chambers. Two trunks were laid open, and clothes were strewn on every surface of the room as if a hurricane had run through the manor. Or maybe just Mother's mind.

"Leave?" he asked. "Where?"

She ignored him at the doorway and folded another dress into the smaller trunk. He trailed her to the dresser, where a letter caught his eye, and he picked it up. His eyes scanned over the document.

Mother snatched it from his grip. "We're leaving Paradise."

"Three," he murmured. "You, Addie, and...?" Could Wynne have made it here before him? He almost wished he could ask, but her name stuck in his throat as guilt squeezed the breath from his lungs.

"Morgan." Mother folded a shirt into the bigger trunk.

A flicker of hope ignited in his chest. Morgan was alive. And Ryder could still spare him the responsibility that should have never been his. He could step in Morgan's place, making it easier for Morgan to leave.

His heart twisted at the thought of not seeing Addie, but if Mother was leaving, it had to be for good reason. He steeled his resolve. "Where is he?"

Mother paused. "Don't interfere, Ryder. It would be best if you got on your ship and left."

She didn't even meet his gaze. Just as when he'd been put on trial and sentenced. She'd known the truth of his innocence and kept her silence anyway. Let him take the fall for murder when it had been a man's own dragon that had killed him.

He'd often seen Mother's indifference flash in his mind, followed by a surge of bitterness with every wave of the ocean crashing against his prison ship. He used to drink to numb the sting of anger, and he waited for it to rise up in him now...but it didn't.

Only pity filled him. His arms dropped to his sides. "Where is he, Mother?"

She must have heard something in his tone because she looked at him. "The Temple. He left to meet with the Prince. When he returns, we're leaving to Symara—"

Whatever else she might have said was lost on him as he raced out the door and onto the streets.

20

Wynne tensed under her dragon's dangerous gaze. Her hand went to her side, but only clutched the flask, heavy with water. Armor growled, and the hairs on Wynne's arms stood up.

Would Armor attack her as she had in the Temple? Her thoughts jumbled together. A few days ago, she would never have thought Armor would lift a claw unless in Wynne's defense. But those same claws had sliced through her skirts and into her leg. It was now healed, but the icy wind still bit her through the unmended tears in the wool.

She let the flask slip from her hand, and Armor silenced.

She took a slow backward step toward the capital. Grass rustled as Armor mirrored her step. Her dragon's blue eyes watched her every movement, but Wynne forced herself to turn fully toward the capital.

As she walked, her eyes roved the barren fields, overshadowed by the reaching arms of the forest. Red and gold leaves spilled like blood over the ground and swept by her feet in lonesome gusts of wind. The same leaves crunched underfoot and behind her like an echoing moan, and she found herself wishing it was a two-legged gait behind her and not four.

She reached the gates of the city as the sun crested over the fortress wall.

"What's your business?" a guard called down from the allure.

Wynne glanced up, but the sunlight dazzled her. "I'm traveling through," she said, her fingers going to the papers tucked in her pocket. "Catching a ship to Mandor. We leave this afternoon."

"Show your dragon." Silver flashed as the guard drew a sword, and the hostility in his tone startled her.

Wynne glanced over her shoulder and spotted Armor a few yards behind her. "She's right here. You'll see she's not Armynian."

"Come forward," the guard called, and thankfully his sword was sheathed. "You may pass."

The gates opened, and Wynne stepped into the city, waiting just long enough down the street for Armor to pass into the gates. She almost expected Armor to bound up to her side, like she might have just a few days ago, but her dragon kept at a steady distance, if just a bit closer than in the fields.

Wynne started through the city. Her feet carried her down familiar paths, her toes tracing the cobblestones. Shuttered windows closed their eyes to the rising run and passersby eyed her from downcast gazes, their dragons pressed closed against their sides.

All too quickly, charred stones greeted the soles of her feet, and she spotted the shell of what had once been her home.

Wooden posts were roasted and snapped like toothpicks, which once had held up the roof under which she learned to walk, run, dance. Her heart drummed in her throat as silver peeked at her from the rubble—the glint of Papa's blades—and she could almost hear when he had patiently tried to teach her how to parry. Her feet paused at the edge of the carnage, sure that it had been picked through for valuables. Whatever worthless things remained were an aching reflection of her own life.

Tearing her gaze away, she turned and walked down the street.

She took the roads to Morgan's house, weaving through the alleys to avoid the bustle of voices that she was sure would be convening in the square.

When she reached the manor, she knocked. Armor now settled a few feet behind her, like a shadow over her shoulder. Though once her loyal companion, Wynne guessed her dragon would not obey her if she asked.

The door didn't open. She glanced at the windows, all draped closed, and her heart twisted with grief.

She moved around the manor to the back door, where she snuck in through a servant's passage, leaving Armor outside. She'd become too big to pass through the door.

Her feet moved quietly, practiced from the times where she would sneak by to meet Morgan in his study or surprise Addie, and she couldn't help the tug of a smile. But pain speared her heart at the thought of Morgan, and she scowled.

She passed the darkened doors to Addie's room, Morgan's room, and paused when golden light kissed the hem of her grimy skirt.

She stepped into the study, her heart twisting in her chest. Morgan's desk remained as if he had just left it unattended. Smoky candles filled the space with a decadent peppermint scent, and gentle breaths reached Wynne's ears.

There, nestled in an armchair, was Addie, her face twisted with pain even as she slept. As if nightmares plagued her.

Perhaps they were the same nightmares that plagued Wynne even as she was awake. The rockslide, and how Morgan could never have survived. Tears came to her eyes, and she clutched her arms about her.

She went to Morgan's shelves. How often had he pored over those tomes to understand more of Paradise? What existed was little, and it seemed Morgan would spend more of his time studying his father's Symaran books. Her fingers passed over an empty slot among the books, and at a glance, she spotted a book on Morgan's desk. Curiosity prickled in her and she neared to inspect its pages.

Then she gasped, stumbling back a step. She hurriedly close Morgan's book, fishing her own out of her bag. She laid them side by side: the worn leather, the gold lettering on the front, even the title was the same.

Psalms.

She flipped open to a page on her book, her heart drumming in her ears. She could still make out the words. She opened Morgan's book to the same page. Where hers was untouched by the elements or handwriting, Morgan's book was marked with the hand of a careful reader.

> *Those who live in the shelter of the Most High*
> *will find rest in the shadow of the Almighty.*
> *This I declare about the Lord:*
> *He alone is my refuge, my place of safety;*
> *he is my God, and I trust him.*
> *For he will rescue you from every trap*
> *and protect you from deadly disease.*
> *He will cover you with his feathers.*
> *He will shelter you with his wings.*
> *His faithful promises are your armor and protection.*

Tears pricked her eyes as she read the verses, the words weaving through her mind like song. Who really was this God that would protect her? If none of Wynne's offerings were enough for Papa's curse, then it was impossible that this God would shelter her without something in return.

The reader had carefully marked the passage, and she knew it was Morgan's father's script. Delicate and looped compared to Morgan's quick scratch.

Her mind whirled as her thoughts flew back to her conversation with Morgan in her kitchen. He'd mentioned his father's sickness to her, the way his mind was taken...but could it be that his father had been sick with the same infirmity as Papa?

And if Morgan's father hadn't been spared, what would be enough to save Papa?

"He's in the Temple," a voice cut over the stillness, and Wynne's eyes shot up to see Diane Delmar in the doorway. "Elwin has been taken for final mediation."

The breath fled from her lungs. "When?"

"Two days ago," she said.

"And...Morgan?" Wynne breathed. "Was he...when he..."

She trailed off, but it didn't appear as if Diane was listening to her anyway. Her gaze was fixed on a point over Wynne's shoulder, though her gaze was far away. "I always wondered why Morgan would pick someone like you," she said quietly. "He never listened to me. Too stubborn like Stefan."

Morgan's father, Diane's husband. Something like pain flickered over Diane's features.

She might have once been offended at Diane's words, but now only hot tears pricked her eyes. Morgan was dead. Because of her. Her throat cinched tight.

"Now I think I know," Diane said. She studied Wynne and seemed to see something that Wynne did not. "You know who he is, his struggles, and yet you don't look away. You would follow him anywhere." Diane nodded in what Wynne recognized as approval, and something unfurled in Wynne's chest. Surprise.

Relief.

Anger.

"A little too late. He—" She choked.

"Would you follow him now?"

Wynne blinked. "I—"

"We are leaving, Wynne. I have secured passage to Symara. It would be treacherous, and we wouldn't be safe even across the border, but you could start a new life. With my son."

Wynne's knees almost buckled, and she caught herself on the desk. Morgan was alive.

He hadn't perished under the rockslide.

He was alive, flesh and blood, heart pumping, though probably not racing as hers was at this moment. And they would leave to Symara.

The only person left was Papa. "What about my father?" She couldn't leave him.

"I hope whatever you have found on your journey will be enough to heal him." Diane frowned, eyes glassy as if lost in thought. "Or that my husband's God will hear your prayers...even when He didn't hear mine."

Wynne scoffed, bristling at the mention of God. "You sound like Ryder."

"Ryder?" The interruption drew Wynne's gaze to Addie, who was rubbing sleep from her eyes.

"No," Diane snapped, the guard coming down over her face again. For the first time, Wynne recognized it for what it was: fear. "You were dreaming. You heard wrong."

Addie sat upright and trained her gaze on Wynne. "Is Ryder here?"

Wynne swallowed. "I—I'm not sure."

She seemed to take that as confirmation. "I have to see him." She sat upright and rushed from the room. Diane followed, and Wynne trailed behind.

In the foyer, Diane grasped Addie by the arm. Addie's dragon growled, but Diane's dragon loomed over, and the little golden creature silenced.

"You are not leaving this manor," Diane snapped. "Morgan will return shortly, and we are leaving."

"But Ryder—"

"He'll handle himself."

"Mother!"

"Enough, Adelaide!"

"Wynne!" Addie reached for her, but Wynne was frozen between her friend's pleading eyes and Diane's withering glare. Any other day, she might have helped Addie escape her mother's clutches, but there was a far more pressing matter on her mind: Papa.

"I'm sorry," she said, and ducked out of the manor.

21

RYDER RAN A HAND through his hair as his eyes roved over the scrolls in the Temple archives. He'd made it into the Temple by nothing other than God's grace. He had gone to a back entrance, the same one where he'd been ushered out three years ago to avoid the spectators eager to sink their teeth into the gossip surrounding the 'convicted' Delmar murderer.

Not that being a believer in God would make his image any better. Even Addie might balk at him for that.

But he would deal with that later. Right now, he needed more information. Killian had been a priest in Armyn, and something in the scrolls had shown him the way. What were the Paradisian priests hiding? What did their scrolls really say?

He didn't understand the priests' system of organization, nor did he have time to figure it out. He pocketed a scroll from each shelf and ducked out of the archives just as footsteps sounded at the back.

He'd avoided detection for now, but he still had to find Morgan.

Morgan's face flashed in his mind from when they had faced off in the ravine. The unbridled disgust in the turn of his frown, the tension in his frame as Ryder had pressed the knife to the delicate skin at Wynne's throat. And, worst of all, disappointment. For a moment Ryder had felt that it wasn't Morgan staring him down but Father.

Voices nearby yanked Ryder from his thoughts as he neared the sanctuary. He stepped closer, hiding behind a serpent statue, when he spotted two figures whispering fiercely before the veil in the sanctuary.

"It was only going to be a matter of time," said a nasally voice. Lord Henry Soam. Ryder rolled his eyes. "Better him than me."

"We don't know that yet," Felipe Ashton countered.

"You saw the trial," said Soam. "The King wants a new Prince."

Ryder jolted. A new Prince? Prince Tannin had held the position since before Ryder was born, at least twenty-five years now, and though Father had never hesitated to call out the hypocrisy of the priests, he'd been utterly silent on the Prince and his ways. But it wasn't hard for Ryder to spot the cracks in Prince Tannin's façade, how the revered leader of Paradise was just as bound and tormented as the lowest sinner.

Who would be next to lose their future at the service of the serpent King? And what would become of Tannin now?

Felipe frowned, seemingly unable to argue. "Morgan doesn't deserve it."

"And I do?"

Ryder's breath froze in his lungs. The King wanted another Prince. And Morgan was first in line.

Mother might have known that Morgan was in the Temple, but she couldn't have known this was the King's design. She would never have allowed it.

And neither would Ryder.

"I wouldn't wish it on anyone," Felipe said. "Even you."

Soam scoffed. "You would be the only one."

Felipe's expression turned thoughtful. He opened his mouth, but closed it again and let out a huff.

An expression flitted over Lord Soam's face, and for once, Ryder recognized the nervous, gangly teen he'd grown up with and not the narrow-eyed noble glaring at everyone down his nose. He swallowed, then scoffed, and his expression was steeled once more.

"I'm sure we know how your father would react," sneered Lord Soam, eyeing the chains that wound up Felipe's arms. "He didn't lift a finger in your defense yesterday."

Felipe's gaze hardened, and he pursed his lips as if biting his tongue. He bowed stiffly. "If you'll excuse me," he said. Felipe exited the sanctuary, going out to the Temple square, and Lord Soam was left, glaring at the stone-faced serpents guarding the veil.

His dragon, a large creature that loomed over his shoulder, nudged him and let out a lamenting growl.

Lord Soam shoved his dragon's snout. "Be quiet," he snapped.

Soam started down the hall. Ryder held his breath as he approached. But he never got to Ryder's position, instead turning right down a corridor. The curtains swished closed behind him and his dragon.

He started after Soam, ducking through the curtains of the corridor.

Candles lit the long hallway, frames on either side of the walls showing portraits of the past Princes. Lord Soam regarded the painting of his father, an unfamiliar expression on his face.

"Would it really count as losing him if he was never really my father?" he grumbled. He swiped a hand over his face, and now

Ryder understood the slight tilt of his frown and the furrow of his brow as fear.

"Henry."

Henry turned, whatever expression was on his face disappearing. His eyes widened with shock. "Ryder?"

"I need your help."

Henry's eyebrows shot up. "Are you on trial again?"

Guilt washed over Ryder at the sudden sharpness of his voice. No doubt he questioned Ryder's motives. He believed, as everyone did, that he was a killer.

Ryder steeled his resolve. He knew it was going to be hard facing the reality of his reputation, but he had to push through it. "I'm looking for Morgan."

Henry scowled. "So is everyone else."

"I'm here to take his place." He swallowed. "As Prince."

He tensed. "Don't pretend you're such a saint, Delmar," he spat. "Why would the King want you anyway?"

"I'm not worthy," he said, "but Morgan doesn't deserve this fate. And neither do you."

Henry's eyes narrowed. "You were listening."

"Yes."

"You don't know what you're asking for, Ryder. Go. You have no business here."

Ryder straightened. He couldn't let Morgan take the consequences that should be his.

"I must do this." Ryder stepped forward. Not only to take his place, but to say something—anything—to ease the burden that had been crushing his chest ever since he saw Morgan disappear under the rockslide. "The King will take me over you or Morgan," he said, mind whirring with any way he could convince Henry to take him to the Prince. "He spared my life when I should have died on the scales. Why would he have done that if he didn't have a bigger plan for me? What if my punishment has been to teach me discipline?"

Every word he spoke was a lie, but Henry's brows furrowed in thought. "You really believe the King would take you in Morgan's place?"

"I will be the only choice."

He nodded. "Come with me."

Wynne pushed into the bustling Temple square and cursed under her breath. Some people sat on the Temple steps as in the season of penance, as if awaiting judgment for their deeds. Others hung about in groups and watched the passersby for their dragons. A tension seemed to hang in the air, like the electrified breeze before a hurricane on the horizon.

She gripped her flask at her side and wove through the crowd. A few eyes roved over her and the empty space Armor did not occupy, but she ignored them.

They may not have seen her dragon, but she did.

Armor walked about thirty paces back, her blue eyes just about boring holes into Wynne's back.

A few priests stood at the top of the Temple steps. One seemed to be praying for a young couple, while two more watched the crowds with suspicion, as if searching for the flitter of dragon wings or the glow of a revolutionary sword.

Wynne's heart twisted. How was she going to get through?

"Wynne Mayweather?" a voice called her name from a few yards away.

She looked over at a familiar young man. His brown eyes shone with kindness underneath an unruly mop of red hair, and he smiled tentatively. "It is you, isn't it? Addie's talked so much about you and Armor." His eyes flicked to Armor a few feet back.

"Yes. Felipe Ashton?" She forced a smile, hoping he wouldn't ask about her dragon.

His eyebrows rose in surprise.

Now she really grinned. "Addie's talked about you, too," she said.

"Felipe!" a voice called from the crowd, and Addie appeared between them, grasping Felipe's arm.

His face fell in concern. "What's the matter?"

"I need to get into the Temple," she said. "I need to find my brother."

Felipe nodded. "Come on." He glanced at Wynne sheepishly, and Addie looked over her shoulder now.

For a moment, Wynne worried that Addie would hold a grudge and leave her here, but she stretched out a hand. "Wynne comes, too."

Wynne mouthed a silent 'thank you' while Addie looped her arm through hers, and they fell in step behind Felipe. At the top of the steps, the priests stepped aside at Felipe's request, and two guards opened the doors of the Temple.

As soon as the doors shut behind them, the panic that had been building in her chest constricted now. She needed to get to Papa. Wynne shot forward down the hall. "I'm sorry!" she shot over her shoulder. "I'll find you later!"

The coughs and moans of the sick reached her ears, and she turned to a staircase. She flew down the steps and pushed through a black curtain.

The dismal darkness oppressed her senses. Flickering candles cast a ghostly pallor over the people lined up on straw cots along the walls. More curtains divided the space, and though hearths flickered with hesitant fires clinging to life, a cold dread filled the air. A few attendants milled about, but by the pinched looks of worry, she knew the sick didn't have long.

One attendant caught Wynne's eye. "What do you want?" Her eyes glinted with distrust, and with a shock, Wynne realized this attendant was no older than Addie.

She cleared her throat, which was suddenly dry as the Symaran desert. "Where is Elwin Mayweather?"

The attendant's grimace only sent a shard of fear into Wynne's heart. "This way. But you'll owe me."

"Whatever you want, you can take it," she answered, muttering under her breath.

She followed the attendant to the back, where, through another black curtain, more cots stood in neat rows. Dragons of all sizes and colors lay out in between the cots, some rumbling with a rattling cough, others still as death.

Wynne's hand went around the flask as she spotted her father. She wouldn't have recognized him if it wasn't for Miro's bright yellow gaze fixed on hers from across the room. She was at Papa's a moment later, tears blurring her vision.

Dimly, she heard a voice behind her, but she couldn't make out what the attendant said as she walked away.

"Papa," she whispered, weaving her fingers through his. So cold. "It's Wynne. Can you hear me?"

A rattling breath. A sliver of white as his eyelids parted. He took in a breath but let out an awful cough.

"It's okay," she said, "you can talk to me later. Just drink this first."

She unlatched the flask from her hip and unscrewed the cap. A flash to her left caught her gaze. Miro fixed her with a wary look, letting out a rumbling growl.

"Wynne..." Papa's voice snapped her attention to him. "You look so beautiful, like your mother..."

Her eyes filled with hot tears. Anger unfurled in her chest. Would he ever see her as anything else?

His hand reached up to her face, his rough thumb wiping tears. "Don't cry, starling..." he whispered. "Fly, don't let sin's fangs pierce you as they have me..."

Wynne pressed a kiss to her father's cold hand. "Tell me about it later, Papa." She held the flask to his lips. "Drink first—"

Pain seared across the back of her hand. The flask went flying, and Miro's tail whipped back for another attack.

Wynne fell to her knees to catch the flask. Water spilled when it fell, splashing a nearby dragon, who hissed when the water touched its skin.

She held the bottle upright. But now it was empty.

Miro whipped his tail back and forth, staring at her. But she didn't care. This had been her only chance. The life-giving water was gone.

She had failed.

Papa gripped her wrist with a startlingly firm hand. "Tell me, starling. Tell me the truth. Where is my God?"

Her throat cinched tight. "I–I—"

Papa let out a rattling sigh. "So that's it... He has not answered me because He lost...and so I must pay the price I set."

"Papa—"

"The King's law is firm on this, starling," he gasped. "If I must—"

"No." She found her voice, trembling.

Words echoed in her mind:

No...our acquittal is not based on obeying the law. It is based on faith.

She took a deep breath. "You're wrong. God didn't lose against the dragons."

"But they live—"

"And who feeds them?" Hot tears pricked her eyes as a sudden warmth enveloped her. She wasn't even sure she believed it back in Armyn, but a sudden conviction pressed on her heart, and she knew that what she told him was true.

The walls she'd seen in Papa's expression when he'd spoken with Killian were gone. Just sincerity—and a glimmer of hope.

Miro's growl deepened, his claws scraping against the marble floor, but she went on.

"God paid the price for our sins," she said. "His Son gave His life to free us, but it's our choice to accept him... The King of Paradise won't save you, Papa, but Jesus will. All you have to do is ask."

Papa let out a rattling breath. "If He has broken through your armor, how can I deny it? Yes, Wynne. Yes, Jesus, I—"

Miro snarled and pounced toward Wynne.

She braced herself for an impact that never came. While in the air, Miro's form melted into the shadows before ever touching Papa. Wynne grasped Papa's shoulders. "No!"

She shook him, but his eyes were glazed over, lifeless. His face was cast in white pallor. "Papa!"

Wynne buried her face in his shirt, in the soft touch of cotton that he wore, not at all like the calluses on his weathered hands. Her body shook with sobs, and dimly, she felt a hand across her shoulder.

"No," she snapped tearfully. "Leave me here."

The hand gripped her shoulder tightly. "Get out," the attendant snapped. "Now."

The attendant didn't ask again, but yanked her from the cot. All around her, the voices of the sick rose in desperation, even as dragon growls and snarls rose to meet them.

"God, help me!"

"Jesus..."

The attendant pushed her through a black curtain. Wynne held a pillar for support, trembling.

"What did you say to them?" The attendant scowled, and a low rumble emanated from her dragon at her side.

"I—I need to go back." She tried to sidestep, but the attendant blocked her.

"No," the attendant snapped. "Where is your dragon?"

"Please, my Papa..."

"What did you say about that God?" Now the attendant's dragon growled at her, but she ignored it. The attendant's words snapped something in Wynne as the shouts and voices rose beyond the curtain.

Papa was gone, but she could still get to Morgan. Then they could escape, just as Diane had said.

Wynne started down the hall, the attendant letting her go.

She didn't know where to go, but if she stopped, Wynne thought she might crumple to the floor again. On she went, up a flight of stairs. Down two doors. Up again.

She should have reached the sanctuary by now. Or some familiar statue. But only twisting passages and corridors sneered at her. She squeezed her eyes shut, her throat tight. "God, please, show me the way..." She couldn't lose Morgan, too.

Dimly, she heard voices to the right. She pushed through a curtain. Darkness enveloped her, and by her fingertips, she felt another layer of curtains ahead. Now closer, she heard clearly the words that had been muffled before.

And she heard Morgan.

22

Wynne's heart drummed in her ears so loud she could barely make out the words. A small sliver of light filtered in through a gap in the curtain, and she crept up to it until she could see into the chamber. A confession room. Orgul's large black form partly blocked her view, but she could spot three figures: the high priest, the Prince, and Morgan.

"We will conduct the ceremony at noon," the high priest was saying with an air as of relishing newfound power. The tone sent a chill up Wynne's spine.

"It would be best if the moment were delayed," said the Prince, voice sharp. "The people may take it as a sign of weakness."

"The King has decided, and so it must be done," the high priest answered with a smug smile.

"The King does not understand his people, then," the Prince snapped. "It is not the time to evaluate whether or not we should select the next Prince. The people will get worked up and worried...only for everything to stay the same. It is not wise, Anias."

Wynne almost gasped. The King was picking another Prince? Dread sank heavy in her stomach.

"The time is running short." Prince Tannin stood, his chair screeching across the marble floor. "Get out, Anias," he ordered. "I must confer with Lord Delmar alone."

Anias bowed, though not without a smirk at Tannin, and left the room, his dragon trailing behind him. Wynne wondered at the tension between the two, but she focused on Morgan, her heart pounding in her chest.

Morgan was the only one left around the table. Orgul was only a foot behind him, eyeing the Prince as if he were a wolf about to strike.

"What would you say, Morgan? Do you have the heart the King seeks?" The venom in the Prince's tone was unmistakable.

Morgan was silent, though there was something of a resigned glint in his gaze.

This couldn't be happening. Not Morgan. He could rule the people of Paradise with ability, but at what sacrifice? She'd heard little of what it meant to be Prince, but enough to know that Morgan would not be the same.

"Well?" the Prince prompted, voice cold like shards of ice.

Morgan let out a breath. Wynne's stomach twisted at the sigh that escaped Morgan's lips. Despite the stubborn set of his shoulders, Morgan would agree with the Prince. He had little choice in the matter.

But she did.

At the bend of the corridor, Henry suddenly shot a hand out to stop Ryder. "Wait."

Two figures pushed through the curtain of the room in front of them. The high priest and his dragon. They left and disappeared down another hallway.

Ryder stepped forward, but Henry grasped his arm. "Ryder."

"What? Are you getting second thoughts about trading my future for yours?" He offered a grin, but he was sure it was more of a grimace.

Henry shook his head. "Your father," he started. "He was a hard man, but did—" He hesitated.

"Ryder!" A female voice gasped and Ryder turned, shaking free from Henry's grip.

A face came into view, and Ryder froze in shock. Her hair was a mess, and her golden dragon was just a few inches bigger, but even though her face had lost its youthful impishness, her eyes still flashed with familiar fire below the tears brimming on her lashes.

Addie.

She launched herself at him, wrapping her arms around his middle, and he caught her, stumbling back a step.

"I missed you," she mumbled into his shirt, then pulled back. "You stink," she said, laughing.

He brushed a tear from her cheek. "An unfortunate consequence of making it here," he said, grinning, blinking rapidly to dispel the tears in his own eyes.

"Your hair is longer."

"Distinguished, no?"

"It would help if it wasn't greasy," she quipped. Then she grasped him around the middle again in a tight hug.

Ryder caught a glimpse of Henry's surprised expression. "She knows what you did and she still loves you?" he whispered.

Addie tensed and pulled back, her eyes flashing. "He didn't do anything." she snapped. "And I would love him even if he did."

Henry blinked, then something in his gaze shifted. "Of course."

"Don't you dare judge him."

Henry's expression hardened. "I hope you can extend to me the same mercy."

Something like dread twisted in Ryder's gut. "Henry. Let's go."

Henry waved a hand, and his dragon at his side disappeared through another set of curtains. Ryder's eyes flickered over to another rippling curtain as Felipe and his dragon entered. But Addie didn't spare Felipe one glance as she fixed narrowed eyes on Henry. "Where are you going?"

Ryder shot Henry a look. "We must speak with the Prince."

"I can't let you." Henry's voice was low and dangerous. "Not anymore."

"I should have known better than to trust you, Soam," he snapped.

"You lost your father, Delmar," Lord Soam said. "I will not lose what I have left of mine."

Ryder scowled.

Two guards burst through the curtains, flanking Ryder.

"Take him," Lord Soam spat. "He's a traitor to the King."

The guards grasped Ryder's arms, pinning them behind his back.

Addie let out a scream as she was shoved roughly by a guard. "No!"

"Addie." Felipe stepped forward, concern etched on his face, and Ryder wished he could thank him for trying to keep Addie back.

She flinched, turning her anger on Felipe.

Good.

"Take him to the dungeons," Lord Soam said.

"No!" Addie struck at Lord Soam, but he grabbed her wrist, and she let out a yelp.

"Take her, too," he snapped.

"Wait, Henry," Ryder fought the guards. "She's innocent—"

Blinding pain exploded against his skull, and suddenly all he knew was darkness.

Morgan's heart drummed in his ears.

"Well?" the Prince asked again, and his voice could have been the hiss of a serpent for all Morgan heard.

When he'd received the Prince's summons, he had thought it might have been to finally remove the chains. But his hopes had been dashed, then trampled, and now bled out on the cold winter earth.

He'd hoped he might still have been able to leave Paradise. Find Wynne. Catch another ship to anywhere else if it meant they wouldn't have to stay in Paradise anymore. But even if the Prince wanted Morgan gone, there was only one creature who really had a say. And the King would never let Morgan refuse.

A voice cut over his thoughts. "No, he doesn't."

It was all Morgan could do not to stare as Wynne emerged. Despite the dust on her face and the hesitation in her step, seeing her sent a wave of relief through him.

But she didn't run to him as before in King's Pass. No, her blue eyes were locked on the Prince in challenge.

Prince Tannin let out a chuckle. "A lover? My, my, Delmar, I wouldn't have expected you to pick from the common folk."

The smirk on Tannin's face left no room for Morgan to mistake his intent for anything but malice.

A cold realization had dawned on Morgan in their conversation, and the Prince's reaction now confirmed it: having the King's favor wasn't something to be coveted and leveraged for a blessing, as so many Paradisians believed. No, it meant that Morgan's life didn't belong to him anymore but to the serpent King.

And Morgan couldn't subject Wynne to a life of misery as the wife of a wretched puppet.

The Prince would try to disqualify Morgan from being selected by making him choose otherwise, but that would never work. The King's outcome was guaranteed, at whatever cost.

"It must be in the Delmar blood to attract those of lower stature," Tannin went on, dark eyes trained for any weakness in Morgan's expression. "I guess there's something exciting to having a woman who can't refuse."

Morgan fought the rising ire unfurling in his chest at the Prince's insinuation. He couldn't lose his composure, or the Prince would know exactly where to twist the knife to force Morgan's hand. Morgan's fate was sealed, but Wynne could still be free.

He knew what he had to do. He sneered. "Exciting is one word for it." His words tasted like bile.

Wynne froze. She was on the other side of the room now.

Tannin grinned widely. "Your loyalties are divided, Morgan. Love for a woman has overcome your love for your country. Are you sure you could handle the mantle of Prince?"

Morgan swallowed, not breaking his gaze from Wynne. "I assure you," he said. "I am single-minded when it comes to loyalty." He looked over at the Prince. "Let the King decide my fate, Tannin, if he so favors me as you say."

"If you are to be wed," Tannin prodded further, "then your wife is also tied to your fate. Perhaps it would be best if you two disappeared." He smiled and lowered his voice to a whisper. "I wouldn't breathe a word."

Fear tightened Morgan's throat, squeezing the breath from his lungs.

"Don't you want her by your side?"

He did, but not like this. Not if his life would be under the thumb of a wretched serpent.

Morgan forced out a laugh. "Hardly."

Wynne winced.

He scoffed, but his head pounded. "Barely enough decorum to be the wife of a lord."

Wynne's eyes widened at his words, and he knew he'd cut her to the core.

If she didn't hate him now, she would by the end.

I'm sorry, he wished he could say.

Instead, he extended his hand for the final blow. "I assume you still have it? My ring?"

Her expression hardened in disbelief, but her hand went to her side anyway. "No, I don't."

Morgan's lungs tightened, his breaths sharp and shallow.

The Prince glanced between them with a note of intrigue. "This isn't befitting of the future royalty of Paradise, is it?"

Wynne looked at him, eyes bright. "I think not."

She let out a shaky breath, which hurt Morgan more than any response she could have given. She moved around the table, not breaking her gaze from Morgan as she spoke.

She paused less than arm's length away from him. Up close, he could see the tears sparkling in her eyes behind her grim determination. She reached a hand toward the purple bruises he knew crawled up his neck. Her breath caught. "You're hurt—" Then she stopped herself, pulling her hand back to her chest.

"Wynne." His voice cracked as he spoke her name.

She grasped his hand, and his fingers automatically tightened around her grip. A squeeze.

It said far more than he could ever speak, but he hoped she would understand the impossible choice.

"I know I am not worthy of such an honor," she said, her voice barely above a whisper, "but might I give a blessing for the future Prince of Paradise?"

Neither of them looked over at the Prince, but by his silence, Morgan took it as acceptance.

Wynne enveloped him in a hug, and he held her close, breathing in her presence for the last time. She pulled back enough to kiss his cheek, her breath curling around his ear.

She was so close that a stray tear fell from her lashes to his collar. He ached with the longing to brush it away, to comfort her, but he was trapped.

"The King," she whispered in his ear, "has no power. Morgan, believe me, there is more—ah!" She gasped, dropping her arms and stumbling back at the sword that swiped between them.

The Prince glared at Wynne. "You are deceived."

Wynne met Morgan's gaze, her eyes pleading.

Crimson beaded on the silver blade from where it had nicked Wynne's shoulder in a fine line across her sleeve. The blood jolted Morgan, and he shoved the Prince back. "Enough, Tannin. You've made your point, but it is not for you to decide. I will submit to the King."

But that didn't seem to pacify Tannin. His eyes flashed green as he glared at Wynne.

"She is dangeroussss," said the Prince. Wynne tore a strip from her skirts to stem the trickle of blood from her arm. "You are one of them."

"No, she's not." Morgan rounded on Wynne. "Tell him."

Wynne fixed her gaze on the Prince in a fierce glare. "You have no power over me."

Wynne's lips moved as if she were whispering a prayer. A bolt of light shot out from her hand. Morgan's eyes widened. It was the same dagger Killian had, only larger. It flickered in her grasp.

She leveled it to the Prince.

Tannin laughed. "Go on." He put a hand to his heart. "Kill me. Morgan will ascend to the throne that much faster."

She hesitated.

The curtains parted, and the high priest entered. "We must advance. Two intruders were found in the Temple and—" He froze as his gaze fell on Wynne and her weapon. "Is this another revolutionary?"

"Take the girl to the dungeons," Tannin ordered.

Morgan wished he could reach for her, but he was frozen in place as the priest's dragon stepped to Wynne. Smoke billowed from its nostrils in a silent threat of deadly flames. The dagger flicked out of Wynne's hand as she surrendered.

The look she gave him broke his heart, like she was looking at a dead man, and he couldn't help but feel so as two guards came to her side, restraining her arms.

Morgan stepped forward, but the high priest's dragon growled, baring its yellowed teeth. Fire flickered through its crocodilian snarl. The chains on Morgan's arms warmed in warning.

"Enough." The Prince flicked a hand and the dragon relaxed, the snarl replaced with sudden obedience.

Despite the fact that the Prince had just exerted reign over Anias' dragon, the high priest smiled. "We must begin the ceremony. The King grows impatient to pick another," he said with a smug look. He waved at his dragon, but the creature remained placid, its eyes fixed on the Prince.

"No, please!" Wynne struggled against the guards pinning her, a wild desperation in her gaze. "Morgan," she said, "I—"

A crack sounded as the Prince struck his staff across Wynne's temple. She crumpled, her skirts pooling on the marble like a spill of crimson.

23

Wynne woke up to a pair of soft, warm hands pressed against her face.

She jerked, remembering the Prince's staff as pain exploded over her skull, but her hands only met cold stone.

"Please wake up, Wynne."

Her eyes flew open at that voice. Her vision swam with golden light, and when she breathed, she sucked in humid, musty air. A cold weight wrapped around her wrists, and her stomach sank. She was in the dungeon.

Blinking hard, Wynne forced her eyes to focus on the voice tittering just above her. She stared into a set of concerned green eyes. "Addie?"

Her friend attempted a smile, but it was more of a grimace. Though her eyes remained their vibrant green, her face was white, and her lips shook as if she was trying to hold back tears.

Wynne tried to sit up, but Addie held her down. "Let me take a look at your head first."

Addie's fingers traced her hairline, and blinding pain shot through her skull. She hissed and pulled back, her stomach roiling. She gulped in deep breaths until she could see straight and grasped Addie's hands in hers. "What are you doing here?"

Addie grimaced. From the shadows, a scoff cut her off.

"She shouldn't be here at all," a voice said. Wynne glanced over and jolted. Ryder was chained just a few feet away, his gaze fixed on Addie. "That's my fault."

"Stop it, Ryder," Addie said. "You can't blame yourself for Morgan—"

"He wouldn't even be considered by the King if I hadn't been exiled," he said. "I should be the next Prince." He spat the last words with bitterness.

"Exile's not your fault either," Addie insisted. "You tried to stop that man's dragon."

"And I failed." Shackles clinked as Ryder ran a hand through his hair. "Why do you argue, Addie? My dragon alone tells you everything you need to know about me." He sounded as despondent as he had in the Armynian Temple, only now his voice had lost any trace of hope.

Across the wide corridor, a black chain anchored Addie's dragon to the wall. Whisper chirped mournfully in Addie's direction.

Wynne's mind spun with her last moments with Morgan. Even though she knew he was trying to protect her, her heart ached with the words he'd spoken and how his chains had not seared him.

The man that had said those words to her was not Morgan. That man, that Lord Delmar, was unrecognizable. But then his cool voice betrayed the turmoil within, and she caught a fleeting glimpse of Morgan. Her Morgan.

She let out a breath. "Morgan isn't gone yet," she said. She pulled pins from her hair and set to work unlocking her shackles. She was free a few minutes later, then she followed by freeing Addie and Ryder.

Even when the shackles fell from his wrists, Ryder didn't stand. He glared at the ground as if he wished it could swallow him up.

Anger unfurled in her chest. "What were you saying about taking Morgan's place?" Wynne crossed her arms. "If you want to wallow in self-pity, go turn around and get back on a ship. But that's not the Ryder I've come to know."

His gaze shot up at her words, and she pursed her lips.

"That's right. Don't let it get to your head."

He gave a weak grin and stood. "I see why my brother loves you," he said. "If you said all things with such conviction, I'm sure he'd believe anything you say to be true." Ryder rubbed his wrists.

Wynne nodded, shoving his shoulder. "Let's get back to him."

"Wait!" Addie rushed across the corridor to her little dragon. "I can't leave without him."

The little dragon lifted his head as Wynne and Addie approached, but no sympathy stirred in Wynne. She could still feel Armor's blue eyes boring into her back as she stalked her through the field and across the city.

"I can."

"Wynne!" Addie begged, eyes bright. "Set him free!"

Wynne crossed her arms. "Really?"

Ryder elbowed her. "Do it, or they'll hear us."

Wynne knelt down beside Whisper and unlocked the silver shackle around the dragon's neck. Whisper leapt into Addie's arms, and they had to walk quickly to catch up to Ryder, who had already started down the corridor. He yanked a lantern from the wall and quickened his pace further.

In the darkness behind them, Wynne could hear the slithering of a giant serpent roaming the corridors. The King.

The cool, musty air was broken by the occasional breeze. With every turn Ryder made, the breeze seemed to strengthen, carrying the salty tang of the ocean. Hope surged in Wynne's chest.

Ryder and Addie turned the corner, and Wynne hurried to catch up. By the time she made it around the corner, darkness gaped at her.

"Ryder? Addie?" she called, but her voice echoed back to her.

She felt the sudden pressure of eyes on her and turned. Blue serpentine eyes glared at her from out of the gloom as Armor crept from the shadows.

A vision pressed on Wynne's mind. The sanctuary. The scales. The green snake form of the King, and beside him, Morgan clothed in black, a golden crown glittering in his dark hair. Then another figure, golden hair cast about her shoulders, a cold expression on her queenly face. And beside her, Armor draped in the finest of the garments.

"You cannot save him alone."

A voice shattered the vision, and with a start, Wynne saw her own reflection stare back at her. Whatever wraith of herself she had seen in the well's water—and now—stood before her in royal regalia. As Wynne stared into the reflection's piercing blue eyes, she recognized her dragon's slitted pupils.

The wraith raised a delicate hand. "Let me lead you to him."

Wynne looked back to the way she came. Darkness gaped at her.

Now Armor stretched her arm out to her side, and stones rumbled. The wall became a passage. Inviting lanterns blinked awake, winding away back into the dungeons toward the Temple. "Come with me, Wynne. I know the way."

Wynne scowled. She faced the darkness to her back, the way she'd come. The inky blackness seemed to writhe and crawl, and a deep chasm seemed to open up just one step away.

With a breath, she steeled her will. "I'll find Morgan myself."

She took a tentative step into the gloom. When the ground didn't fall away beneath her, confidence surged through her. One hand to the wall, she started back down the way she had come.

The wall at the edge of her fingertips ended. Wynne stepped out into absolute nothingness, only the ground beneath her feet. A chill blew through the air, making her shiver. Behind her, the orange lanterns radiated the warmth of a hearth in winter. She could feel Armor's gaze on her, expecting her to turn around and follow her.

No.

She put a hand to the wall and followed its curve around the bend to the right.

Maybe Armor's way would get her to the Temple, maybe even fast enough to save Morgan, but what victory would it be if Armor's hold on her was fastened forever? Cold gripped her throat, her arms, her ankles so she felt as if chains were weighing her down.

Words came to Wynne's mind, like a hopeful whisper of a breeze.

He alone is my refuge, my place of safety;
he is my God, and I trust him.
For he will rescue you from every trap...
His faithful promises are your armor and protection.

She mouthed the words, an echo that seemed to carry down far beneath the silent dungeon, and light beamed forth from her hand in a radiant arc. A shield. Wynne held it up, and its crest—a lion—seemed to glow like white fire.

A sudden crossroads opened before her. Darkness on either side and in front, and the ever-present orange lanterns behind.

Wynne stepped forward. Darkness receded. A glance behind showed Wynne that the orange had not dimmed nor grown far away.

She steeled her nerves and went on to the right, raising the shield as the darkness cowered. Wherever the light banished the darkness, she stood and crept forward, first slowly, then striding.

The footsteps that had echoed behind her, now started once more, but in the tell-tale rhythm of a dragon. Now where she saw the edges of the dungeon corridors closing in, reptilian eyes seemed to smile grimly back at her. Shackles dangled from a few places.

Wynne went on. The footsteps grew louder.

A solid grate loomed before her. Locked. The light that was the shield in her grip faltered.

Orange blossomed behind her.

Come with me. Hearing her own voice sent shivers down her spine. She spun to see Armor once more, in reptilian form. *If you don't, it will be too late.*

It may have been too late anyway. And though a desperate piece of her wanted to believe her dragon, trust in all the times that Armor had helped her, saved her, something deep within her heart made her hesitate.

Wynne lifted her shield as her dragon neared. Armor paused at the edges of the brightest light.

"You have saved my life before, Armor, but now you have tried to kill me twice."

Kill? She let out a growl. *You are already dead to me. What you seek will not give you life.*

Armor's silver talons glinted, ready to slice through her throat.

"No." Wynne lifted her shield and it seemed to grow in height. "Not anymore. I won't be weighed by you. I'm done with the King and his scales."

Then you will die on them. The voice was a vicious snarl that seemed to pound in Wynne's head.

A force struck the shield. Like with the revolutionary on the bridge, Armor went flying back, her silver body arching backward toward the orange torches still so near, so deceptively inviting.

The shield slipped from Wynne's grasp as it suddenly had weight, becoming metal. It clanged on the stone floor.

Armor righted herself, lowered her head, and charged.

Wynne barely had enough time to breathe, but in a flash, a bright sword was in her hand. Armor leapt, and Wynne couldn't duck or run.

No escape now.

The light sliced through Armor's chest like water. Hot drops of blood steamed and boiled mid-air, erupting a foul stench even as Armor's body became wisps of darkness, devoured by the shadows.

24

THE WHOLE OF THE council was adjourned in the sanctuary of the Temple by the time Morgan was thrust into the room, escorted by two guards. He could hardly believe he was walking toward this fate.

A large stone table had been placed before the scales. The sun's angle through the stained-glass windows cast the area in a bloody shade of crimson.

Council members seemed caught in the flurry of whispering conversations around the room. Lord Soam shot barbs over his mother's trembling frame as Morgan stepped further into the room. Felipe stood at his father's side, and he cast Morgan a worried glance from where he was rooted. By the scales, Captain Corl nodded solemnly at Morgan, hand resting on the sword at his side.

Addie stood at the far corner of the room at Mother's side. At least she had bothered to make an appearance now. Orgul had taken up a spot behind her, so she looked for all the world to have two obsidian black dragons. The only difference was Orgul's glowing amber gaze to Elya's ice-toned eyes.

And right beside Mother, engaged in a heated conversation, was a figure he would've recognized even if he hadn't held a knife to Wynne's throat.

Ryder.

He ran a hand through his hair, and Morgan almost staggered in shock. His signet ring. The one that had carried so much of his life in the last three years. It was simultaneously the gold shackle that tied him to the King's service, and also what he had given to Wynne to show she was worth more than all of Paradise and its serpents.

Now it was in Ryder's hands, the same way it had been before he'd killed a man and been tried on the scales, but something was different. He still had the same determined hunch to his shoulders as he argued with Mother, but the expression on his face was altogether new.

The anger that flared through Morgan dimmed as curiosity spurred him closer. What had happened to his brother?

"...Mother, I must do this," Ryder was saying. "He doesn't deserve it."

"None of you do," she hissed, pressing papers into Ryder's hands. "You must go. All of you." Her eyes flickered to Morgan's as he approached, but if Ryder noticed, he didn't glance over. "Forgive me, Ryder."

"I'm not running anymore," Ryder said, his gaze fixed on Mother. "I should be the one to bear this."

"No," Addie spoke up, her eyes bright with tears as she clutched at his sleeve. "You can't—"

"Ryder."

His brother turned, his shoulders rising as if preparing for a strike. His eyes studied Morgan warily, but then he dropped his arms to his sides as if resigned to whatever punishment Morgan would dole out.

And yet, something shone in his brother's eyes that surprised him. A humility that hadn't been there before.

Morgan let out a breath. "I appreciate the sentiment, Ryder," he said, "but my fate is sealed." He raised his arm and pulled down the cuff of a sleeve so the chains could catch the light.

No matter what he did, Morgan knew he couldn't be free. These chains would always bind him.

"No, it's not," Ryder said.

Before Morgan could answer, the Prince appeared, behind him the high priest carrying a bundle of cloth. Tree leaves from each province. Four piles were laid out on the altar.

"Today we will stand before the King's presence as he breathes judgment. Each house will bring forward a worthy offering, and if yours is untouched by the King's fire, you will be found worthy of being at his side. Should none be found worthy, all will remain as it is." The Prince's eyes flashed. "Bring forth your token."

Icy fear crept up Morgan's spine.

Lord Ashton went first. His footsteps echoed as he walked to the altar. Removing the Ashton house emblem, the symbol of harvest, from his shoulder, he nestled it among the oak leaves. Another province leader all but threw her token—a diamond fastened to her collar—on the pine needles. Lord Soam tore away from the clinging hands of his mother to present the silver ring of a snake coiling around his finger.

A few of the council looked to Morgan expectantly, and he caught their shocked expressions when they noticed Ryder at his side. Lord Soam only crossed his arms and scoffed.

Mother stepped forward, but Morgan gently grasped her shoulder. "Let me," he said, opening her fist to reveal her own signet ring.

A strangled sort of sound reached his ears, and Morgan knew without looking that it was Addie. His heart pinched in regret but resolve as well. He met Ryder's gaze, and an understanding seemed to pass between them. Protect Addie.

Morgan strode forward and nestled the ring in the leaves.

The floor rumbled. Smoke crept from the chasm in the floor. Nausea twisted in Morgan's stomach at the memory as the King emerged. Bright green eyes still poisonous as ever, with sharp fangs and the rattling hiss that he felt down to his bones. The King circled the room until Morgan couldn't see over the great green scales, and at last, his tail emerged, rattling like the shaking of dry bones.

To his left, Ryder sucked in a breath, and Addie clutched at Ryder's arm.

The King settled his head by the scales. His pink tongue flicked out before Prince Tannin.

My my, the King hissed, *you are a wretched one, Tannin. Isn't your son proud to see you?*

A few eyes went to Lord Soam, but his expression only hardened even at his mother's quiet words of consolation. Fear dug deeper into Morgan. How would Mother and Addie react if he was the next Prince?

"It is always a pleasure to be in your presence, my King." Prince Tannin bowed stiffly and extended an arm to the altar. "Breathe your fire. And seal our fates."

The King lowered his face to the stone table, then breathed a plume of fire. Red flames burned as all was consumed. Morgan felt the heat even from where he stood by the veil. If a pile was unscathed, it was impossible to tell from the distance.

The flames stopped. The King turned his serpentine face toward Tannin and the high priest.

The high priest stepped forward. With the blade of an ornamental dagger, he brushed the ashes aside. At last, he held up something gold and red and Morgan's stomach twisted.

I have spoken. The King lowered his head to Morgan's height. *You, Delmar, are my chosen vessel to destroy this God and his revolutionaries.*

Morgan swallowed.

"What if I accept?" Ryder shouted.

All the eyes of the council turned to him.

The King made a noise as if hissing a laugh, and it turned to a snarl. *You are tainted, Ryder. Though perhaps you may be of some use yet when you realize your God can't save someone like you.*

Morgan's gaze shot to the Prince, who was ghostly pale. His wife had come to his side, grasping his hand with a white-knuckled grip. Across the room, nobles and their dragons shifted. Mother had a grim expression on her face, as if she was pained, but Morgan was alone.

As he always had been.

The King's serpent eyes fell on Morgan. *I have blessed you,* the King hissed. *And yet you know not what you have.*

Anger flushed through Morgan, as hot as Orgul's searing fire. "Blessed?" Morgan spat. He threw his hand out to the scales. "Your gifts have been nothing but a curse."

Would that you could see the power inside your dragon. The King's eyes flashed. *I bestow glory in this life, power over judgment, freedom from all. Would you say that you have no one you'd wish to protect?*

Wynne.

Addie.

Mother.

Elwin.

Morgan was reminded of his conversation with Killian at King's pass and the revolutionary's quiet question: *Who do you look to for redemption?* Morgan had no one in which he placed his faith, certainly not himself, but what if the King's offer could give Morgan that power?

The King's voice rumbled through the floor. *It is a shame*, he said, *that you would not accept me. I can offer you a power greater than any poisoned water.*

His last words dripped with disdain, and Morgan heard the hiss of warning.

He would never be able to escape the King's clutches.

But if he stepped forward, Mother and Addie and Wynne and even Ryder would be spared this misery.

Morgan forced himself to meet the King's slitted gaze. "I accept." He stepped forward. "What must I do?"

The King swept the ash off the altar with a flick of his tail. *Bring your dragon.*

Orgul, head low, came forward, climbing up on the stone as if anticipating a final blow.

With this offering, Morgan Delmar, do you accept me as your own, forever, until death claims your soul?

The declaration, so similar to the vows of marriage that Morgan had hoped he could one day exchange with Wynne, sent ice through his veins.

Lord Soam was looking between Morgan and the Prince, anguish plain on the scowl on his face. What must it have been like to have a father whose mind was controlled by a serpent? Whose very existence was determined by the hiss of a ground-dwelling creature? Whose love, if given, could mean little. The Prince would not have loved his son like a father, constant and unconditional, but harsh and demanding and lawful beyond any depth of grace even after asking for forgiveness.

How much of Morgan would be left? Would Wynne feel obligated to love him?

He knew the torment that Wynne would have to suffer, tied to him. And though he had imagined a hundred different futures with her, he would spare her this ending.

Morgan swallowed and nodded.

The King clamped his jaws around Orgul's black frame. Bone crunched. Orgul let out a roar, but it was futile. Morgan tore his gaze away as his dragon was consumed. All he heard was his heart in his ears over the bones.

The Prince fell to the floor, lifeless, and Lord Soam dropped to his knees. Lady Soam's screams echoed through the sanctuary, joined by another shriek.

Morgan spun to see Mother clutching her head. "Mother, what's—"

Before he could reach her, a solid mass flung into him, and Morgan staggered. Amber flashed in the black dragon's eyes. Orgul.

The realization dawned on him.

Impossible.

"No!" Morgan knelt beside Mother as she lay on the floor, clutching her head. Her face contorted with pain.

Orgul had not stepped up to the altar, but Elya. Guilt twisted his insides as he finally saw Mother's heart. How many sacrifices had she made for them? For him and Addie and even Ryder? How many of her offerings adorned the priests' necks and fingers?

Footsteps sounded beyond the veil. A guard pushed through the curtain. His gaze searched for Prince Tannin, only to fall on the King. He swallowed. "M-my lord, the Armynians attacked the western wall! They're coming for the Temple!"

The King's hiss reverberated like a boiling kettle. *Go,* he snarled, *prepare the people to fight.*

"We can't beat their weapons, sir!" he said, trembling. "They can take down our dragons—"

You fear death? the King hissed. *Do as you are ordered, worm.*

The guard screamed as the bands on his arms seared white-hot.

"I can't!" he shouted. "They'll kill me."

Then death shall be your wages, said the King. *Go.* Now the King's gaze fell on the guard's dragon and the creature stiffened. It turned and darted from the sanctuary. As if tied by some invisible string, the guard turned, trembling, and followed his dragon.

White shifted and another dragon moved. Dread cinched around Morgan's throat as Felipe's dragon bounded from the room. Felipe's sleeves smoldered as the chains seared his skin, but he kept silent even as he marched out of the room in pained obedience. Addie's voice rose over Lord Ashton's shouts pleading with the King, but Felipe was gone.

A few gazes turned to Morgan as his chains glowed, searing his flesh. He winced. Wynne's words echoed in his mind:

The King has no power over me.

He has been defeated.

Morgan couldn't imagine who would be powerful enough to make the serpent King bow, but only one name came to mind.

"God, please," he whispered. "Help me."

The searing pain of the chains dulled to just tolerable. The King let out a hiss, his breath carrying the scent of death over Morgan, but he didn't flinch.

Lord Soam moved first. Dragging his mother, he fled from the sanctuary. Lord Ashton cast Addie a scathing glance before stepping through the veil. "Addie, let's go." Morgan heard Ryder's voice over the chaos, but she joined Morgan at Mother's side.

Then the priests emerged. They fled from the archives, bundles slung over their shoulders.

"Get out of here, Morgan." Mother's voice was hoarse, her hands trembling so much that he almost shook with the force of her grip around his.

"Not without you." He stood and pulled her with him.

Her free hand went up to his shoulder to steady herself, but her hands suddenly clamped around Morgan's neck. Her eyes flashed, the pupils now fine slits.

"Mother—"

Her fingers dug deeper, even as Addie clawed at her arms

Shouts echoed in the city far beyond. Growing now.

Regret flickered in Mother's gaze. Her hands fell to her side. "I—I'm sorry."

He clasped her shoulder. "It isn't you—"

Pounding cut off his words. The marble seemed to shake as voices rose in rebellion outside of the Temple. The Armynians. Captain Corl's gaze went from Diane to the King, his hand resting on the hilt of his sword.

Come, Diane, said the King. *You know the path you have chosen.*

Mother stiffened.

"Stop it." Morgan glared at the King. "Let her go—"

Mother doubled over, clutching her head. "Agh!"

No. The King spoke, and Mother screamed.

Ice ran down Morgan's spine.

Mother straightened, but she didn't look like herself anymore. She moved past him as if a ghost, to the scales, the echo of her screams reverberating in his skull.

She leaned down to Tannin's body and pulled a dagger from his belt.

"Join us, Morgan, and live." She trained the blade on him. *"Because if we perish, you will die with usssss."*

Wynne dropped to her knees, her mind whirling.

Weightlessness was all she knew now, not the stones digging into her palms or her heart pounding in her skull or the fear still coursing through her like electricity.

Armor was gone. And with her, a burden had lifted from Wynne's shoulders. The weight that had dragged her down vanished, as if she had been under threat of punishment for so long but now she was free.

Her sword had slipped from her grasp, but it remained. Its brilliant light had dulled to a white tone. Like Killian's dagger.

Words echoed in her mind:

Yet God, in his grace, freely makes us right in his sight. He did this through Christ Jesus when he freed us from the penalty for our sins.

The icy chains that wrapped around her limbs were gone. Freedom.

Shouts reached Wynne's ears. She spun and slashed the grate. The sword sliced the bars like scissors through ribbon, and the bars fell away. Wynne stepped forward, and familiarity greeted her so she almost cried.

The Temple.

She could find her way to Morgan from here, if he was in the sanctuary. She found her shield—smaller than before, but comfortable—and strung it on her arm.

More shouts. Guards rushed by...then priests, clutching scrolls and heavy coin purses.

She pushed past them. A few glanced at her, but most ran, fear in their eyes. In the sanctuary, the veil rippled like the waves of a lake. The folds parted, revealing flashes of emerald. Wynne's blood went cold. The King.

She tightened her grip on her sword. She would not be swayed.

"You, stop!" a voice cut over the shouts. Eli rushed toward her, his dragon lumbering behind him.

Wynne stepped closer to the veil. The dragon growled. She raised her sword, the metal glowing faintly, and the creature silenced.

Eli blinked at her, his face red with fury. "Now you're truly lost, Mayweather."

"And you are blind," she spat. "You're leading the people to hell."

He flinched at her words, and realization dawned on her.

She frowned. "But you knew that already, didn't you?"

He scowled, clutching a glowing scroll in his hand, and spun on his heel, disappearing into the Temple. The priests had lied about the truth, keeping the Word of God hidden... How many more lies had she believed?

She faced the veil, steeling her shoulders, and strode through the parting. A darkness clung about the walls so only the sheen of her blade showed her the massive wall of rippling green scales too vast to climb.

Her heart drummed in her ears as she stepped around one way, until the green scales pressed fast against one wall. The other wall was no better. She heard nothing but the rustle of scales before her and shouts all around.

"Morgan?" Her voice sounded high and clear to her own ears.

No response. At least, not one she heard. Silently, the ripples of green flesh moved like a receding tide and the sanctuary opened before her.

All she saw was Morgan.

Before she knew it, she was running, charging, caring nothing beyond the elation that surged in her chest as she spied his face and the dark blue of his eyes. There was no green cast over his expression, not like the eyes of the Prince or of the—

Whoosh. The ceiling flew up before her, and suddenly Wynne was on her back. A solid mass had knocked her off her feet. Cold fear gripped her as she struggled back to sitting, blinking away tears, and stared into the eyes of Diane Delmar.

Her shield clanged as it skittered along the floor to the dragon who had knocked her over—the red Armynian one. But a cruel laugh stole Wynne's attention to Diane, who regarded her with coldness in her green eyes.

"We expected you to come, Mayweather, but not as a traitor."

A hiss filled the room at the last word, and far beyond, hovering just above Morgan, was the King. Diane spoke again, but it seemed to be carried by a slight hissing. *"Stand up. You may find redemption yet."*

Wynne stood, leaning on her sword after her ankle buckled. A captain stole her shield off the marble and lifted it. His crimson-scaled dragon crept around her other side. With a flick, its tail whipped against Wynne's knee and searing pain shot up.

She balanced and raised her sword to the Armynian captain, though her gaze went to the King's head hovering just beyond Morgan.

If she would need to fight her way out, she would.

Someone had defeated the King of Armyn once. She could behead this wretched serpent.

At Morgan's side, she spotted Ryder, his expression twisted with pain as he clutched Addie in his arms. Addie clawed at his grip, anguish plain on her face.

The Armynian captain swung his sword, and she stepped back. She stumbled over the red dragon, her weapon slipping from her hands. Then the captain was restraining her, barring her from freedom with the blade of her own sword.

"Enough! I'll do it. I'll take Mother's place." Morgan's voice cut over her pounding heart. "Whatever you ask, but set her free. Let her go, Corl."

"Morgan—" she gasped.

The sword pressed against her. A warning.

"Shut up, Ly—Wynne," the captain whispered.

The blade dug deeper, slicing the side of her dress.

Silence reigned over the sanctuary before the King's rattling hiss came from above them all.

You can change your circumstances. The King hissed. *Accept your fate, as has been decreed. Defeat this false God and take for yourself the power of life and death. Life for your family. Life for yourself.*

"Morgan!"

But he hadn't seemed to have heard her.

The sword pressed deeper. Fire seared where her glowing blade touched her skin. "I'm trying to help you," the captain hissed.

Morgan's gaze was only fixed on his mother. "If I accept, this will kill you, too."

"*For a moment.*" The King and Diane spoke at the same time. A chill ran up Wynne's spine. "*You would hold all things in your hand. You could bring her back. And you could have peace with your partner. Bring her forward.*"

Wynne eyed Corl, the unreadable gleam in his eye. The Prince's crumpled body lay before the altar. Diane would be next, and Morgan would only ever be one in a long line of death and destruction.

"God, please..." she whispered, then her words cut off in a gasp.

The captain's sword dug in once more, pressed into the bone of the corset. He grasped her roughly by the shoulders. "Your God won't save you now, so keep quiet," he spat.

Now Wynne was dragged to stand in front of Morgan. She looked up at him, the pain in his face. The anguish she'd seen so many times, when he'd come from the council burdened with what he shouldn't have had to bear.

The captain released her.

She took her chance.

Wynne flung her arms around Morgan's neck, pulling him down as his arms wrapped around her. She made as if to kiss his cheek but whispered in his ear. "Don't give in. The King has no hold on me. I'm free, and you can be, too—"

She bit back a scream as the captain yanked her back, his fingers pressing painfully around her ribs. Morgan's eyes widened, then anger flared in his expression.

But Wynne twisted, having stolen Morgan's dagger from his belt, and plunged it into the captain's leg. He released her with a string of curses and clutched his leg.

She scrambled, lunging for her shield. Her fingers caught the beveled edge, but she couldn't control her momentum, and her head slammed against the marble. Black dotted her vision. Claws scrabbled on marble, then ceased as the captain's dragon leapt at her—

A black shadow struck the Armynian dragon like a tidal wave. The dragons went tumbling, Orgul on top, while the red one snapped and scrambled for freedom under his gargantuan mass. It was like a cat pouncing on a dragonfly.

"Get up!" A hand yanked her to her feet—Morgan.

Morgan swept her shield up from the floor and brandished it to the King. His head hovered only a yard away, enough to swallow them both whole if he so dared. Morgan's grip around her tightened, and she winced as his hand pressed against her side. She forced herself upright at the dawning horror on Morgan's face.

A muscle in his jaw twitched as he stood, stone-faced, facing the one who would pronounce their doom.

You wish to be deceived. The King's dreadful hiss shook the floor. *So be it. You will face the scales at the end of your life, and how will you measure then?* He flicked his tail, sending Orgul off of the red dragon. The captain limped to his companion.

Orgul, the King hissed.

The black dragon straightened.

Come forth.

Orgul moved as a puppet on strings. His amber eyes stared, unblinking.

The King's voice hissed again. *Your companion has been a blessing that you reject. For a time, you ruled him, but now he will rule you. He will be at your side no longer.*

The pink tongue flicked forward, then retreated. Green eyes flashed, then fangs as the King seemed to smile.

Until we meet again, Morgan Delmar.

A sudden flash caught Wynne's attention. The captain rushed to the King, Wynne's glowing sword arching over his head.

As quick as a whip, the King's tail struck Corl in the middle, sending him flying across the room. He hit the wall, Wynne heard the crunch of bone, and he crumpled.

The King turned his gaze on Corl, and Diane mirrored the gesture.

"You are a wretched one, Corl," said the King and Diane. *"Did you really think I would not recognize you?"*

Corl grasped the wall, staggering to his feet, his arm bent at the wrong angle. Shock registered on his face amid the pain.

Morgan grasped Wynne's arm, and he whispered for them to leave, but she couldn't tear her gaze away.

"Worry not, captain," Diane hissed. *"Your wife's soul is safe in my care. You will meet her yet, but not today. You have not served your purpose."*

With a final hiss, the King disappeared back into the abyss from which he had emerged. The High Priest rushed to Diane's side, shouted something to her, and they disappeared past another section of the Temple curtains.

"Mother!" Addie shouted, but Ryder hauled her over to them.

Morgan removed his arm from around Wynne's waist to retrieve her sword, and her balance swayed, putting pressure on her ankle, which sent a searing pain up her leg.

She let out a hiss of pain. "Morgan—"

"Let me." Morgan was back at her side, her sword at his hip, as he bent and swept her into his arms. He took a step and paused. "Where's Elwin?"

At mention of Papa, Wynne's throat tightened so she could hardly breathe. Hot tears sprang to her eyes, and she swallowed. In his face, she saw all the hurt he must have felt when he lost his father.

"I'm sorry. We need to leave." Ryder's voice cut over them. Though his tone was firm, when she met his gaze, his mouth was pursed in a tight line.

They were just out of the sanctuary when wood splintered, the Temple doors broke open, and a harsh voice made Morgan freeze, his arms tensing around her.

An Armynian held a glowing sword pointed toward them. "Who are you?"

25

Wynne eyed the soldier, a gray winged dragon at his side. Armynian. They had invaded the Temple.

He raised his sword. Wynne raised her shield.

"They're with me." Wynne spotted the Armynian captain limping past the veil, supported by his red dragon. "I recruited them," he said. "They need to get to Kyrn before they join the fight."

To Wynne's surprise, the first Armynian lowered his weapon and scoffed. "Paradisians. You really have all the bright ideas, don't you, Corl?"

Captain Corl straightened. "They may not be able to fight," he said, "but they hold value in other areas. The King of Paradise has not fallen yet."

"And it won't if you keep recruiting nobles," the Armynian said, glaring at Morgan.

"Go after the King," Corl ordered. "He may be in the dungeons still."

The Armynian grumbled something else but disappeared down the hall.

Captain Corl and Morgan exchanged some kind of glance that Wynne didn't understand, and Morgan nodded.

Morgan carried her out of the Temple, down the steps, and through the square, but her mind whirred all the while.

Ryder and Addie trailed them, having some kind of argument, but Wynne couldn't discern any of it. The crowds were pushing them apart.

"Go to the western gate of the city!" Morgan shouted back to them. "We'll meet you there!"

Then the crowd surged between them and Ryder and Addie disappeared. Wynne clutched Morgan tighter as they wove through the crowd in the same direction.

It was only by the grace of God that they had made it out of the Temple. What would the Armynians have done if they had captured Morgan? They could barter for much with the life of a Delmar on the line.

Something that she could never live up to.

Her stomach twisted, and she wriggled in Morgan's grip. "Morgan—"

He didn't seem to hear her as he pushed past the crowds that pushed on toward the ports, where a single ship bobbed. One ship that could never hold the thousands clamoring for a spot.

A Paradisian guard passed them, and Morgan called, catching the man's attention. He shouted some kind of instructions to the man, but she couldn't listen past the blood pounding in her ears and the panic that threatened to claw up her throat.

"Morgan, wait."

He let her down, worry pinching his features. "We need to go," he panted. His hair was in his eyes, looking disheveled like when he'd spent all day in his library absently mussing it while he was thinking. But her eyes fell to his clothes, the silk and gold, and her fears coiled around her throat like a snake.

His words echoed in her mind.

Barely enough decorum to be the wife of a lord.

This isn't befitting of the future royalty of Paradise, is it?

No, I think not.

Hot tears spilled from her eyes, burning her cheeks. Through the blur of the world, she saw Morgan's face fill her vision. His expression softened, eyes searching hers as if he could read her thoughts.

"I didn't mean any of it."

She glanced down at his outstretched hand, her breath catching in her throat.

"I love you, Wynne."

The truth in his words, quiet but warm, rang in her head, drowning out everything else. She swiped tears from her eyes, and when she looked at him again, she saw her Morgan. The one she'd fallen in love with all that time ago. The one that would give anything for her, that she would follow to the ends of the earth.

Paradise was empty now. Papa gone.

But the world was open before her, held in Morgan's outstretched hand.

With a trembling breath, she grasped his hand. "I have another idea." She reached in her pocket, wincing with the movement in her corset where the sword would have left a bruise. "Take this."

Someone jostled them, and she teetered to one side, but Morgan caught her around the shoulders. "It's okay." He brushed the hair from her face. "I'll get us out of here."

"Yes... You did." She pressed the parchment into his hands. Their papers, identification cards. Mr. and Mrs. Belrose.

Morgan's expression was pure shock, and she couldn't help but laugh—though it turned into a groan as her head pounded.

"You're brilliant!" He swept her in his arms, but then his face fell. "But Ryder and Addie..."

"We can find them," she said.

He nodded.

The rush of joy that filled her with energy dissipated with the flap of wings overhead. Armynians. Then the first one swooped down to strike.

26

RYDER CLUTCHED ADDIE'S HAND with such a strong grip that she wriggled free from his grasp.

"I'm not going to disappear, Ryder," she snapped, her face red with exertion as she ran. He didn't take her tone personally. She was just exhausted. Upset. Worried.

Just like he was.

"I know," he answered.

She kicked at her skirts as she ran, muttering something under her breath. Her hair had come undone from whatever hasty method she'd pinned it up, and her skirt bore a few stains from the dungeons.

She was only two years older than when he'd left—fourteen now—but she carried herself with gravity. Maybe she also felt the weight of what he'd left behind. Guilt twisted in his stomach.

He paused in a quiet alley and pulled her into a hug.

She let out a few protests about getting sweaty, but then her arms wrapped around him so hard he couldn't breathe.

She was trembling.

"Come on," he said, "let's get you safe." He pulled back only to be met with her expression of anguish. Tears brimmed her bright green eyes.

"Why—why did you have to go?" She hiccupped between sobs. "No one believed me. I saw, Ryder; I swear I did. I believe you."

He squeezed her tight, then let go. "Can you keep another secret?"

She nodded, swiping at the tears on her face.

He reached into his pocket and pulled one of the scrolls. "Keep this safe for me."

Her eyes widened at the crimson ribbon wound around the scroll. "I've seen those in the Temple! Did you—" Her hand went up over her mouth, and her gaze fixed on something high above them.

A monstrous shape hovered over the city, the breadth of its wings like a giant thundercloud. Then sunlight cut through it, and Ryder realized what it really was—

Armynian dragons in formation.

A few dragons released a load, sending a rain of rocks down on the northern wall. Fires went up as the earth-bound Paradisian dragons retaliated. Projectiles whistled as ballistas fired shots, downing a few of the Armynian dragons overhead.

Addie had grasped his sleeve as they ran. They jostled the crowd of people as their dragons fought to get to the pier. He spotted nobles and the sick alike pressing against them, but no one seemed to notice their presence after they were out of the way.

Addie's hand now clasped around his wrist, grounding. He went faster, ducking low, praying no one would see them.

Whisper was wrapped in Addie's cloak, so at least the dragon wouldn't get trampled.

Ryder pushed through the crowd, straining to see over the buildings to catch a glimpse of the gates. He needed height.

Armynian dragons sailed overhead.

"Stay here." He ordered Addie, pulling into an alley. "I'm checking the best route."

He stepped up on a windowsill, then reached for the next one. A moment later, he was on the roof.

Flames licked the fortress walls. Black smoke came up from the fire, coming down again on the city like ash rain. All the gates were either blocked, torn down, or aflame.

That was not an option.

Despair snapped Ryder like a snake's bite. How in the world would they escape?

He climbed back down. Addie grabbed his hand in a grip that made his fingers numb. But at least he knew she was there.

If only they had a way through the walls, some chink in the Armynian plan, an entrance—

Entrance.

Ryder halted, and Addie almost ran into him. God had spit him out at the fountain just this morning. Perhaps they could go through again.

Ryder pushed against the throng of people fleeing toward the ports to board the last ship. Even some carriages flew past, carrying people's belongings and dropping boxes along the way. A few guards patrolled the roofs, their dragons sending bursts of fire at the shadows in the clouds.

Ryder pulled Addie to his side. Too many were being toppled. Too many trampled.

Panic singed his throat like bile. A dragon shoved him.

"Watch it," he snapped at the owner beside it.

Now some people were screaming and pushing back in the same direction they were going. Ryder glanced back.

His breath caught.

There, on the next street, Jessie was clawing her way through the crowds. The massive sea dragon seemed to take lungfuls of air before coughing up a fish on the cobblestones.

The main square overlooking the Temple opened up before Ryder.

He led Addie to the fountain, where the stone ox looked ready to trample them.

Ryder stepped into the water. He had to bite his tongue to stifle the gasp at the cold water that rushed into his boots. Far colder than the ocean. His sole slid along the bottom against the coins, but he put another foot up just the same.

God, please let this work.

He extended a hand to Addie. She glanced over her shoulder, face white. "Shouldn't we be going—"

"Come on." Ryder reached for her. "This is our way out."

Whisper, who'd crawled to Addie's shoulder now, snapped at him. His tail flicked in warning.

Ryder grasped Addie's arm, but the little dragon struck like a dart. His claws drew across the back of his hand, drawing blood. Red drops dripped down his fingers, to the water below.

Addie gasped. "Whisper!"

He scowled. "If he doesn't want to come, leave him."

Addie looked at him with horror, but Ryder didn't care. She couldn't stay here, not with the danger.

Mother had not been able to protect her. But he would. He needed to. He pulled a scroll from his pocket, fingers gripping the paper tight. One of the scrolls from the priest's archives.

It wasn't like a memorized prayer, not like the ones Father had taught, but like the heartfelt words of a letter. Full of life and light and power. God's promises.

The Lord says, "I will rescue those who love me.
I will protect those who trust in my name.
When they call on me, I will answer..."

A sword materialized in his hand, the metal light and wieldy. Whisper hissed, and Addie took another step back.

Her eyes were fixed on the blade, face pale. When she looked back at him, something hard had settled in her features, like an impenetrable wall.

"We have to go, Addie."

"Go where?"

"Just trust me."

Ryder dunked his hand in the water, wincing at the icy pain, but when he drew it back, pink tissue was already knitting the marks back together. "I know Someone who can help us. Look." He showed her his hand.

Her eyes widened. "How did you—"

"We have to go." He held out his hand, palm up. "Now."

She glanced at Whisper on her shoulder. "Whisper comes, too." Addie eyed his sword.

Ryder lowered it to the fountain's edge.

When he did so, Addie relaxed and stepped forward. She put a foot on the stone lip of the fountain.

"Ow!" Addie backhanded Whisper with her hand, almost knocking the creature off its perch. When the dragon moved, Ryder caught a glimpse of the red welts on her neck from a claw mark.

Without warning, he picked Addie up around the waist and dunked her feet into the fountain. She gasped and kicked, her skirts drawing up the water. Whisper clawed his way to the top of Addie's head when water splashed up.

But they didn't sink.

The floor didn't go out from under them, and the water didn't close over his head like it had at the well when he jumped down to the bottom. He trusted God, so why wasn't it working?

Addie shivered, teeth chattering, the water up around her knees.

Was it Whisper? If he could grasp his sword quickly, maybe he could—

A huge roar shook the air. Water rippled.

Jessie towered over the square, the top of her head arching over a roof. She slammed her claws on the cobblestones, tearing them up like mud. One black eye was fixed on him, fury in its dark depths.

Her luminescent blue scales reflected the sun in a crimson kaleidoscope of colors.

Ryder reached for the sword, but her tail was faster. It slammed into his middle, knocking him through the air. He hit the front glass of the bakery, the shards falling around him like rain. Addie's screams cut through the air.

Dazed, he shook his head and stumbled to his feet, wincing at the pain that seemed to permeate his body with every heartbeat. Across the square, Jessie advanced on a trembling Addie.

"Ryder! Make her stop!" Her screams were muffled once again by a roar.

Addie ducked as Jessie spun, tail lashing, and shattered the ox statue. It fell and cracked the basin. Precious water started to spill onto the streets. Ryder stumbled out of the bakery, grasping his sword where it had fallen.

He would not let Jessie go any further.

He lifted his sword with one hand.

Jessie's gaze snapped to him, and she studied him with her good eye. His heartbeat drummed in his ears.

With a free hand, he gestured to his sister. "Stand back, Addie." The water in the fountain now fell around her mid-calf.

Jessie huffed. Her breath pushed his hair from his face. An image flashed in his mind, and he knew it was from her.

A fish, small and defenseless, as she charged through the deep waters. It was nothing to her.

Just like he was.

His dragon turned her gaze to Addie.

No.

Ryder thrust the sword into her tail. She howled and wheeled on him. He staggered out of the way as her paw came down on an abandoned cart.

Shouts grew louder. A few small dragons looked down on the square from the roofs of nearby buildings.

Jessie struck out again. Ryder swiped blindly.

Dark blood poured from the slash across her muzzle. She lowered her giant head until it was level with his. A gurgling sound came up from her throat as her teeth flashed.

Worthless.

The voice reverberated through his skull. He might have thought it was his mother's voice if he hadn't watched her disappear into the shelter of the Temple.

Coward.

Jessie turned her head so only her good eye spotted him. She let out a huff of breath as if in disdain.

The realization dawned on Ryder cold and clear.

Look at you. Look how they run. They know who you are, and they are afraid.

People had fled the square in panic, but Ryder pushed the condemnation away. If people feared him, they feared his dragon.

So had he, but no more.

"Stop this." He raised his sword in warning. Blood stained the steel, and its glow dulled, but it only grew heavier in his hands.

You know you cannot protect your sister alone.

Ryder's gaze shot to the fountain, where Addie seemed frozen in place.

"I don't need you," he said slowly, circling his way toward the fountain. Jessie's head followed him like a crossbow readying its target.

The voice seemed to laugh in his head. *And neither do I.* She snarled, her yellow teeth flashing.

He didn't wait for her to move. Gripping the hilt, Ryder lifted it and plunged it into her eye. When she pulled back, he dropped the sword and jumped to the fountain, scrambling to stand beside Addie.

Jessie flailed, tail whipping debris across the square, claws raking the air. Her tail lashed inches from the fountain, but she was blind. Ryder lifted his gaze skyward. If only the well would open.

Addie gasped, gripping his arms as she slipped on the mossy bottom only pooling around her ankles. "Ryder!"

Jessie's head snapped to them.

If I must go, then so will you.

She barreled forward as if to ram the fountain.

"God, please!" Addie's voice cut through the air.

Suddenly the floor went out from under Ryder, and water swallowed them. Addie's grip was the only grounding feeling in the bitter darkness. He opened his mouth, the water sweet on his tongue, and squinted his eyes.

Gold and bubbles flashed in the water as Whisper flailed, raking his claws against his scales as if trying to break through to his own heart. Addie treaded water beside her dragon, and she grasped his tail.

A circle of light grew below them. God's well. The bubbles shifted from going above their heads to pulling down to their feet.

Ryder sank quickly, but Addie wasn't descending. He swam up and gripped Addie's arm to shove Whisper away, but she wouldn't let go.

"No!" Her air escaped in a burst of bubbles.

Ryder's lungs burned like fire, his heart drumming in his ears, throbbing through his whole body. It hadn't been like this before.

Then the currents pulled. Ryder was sinking, faster now, and Addie was being thrust back up. She grabbed onto Ryder with her free hand, panic shining in her eyes. The force of the current pulled Ryder and Addie down. Whisper broke free from Addie's grip and thrashed his way up.

Ryder tugged Addie closer to the circle of the light. The entrance to God's domain. Where they could be free and she could be safe—but the look on her face was one of such fury and betrayal that it sent the air fleeing his lungs. He gasped, but only took in water.

Addie pulled free from her grip on him and swam up.

He took one look back at the light below before he chased after her.

Wynne walked alongside Morgan as they pushed once again through the crowds.

She grasped Morgan's arm tighter as another Armynian came down overhead. They were targeting the crowds, the people. And the ship.

They pushed forward.

The ports were overrun with a throng of people. Some even tried to climb up the anchor chain to the boat. Sailors fought with screaming cityfolk, and dragons tussled. Morgan pushed through, and some of the crowd parted—maybe because they recognized him, or maybe because of the look in his eyes.

"Last call!" shouted one of the sailors.

Morgan raised the tickets. "We're here. Mr. and Mrs. Belrose."

Some people in the crowd taunted, others gave up protests in disbelief.

The sailor stared at the documents in astonishment, then annoyance. He grumbled something under his breath, then let them pass. "Better get comfortable. It's a long stretch to Mandor."

27

Wynne Mayweather woke to the sound of her own screams. She clutched her pillow, her trembling hands grasping at the linen, as her tearful eyes blinked away the memories of Papa's death.

Fabric rustled on the floor as Morgan sat up. "Breathe, Wynne."

His hand grasped hers, warmth seeping into her bones as the moments passed until she could finally sit up and look down at him. She swiped salty tears from her face.

"Was it the same dream?"

Hot tears pricked her eyes once more, and she pressed the heel of her palms into her eyes to hold them back. She grumbled something in response, but she hardly knew what she said.

Floorboards creaked as Morgan got up from his delegated place at the foot of her cot, but she couldn't bear to look up. Creeping shadows filled the cabin as the salty wind stirred the palm leaf curtains, making it seem like clawing fingers were reaching for her from the depths of hell.

Strong hands encircled her wrists, coaxing her out of her ball, and something cold pressed into her palm.

"Water," he said, sitting gingerly on the foot of the bed in front of her. His fingers pushed a strand of sweaty hair out of her face, and she finally met his gaze.

Understanding glittered in the dark blue of his eyes, his furrowed brow reflecting concern. She took the glass to her lips and forced herself to drink. She held it back out, but it slipped and shattered.

"I'm so sorry." The words escaped her lips with another wave of tears. She pushed the bedcovers aside, but Morgan grasped her arms gently. He met her gaze with that same understanding expression, and she reeled.

"Wynne, wait—"

She wriggled out of his grip, sliding off the other side of the bed and hurrying around. By that time, yellow flooded the room as Morgan lit a candle. Water and shards of glass glittered mockingly at her, and Wynne hugged her frame.

"It's my fault," she whispered.

Morgan stepped over the glass to her side. "We can clean it up, Wynne. It's all right."

Papa's face flashed in her mind, and her chest tightened. "No. It's my fault he's dead."

Morgan's frame froze at her words, but she didn't dare meet his gaze again. Her vision swam and she blinked, hard.

"I keep seeing him, Morgan. If I had gotten there faster, if he could've drunk the water, he would be alive, and—" Her words broke off in a sob.

The boat lurched and she stumbled, catching herself against the rough wall of the cabin. Morgan's figure swam before her in the blur of her tears.

The darkness of the cabin made her head spin.

The candle winked out, and Morgan was at her side again, his warmth banishing the cold that had seeped into her bones. He took her in his arms, his voice reaching her ears, though she couldn't make out the words.

He cupped her cheek, brushing away a tear with his thumb. His dark eyes reflected a grief of his own, and worry lurked in the depths of his gaze.

"You did everything you could." He brushed a strand of hair behind her ear and grimaced. "Maybe we should have stayed in Paradise."

Her heart twisted. They'd had no choice but to leave.

"If I'm anywhere, I'm glad it's with you." She grasped his hand, entwining her fingers in his. Her silver wedding band caught the light.

Too bad it was false, a cruel joke meant to hide their identities while they just tried to survive the trip across the ocean.

Her bloodcurdling screams had woken the whole boat below deck their first night. After the second night, people were casting Morgan awful glances, and a few asked if Wynne was all right.

Even now, she winced at the thought of the grumbling she'd be sure to hear tomorrow. She and Morgan didn't need more attention than they already had.

According to her papers at least, she was Wynne Belrose, but she hoped no one would notice her blond hair, stark against the normal brown hair of the Mandorian people. Morgan had only barely convinced her not to dye it, but she would take anything if it meant they wouldn't be discovered.

Morgan's signet ring lay on a chain under his shirt. At least he had hidden it. Only after she'd convinced him not to throw it into the sea.

They were starting a new life—albeit a fake one—not erasing the old one from existence.

She wasn't sure she would ever escape the nightmares clawing at her insides, but with God, she could try.

She leaned and rested her head on his shoulder. "There's no more judgment, Morgan," she said quietly. "No pretending. That means for you, too."

He rubbed his forearm where the chains still bound him. Wynne had tried to use her sword, but it only resounded against the black metal with a loud clang that would have drawn too much attention to try again. They would have to try to remove the chains later. Somehow. Now the sword sat in a chest at the foot of her bed. The wooden chest would have to carry all the belongings they could gather from here to Mandor's second biggest isle, Ila.

At least she wouldn't have to deal with the Mandorian dragons; they were all underwater. She couldn't bear it, seeing the serpents, knowing their beautiful scales hid a horrible wraith within.

Morgan's shoulders rose and fell with a quiet breath.

"I'm sorry," she whispered.

He tensed. "What for?"

Her lips curled up in a grin. "We're not exactly on the most peaceful of fake honeymoons."

He chuckled, sending a rumble through his chest as his shoulder relaxed again. "At least we're not including the mother-in-law."

She rolled her eyes. "Not funny."

"You're fighting a smile, I know it."

His joke really wasn't funny, but the fact that he tried to cheer her up only made her love him all the more.

"If I'm going to be stuck on a tropical island surrounded by carnivorous dragons, I'd rather have no one else by my side than you," she answered, straightening now to look at him. "Even if that's only so they have a distraction if they come after me."

He laughed, meeting her gaze. "Quick-witted and beautiful. You're going to keep me on my toes, Mrs. Belrose."

"Did you expect anything less?"

"You are more than I ever expected or deserved."

She flushed, glad that he couldn't see her all too well in the moonlight. She was about to answer when voices stole her attention.

"Inspection incoming!" came a call from a sailor as footsteps sounded overhead. Doors opened, and more voices joined the ones above.

Wynne slipped her hand from his. "Let's go."

While Morgan brushed the glass shards to the side, she tried to brush out the wrinkles from her dress. Not that it wasn't already wrinkled beyond belief after wearing it for three days straight. Oh well, it hardly mattered since it was the middle of the night. At last, he rolled up the bundle of blankets on the floor that had been his bed for the past three nights and tossed it on her cot. If they decided to inspect their cabin, they could at least deter some suspicion.

At last, she threaded her hand through the crook of Morgan's elbow and they started out of the cabin. Morgan's steady frame grounded her through the narrow halls to the top deck.

Midnight skies with twinkling stars greeted them overhead.

A slight breeze brought the scent of seawater, and if Wynne closed her eyes, she might have still been at home in Paradise–if not for the verdant foliage, palm trees and tropical flowers, waving at them in the moonlight.

The captain directed the ship to a lonely dock, where another Mandorian ship with blue and gold sails bobbed.

"Wait here," directed a sailor to the sleepy crowd around them. "The harbormaster will come aboard to check the logs before we continue the last leg of the journey to Mandor. You will have the opportunity to gather your belongings after. Have your papers ready."

Wynne got her documents from Morgan and stowed them in her skirt pocket.

Sailors launched ropes to the docks, and others on land put up a gangway.

A broad-shouldered man came up in sailor regalia—no doubt the harbormaster—followed by a nobleman dressed in Mandorian blue.

"Good evening, Captain," said the harbormaster.

"Here are the logs, sir." The captain handed him some kind of registry.

He tucked the papers under one arm. "We heard of some reports happening on the mainland that require our King's attention. Would you allow us interviews with your passengers before disembarking?"

"How fast will it be?" The captain frowned. "We must keep going to make it to the port in two days' time—"

"You will wait as long as necessary," snapped the nobleman behind the harbormaster. "Our business must be finished. I will speak with the men at the bow, and my wife will speak with women and children at the stern."

The captain bowed stiffly. "At your command, Duke Arlo."

The sailors started dividing the group.

Wynne clutched Morgan's arm. "Where do we meet?"

"If I'm not on the deck, check the cabin." He freed his arm from her hand and squeezed it.

She chewed her lip, anxiety threading through her. "But what if you don't see me?"

He grinned. "What were you telling me the other day, Mrs. Belrose? Trust who?"

She pursed her lips, but she couldn't fight the way her lips tugged upward into a smile.

She remembered. Trust God. "I get it. Go, I'll see you soon."

He disappeared into the crowd of men at the front of the ship.

Wynne followed the women to the back and stood in line. While she had spoken with Morgan, Duchess Arlo had come onto the ship, and she was seeing women in one of the upper storerooms.

The line moved steadily, and women walked back to the lower decks after meeting their families.

Some took a few minutes. Others were longer.

At last, it was Wynne's turn. She entered into a dark storeroom, alight only with a lantern by the duchess's side. A few wooden planks had been set up across two barrels.

The duchess was reviewing her notes when Wynne entered, and a hand delicately covered her mouth with a yawn.

Wynne caught a glimpse of graying hair under a black hat covering her face. A silver dragon slept beside her.

"Papers?" The duchess held out a hand without a glance upward.

Wynne handed over her papers. "Wynne Belrose."

The duchess laughed, the sound grating against Wynne's ears. "Beautiful name." The hat ducked further as she inspected Wynne's documents. "What isle are you from?"

"You can read it on the paper, Your Grace." Wynne held her breath to avoid the frustrated sigh that threatened to escape her lips.

"Humor me," she said with another song-like laugh, brushing a tendril of blonde hair.

Now Wynne really sighed. "Ila."

"Going home today?" The duchess flipped a few pages, and Wynne couldn't help hide the annoyance that flickered in her at having to organize the papers later. She just needed to get out, get away, before anyone asked too many questions or took another long look at her and Morgan. "I plan on it."

"You're all set, Mrs. Belrose. You can wait below deck until the inspection is completed." The duchess's gaze shot up just when she extended Wynne's papers, but they slipped from her grasp.

Painful recognition twined through Wynne, and she froze, unable to pick up the papers. Her breath caught, and she choked on the word that escaped her lips.

"Mama."

Want more? Sign up for Michelle's newsletter for exclusive updates on the sequel in the Paradise duology.

Check out a sneak peek at the first page of

Found

Washed in blood,
but stains remain, I'm
lost to depths of sin's devices.
Would that
He knew
He died
in vain—
I'm doomed to ne'er see Paradise.

What Is The Gospel?

Maybe you picked up this book out of curiosity, or maybe a friend recommended it to you. No matter how you came to these pages, just know that God has a plan for your life, and that future starts with salvation. Maybe you don't know what salvation is, or you've heard of the concept and don't know why it applies to you personally. I encourage you to read the following statement. It only takes a minute, but it can change your life, just like it changed mine.

So, what is the gospel?

God loves you. God hates sin. Even if you are a "good" person, you have not lived a perfect life, nor has anyone else. Your sin has separated you from God, and your payment for sin is death and hell. But there's good news! A perfect substitute can make your payment, and God loves you so much that He gave Jesus as your substitute. Through Jesus's death, you can have eternal life, and by His resurrection, death is defeated. This gift is free. You could never deserve it, but by accepting this gift, your sins will be forgiven and forgotten. You will be reconciled to God and live with Him forever in heaven.

If you wish to pray for salvation, you can do so by admitting you're a sinner; believing that Jesus came, died on the cross, and rose again; and confess Jesus as your Lord and Savior.

Here is one way that you can pray: *Dear God, I am a sinner and need forgiveness. I believe that Jesus Christ shed His precious blood and died for my sin. I am willing to turn from sin. I now invite Christ to come into my heart and life as my personal Savior.*

After praying for salvation, here are some things you should do to continue your walk with God:

1. Read your Bible to get to know God better

2. Pray and talk to God daily

3. Find a local church that you can connect with, one that preaches Christ and the Bible as the authoritative Word of God

4. Tell others about what Jesus has done for you!

REFERENCED SCRIPTURES

AUTHOR'S NOTE: THESE ARE the scriptures referenced throughout Sin and Scales. The parts in bold are the emphasis I added to reference what was shown in the novel itself. Sometimes the Scriptures trailed off in the novel, but I highly recommend you read the full scriptures for yourself and in context!

NKJV Psalms 103:2-5: **Bless the LORD, O my soul, And forget not all His benefits: Who forgives all your iniquities, Who heals all your diseases, Who redeems your life from destruction, Who crowns you with lovingkindness and tender mercies, Who satisfies your mouth with good things,** So that your youth is renewed like the eagle's.

NKJV Psalms 103:11-16: **'For as the heavens are high above the earth, So great is His mercy toward those who fear Him; As far as the east is from the west, So far has He removed our transgressions from us. As a father pities his children, So the Lord pities those who fear Him. For He knows our frame; He remembers that we are dust. As for man, his days are like grass; As a flower of the field, so he flourishes. For the wind passes over it, and it is gone, And its place remembers it no more.'**

NLT Romans 3:23-28: **'For everyone has sinned; we all fall short of God's glorious standard. Yet God, in his grace, freely makes us right in his sight. He did this through Christ Jesus when he freed us from the penalty for our sins. For God presented Jesus as the sacrifice for sin. People are made right with God when they believe that Jesus sacrificed his life, shedding his blood.** This sacrifice shows that God was being fair when he held back and did not punish those who sinned in times past, for he was looking ahead and including them in what he would do in this present time. God did this to demonstrate his righteousness, for he himself is fair and just, and he makes sinners right in his sight when they believe in Jesus. **Can we boast, then, that we have done anything to be accepted by God? No, because our acquittal is not based on obeying the law. It is based on faith. So we are made right with God through faith and not by obeying the law.'**

NLT Psalms 91:1-4: **Those who live in the shelter of the Most High will find rest in the shadow of the Almighty. This I declare about the Lord: He alone is my refuge, my place of safety; he is my God, and I trust him. For he will rescue you from every trap and protect you from deadly disease. He** will cover you with his feathers. He will shelter you with his wings. His faithful promises are your armor and protection.

NLT Psalms 91:14-16: 'The Lord says, "I will rescue those who love me. I will protect those who trust in my name. When they call on me, I will answer; I will be with them in trouble. I will rescue and honor them. I will reward them with a long life and give them my salvation."'

ALLEGORICAL SCRIPTURES

AUTHOR'S NOTE: THESE ARE the scriptures that were not explicitly referenced but woven into the fabric of the story. I highly recommend you read the full scriptures for yourself and in context!

NKJV Psalms 62:9-12: Surely men of low degree are a vapor, Men of high degree are a lie; If they are weighed on the scales, They are altogether lighter than vapor. Do not trust in oppression, Nor vainly hope in robbery; If riches increase, Do not set your heart on them. God has spoken once, Twice I have heard this: That power belongs to God. Also to You, O Lord, belongs mercy; For You render to each one according to his work.

NKJV Romans 6:20-23: For when you were slaves of sin, you were free in regard to righteousness. What fruit did you have then in the things of which you are now ashamed? For the end of those things *is* death. But now having been set free from sin, and having become slaves of God, you have your fruit to holiness, and the end, everlasting life. For the wages of sin *is* death, but the gift of God *is* eternal life in Christ Jesus our Lord.

NKJV Proverbs 18:21: Death and life are in the power of the tongue, And those who love it will eat its fruit.

NKJV 2 Corinthians 2:15-16: For we are to God the fragrance of Christ among those who are being saved and among those who are perishing. To the one we are the aroma of death leading to death, and to the other the aroma of life leading to life. And who is sufficient for these things?

NKJV 2 Corinthians 3:5-6: Not that we are sufficient of ourselves to think of anything as being from ourselves, but our sufficiency is from God, who also made us sufficient as ministers of the new covenant, not of the letter but of the Spirit; for the letter kills, but the Spirit gives life.

NKJV 1 Corinthians 1:18: For the message of the cross is foolishness to those who are perishing, but to us who are being saved it is the power of God.

NKJV Genesis 3:14-15: So the Lord God said to the serpent: "Because you have done this, You are cursed more than all cattle, And more than every beast of the field; On your belly you shall go, And you shall eat dust All the days of your life. And I will put enmity Between you and the woman, And between your seed and her Seed; He shall bruise your head, And you shall bruise His heel."

NKJV Ephesians 6:11-18: Put on the whole armor of God, that you may be able to stand against the wiles of the devil. For we do not wrestle against flesh and blood, but against principalities, against powers, against the rulers of the darkness of this age, against spiritual hosts of wickedness in the heavenly places. Therefore take up the whole armor of God, that you may be able to withstand in the evil day, and having done all, to stand. Stand therefore, having girded your waist with truth, having put on the breastplate of righteousness, and having shod your feet with the preparation of the gospel of peace; above all, taking the shield of faith with which you will be able to quench all the fiery darts of the wicked one. And take the helmet of salvation, and the sword of the Spirit, which is the word of God; praying always with all prayer and supplication in the Spirit, being watchful to this end with all perseverance and supplication for all the saints—

NKJV Hebrews 4:12-13: For the word of God is living and powerful, and sharper than any two-edged sword, piercing even to the division of soul and spirit, and of joints and marrow, and is a discerner of the thoughts and intents of the heart. And there is no creature hidden from His sight, but all things are naked and open to the eyes of Him to whom we must give account.

NKJV Hebrews 4:14-16: Seeing then that we have a great High Priest who has passed through the heavens, Jesus the Son of God, let us hold fast our confession. For we do not have a High Priest who cannot sympathize with our weaknesses, but was in all points tempted as we are, yet without sin. Let us therefore come boldly to the throne of grace, that we may obtain mercy and find grace to help in time of need.

NKJV Isaiah 9:6: For unto us a Child is born, Unto us a Son is given; And the government will be upon His shoulder. And His name will be called Wonderful, Counselor, Mighty God, Everlasting Father, Prince of Peace.

ACKNOWLEDGEMENTS

FIRST THINGS FIRST, ALL glory goes to God. Not only would I not have written *Sin and Scales*, but I wouldn't even be here if Jesus didn't touch my heart five years ago. Thank you, Jesus.

To my wonderful Dad: thank you for always supporting me in my crazy endeavors. ☺

To Liz: thank you for always encouraging me whenever we met every week to work on our novels. Your accountability in writing helped me get through the tough moments.

To Dorothy: thank you so much for all of your hundreds of questions and comments. *Sin and Scales* wouldn't be what it is without you.

To my other writing friends: Heisy, Chaney, Tayler, and Vincent. Thank you for listening to me and bouncing ideas with me (and for forgiving me when you got to the cliffhanger). Your support has been invaluable.

To my church family: thank you so much for all your prayers and words of encouragement. I love you all and am so grateful to have you as part of my life.

And finally, thank you, reader, for taking the time to pick up this book. I pray that God has used it to encourage you in some way, just as He did for me.

From staunch atheist to born-again Christian,
Michelle Emmanuelli strives to reflect God's love in everything she
does.